Reignited
Book IV

This is a work of fiction. Names, characters, places, and incidents either
are the products of the author's imagination or are used fictionally, and
any resemblance to any actual persons, living or dead, events, or locales
is entirely coincidental.

To order additional copies of this book, contact:
Superi LLC.
www.superillc.com

Superi

REIGNITED

CLINT THURMON;
CHRISTINA R. WILLIAMS

Chapters

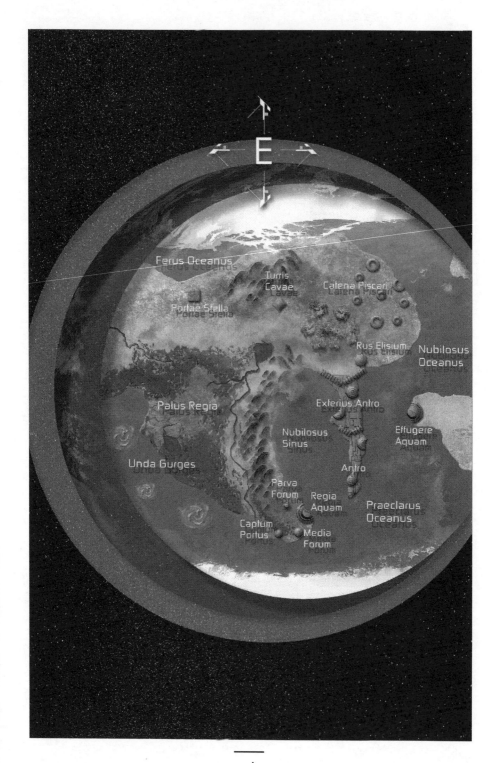

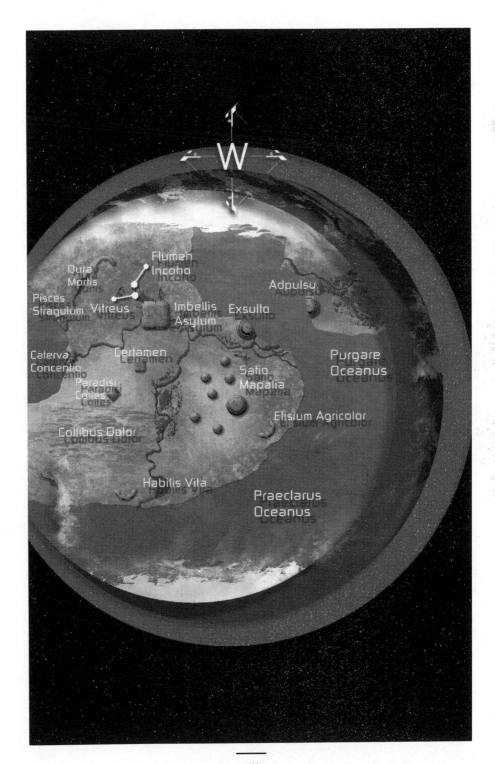

Reference/Dictionary

Malstar Luxson .... (Mal-Star Lux-son)

Calstar Luxson .... (Cal-star Lux-son)

Tristan Matthewson.......... (Tris-tan Matthew-son)

Anliac Aquam .... (An-li-ac A-quam)

Shashara Jacobs .... (Sha-sha-ra Jacobs)

Davad Jacobson .... (Da-vad Jacob-son)

Montilis Aquam .... (Monti-lis Aquam)

Triton... (Tri-ton)

Razoran .... (Ra-zor-an)

Socmoon .... (Soc-moon)

Toy Stevenson............................ (Toy Steven-son)

Shasha Jacobs .... Sha-sha Jacobs)

Inabeth Aquam .... (In-a-beth Aquam)

Superi .... (Sup-ery)

Imbellis Asylum .... (Im-bell-is Asi-lum)

Nubilosus .... (Nub-i-losus)

Pisces Stragulum.................. (Pi-sces Strag-u-lum)

Exterius Antro .... (Exter-ius Ant-ro)

Catena Piscari........................... (Cat-ena Pis-cary)

Caterva Concentio........... (Cat-er-va Con-cen-tio)

Certamen .... (Cert-a-men)

Exsulto Adpulsu .... (Ex-sulto Ad-pulsu)

Vitreus .... (Vi-tre-us)

Antro .... (Ant-ro)

Paradisi Colles .... (Para-di-sy Col-les)

Turris Cavae.............................. (Tur-ris Ca-vae)

Palus Regia.................................... (Pa-lus Re-gia)

———

I

Trifecta

Sulfurous smoke belched from a hole in the aether that overpowered the floral sent wafting from the gardens of Zeus as Hades joined them. His pale, gaunt face was revealed as he removed the helm of darkness and tucked it beneath his arm. In black leather armor, his dark image odd against the background of waterfalls and gorgeous lumbering trees, he stalked forward.

Zeus's long white hair and pointed beard were caught up in a stiff breeze that tugged his white toga against his muscular frame. The glow from his golden skin expanded along with his temper as he said, "Watch your step, Hades," and pointed to the scorched footprints left in the wake of the god through the carpet of lush green grass.

"Sorry, Zeus," Hades said with a grin as he advanced on Apollo. "Twice now, sun god, you have tempted the Fates by showing your face in my presence. If you weren't so pretty to look at I would have killed you by now."

Resisting the urge to reach for his bow, Apollo clenched his fists and bit back a sharp retort to say instead, "The events that are transpiring are of greater importance than our personal feud, uncle. I called for a summit of all the gods, but Zeus will not allow it without a forum of the trifecta."

"I am not interested in false accolades or platitudes." Hades laughed. "Trifecta, indeed."

Apollo grunted. "I should know better than to waste sarcasm on the dim-witted."

"More like the dim-witted shouldn't try to be witty," Hades countered. He turned towards Zeus and asked, "Why have I been summoned? You know I hate coming up here. It's so… bright." He squinted and covered his eyes dramatically.

"Patience, Hades," Zeus said.

Turning his head from right to left, Hades put a hand against his own chest and asked, "Do you know me at all?"

From the pool of water formed at the base of the gentle falls, Poseidon, god of the sea, emerged. His brown hair was held away from his stoic face by a wreath of seaweed. The pale blue toga he wore left exposed his powerful physique as he took in the scene before him with swirling, liquid eyes.

"You're late," Zeus grumbled, as he paced before a golden statue made in his image eons before. "Hades journeyed from Tartarus faster than you surfaced from the ocean. You've grown lazy."

"I see time hasn't improved your temperament, Zeus." Poseidon smirked. "And Tartarus has yet to burn away your twisted sense of humor, Hades."

"Well," Hades replied, "the oceans have succeeded in

drowning yours. Do you see what I did there, Apollo?" His brows wiggled. "Wit and sarcasm."

"Death by boredom," Apollo sneered.

Hades threw back his head and laughed.

"Can we move on?" Apollo said. "Our whole existence may lay in the balance here."

"Ugh, Apollo, we are immortal," Zeus said, "and you are being overly dramatic. In your haste to incite chaos, you have prevented me from showing my brothers the hospitality that gods of their station deserve. The absence of such pleasantries makes this gathering rather dull."

"I could not agree more, brother," Hades said, "but it's never too late. You could conjure a blonde pleasantry for me, preferably one with an ample bosom."

Poseidon chuckled. "The only pleasantries I've enjoyed of late are cold blooded with a tail. I'd settle for something warm, but since we are left in our own company, perhaps we should discuss why we are here."

When Apollo held his tongue, Zeus tossed his arms over his head and gushed, "Well, speak, Apollo. Tell them what you've told me, and see that your concerns are unwarranted, and let this be the end of it."

"This will not be an ending." Apollo shook his head. "It will be a beginning. The angeli of Superi have been reborn."

Fire rolled within Hades's obsidian eyes. "How many have come, and why has Ares not been summoned?"

"Calm yourself," Zeus said. "None are here."

Hades translocated from where he stood next to Poseidon, reappearing before Apollo, to slam a fist into his shoulder. "Scare a god, why don't you."

"Hit me again," Apollo said, grinding his teeth, "and I'll send you back where you came from."

"Careful, Apollo"—Hades grinned—"or I'll take you home with me."

"Enough," Poseidon said. "The rift in the aether that Munsin warned of, was it them?"

"Yes," Apollo answered, shoving his shoulder into Hades's as he moved past him to speak to Poseidon. "I was riding the beams of the sun across the skies of Texas when the crackling of a gateway drew my attention. I caught a glimpse of the damned grove within the purple ring, between streaks of yellow lightning, before the way was closed."

"Is that why you were here with Nike?" Hades asked. "And here I thought you were trying to make me jealous."

"If I wanted to make you jealous, Hades, I would not have to try. We both know I'm prettier than you. Besides, you scare the hell out of women," Apollo replied. "Nike's curiosity drew her here. Her presence had naught to do with me, but on that day, yes, I sought Zeus out."

The scent of sulfur wafting from Hades was made stronger by Apollo's insult, but as he turned to Zeus, his ire cooled. He paused and laid a finger against his chin, and then he said, "It has been ages since the last great influx of souls possessing more than human spirit. A war with Superi might not be a bad thing."

"That was five days ago," Poseidon said. "Why are we only hearing about it now?"

"So it was," Zeus replied with a dismissive wave of his hand. "I have ruled from this mountain for eons, brother. Long has it been since the days when I needed your opinion to act upon a perceived threat. Apollo's fears are unwarranted, and Hades, there will be no war."

"Then you shouldn't tease me with one." Hades sighed. "I swear, Zeus, you're no fun at all."

"The angeli of Superi are no laughing matter, Hades," Poseidon said. "Apollo, are you certain none came through?"

"We certainly laughed when we chased their glowing behinds back through the gateway," Hades snipped.

Ignoring Hades's outburst, Apollo answered, "I waited for hours and then I opened the gateway myself."

"You fool!" Hades cursed as his smile evaporated. "Why not simply release the Titans?" he snarled. "The threat to our reign would be the same."

"Our reign?" Apollo chuckled. "We are weak, Hades! Weaker than we've ever been. Our strength comes from those who worship us, and in case you haven't been paying attention, there are but a handful left who think us more than myth. I did what I had to do."

"Which was?" Poseidon asked.

"I went through the gateway," Apollo answered, "and found a small force of invaders waiting on the other side. They were not without skill, but met their end quickly enough by my hand."

"You claim to have taken on the angeli force alone, on Superi"—Hades's brow arched—"and survived?"

"Those I battled first were not angeli," Apollo said. "They came after."

"There was a reason we fought them on Earth during the last battle," Poseidon said. "What were the conditions like?"

"The gravity of that planet was like a mountain resting on my shoulders. Their twin suns offered me no power. In truth, it drained an immense portion of my strength," he said. "My bow was tainted by their suns' light, and my arrow fell short of its mark. It was with my bare hands that I went forth to eradicate the threat."

"And you failed." Hades chuckled. "You got lucky with the python, Apollo. You should avoid attempts of grandeur without first seeking the aid of your betters."

"I failed because of the angeli," Apollo continued. "I saw the woman, but her male counterpart caught me unaware. I fought them, but was cast back through the gateway as the female angeli gouged forth slabs of earth to speed my exit. The pile of Superian soil still lies in Texas."

Apollo's face reddened, as Hades burst into laughter. "Wait, wait, wait," he said, waving his hands. "Go back to the part where you got tossed, because I have to say, I'm truly sorry I missed that."

"Bite me, Hades," Apollo snarled.

"Can we open another," Hades asked Zeus, "and ask them to do it again?"

"Hades," Zeus said with a growl.

"It's not personal," Hades said. "I'm just"—he shrugged—"looking for a little verification."

Poseidon rolled his eyes. "Are you finished?"

"For now," Hades conceded.

"You." Poseidon nailed Apollo with a sharp glare. "Your action was reckless. Begin again, and this time, share the details you risked Earth to obtain, or I'll send you to Tartarus myself."

Hades's hand shot over his head.

"By the gods, Hades." Zeus pinched the bridge of his nose. "What now?"

"I just want to go on record and say"—Hades smiled—"it would make me very happy if you were to kill him."

"Tartarus is not big enough to hold us both, uncle," Apollo replied. "The day I hand my coin to Charon and cross the river will be the day that Tartarus splits wide." He closed the distance until he stood facing Poseidon. "The woman is truly angelic. She is as beautiful as she is powerful, and she wields her elements as much by instinct as skill. The man, his speed and strength equal my own. I saw him wield no element, but his aggression is like that of Ares. As to Superi, I've told you all I know."

"We should have heeded Ares's advice," Poseidon said. "We should have killed them the moment the curse began to split them in half, as Ares urged us to do. They were weakened. Their minds were twisted. They were defenseless."

"It has taken them this long to crack the gateway," Zeus countered, "and it will take a millennium more before they can open it. Two angeli do not warrant our concern."

"You should not be so quick to dismiss the threat, "Poseidon said. "We don't know that's all that have been reborn. There could be hundreds, thousands. Zeus, something has to be done."

Zeus's countenance darkened. "If you fear them so much, you should have cast a stronger curse, brother."

"Do not lay this blame at my feet," Poseidon said, his chest inflating as he pulled back his powerful shoulders; his trident appeared in his hand. "I did not see you on the field of battle that day."

Zeus shrugged. "Such battles are beneath me. However, I enjoy watching a curse play out as much as the next god. There is a unique pleasure in it."

Slamming his trident into the ground, causing a storm to brew over the Atlantic, Poseidon said, "You pace before your golden image, drawing from it the residue of worship that remains; a sip, a taste, of the power you once drank in mighty gulps from idols much less grand, while your narcissism threatens what is left of us. We are immortal, Zeus. We cannot die, yet we have all but faded from existence. To ignore the threat from Superi is lunacy. Two we can fight. A thousand…" He shook his head. "We would lose."

"That is precisely my point," Zeus bellowed as thunder rattled the sky. Taking hold of his temper, he began again. "Two angeli are like a white-capped wave on the surface of an ocean. The wave rolls; it breaks over and then settles once again. Should we stir that ocean, a thousand tidal waves could crash down upon us, and what remains would be washed away. This gathering was a courtesy"—his chin jutted out—"and I had hoped my brothers would see the fallacy of inciting an unnecessary war."

Hades, wide-eyed, looked askance at Poseidon. "Truly, he has forgotten who we are."

Angered by Hades's flippant attitude, Zeus shouted, "I will not sanction an invasion of Superi, and to act against my word without a full forum of the Pantheon would have dire consequences."

Hades's head lowered until he glared at Zeus from beneath his brows. "If you say there is to be no war, then so be it." An ever-widening circle of grass began to burn. "But you take things too far, brother, when you turn threats upon me." Opening a pit to Tartarus, Hades said, "Later, pretty boy," and then dropped into it.

"Come, Apollo," Poseidon said. "Let us leave Zeus to his naïve notion of reality. There is no reasoning with one who is blind to logic."

"Heed my words, brother," Zeus said. "Do not kick this anthill, or the swarm will devour you."

Apollo leapt upon a beam of light chased the moisture in the air as Poseidon used it to return to the ocean. On a white-sanded beach, the two reconvened, as dolphins danced upon the waves to greet their god's return.

"They are beautiful creatures, Poseidon," Apollo praised.

"If only humans were as loyal," Poseidon replied, "our strength would be beyond measure."

"We cannot conjure strength through will or dream," Apollo said, "but power is what we need. Hades will not act against Zeus, will he?"

"No, he will not."

"What of the others? Perhaps we should summon them. If Zeus demands a forum, I say we call it and let the different Pantheons decide."

"I fear that without verification of an impending threat, their responses would be the same as that of Zeus, if you were lucky."

"You know that I am more than the god of the sun, Poseidon. I am a god of prophecy and I swear to you, uncle, either we invade Superi, or they will invade Earth."

With a sigh that pushed the waters away from the coastline, Poseidon asked, "Can you see which path leads to victory?"

Apollo's broad shoulders slumped. "I cannot."

"Then neither can we be sure which action to take, and Zeus cannot be faulted for wanting to avoid a fight that even you fear we cannot win."

"Of all the gods, you have as much reason to hate them as I do. They confused our worshipers. They defiled my temple."

"And they destroyed my city." Poseidon nodded. "I know, Apollo."

"Then how can you stand for Zeus's decree?"

"His threat of dire consequences was not an idle one," Poseidon said. "To invade Superi by force would be folly."

"Ugh," Apollo sneered, turning his back on the elder god. "If you will not fight, then I will take my cause to Ares."

Poseidon caught his arm. "And he will betray you to Zeus."

Apollo yanked his arm away. "Then I will go alone."

"Such arrogance." Poseidon smirked. "You get that from your father."

"It is not arrogance you see," Apollo replied. "It is desperation."

"There are five gateways that link Earth to Superi," Poseidon told him. "Opening any one of them will alert not only the Greek Pantheon, but every deity that is connected to the aether. Even if we cloak our location, we would have less than a day before we were hunted down, and those dire consequences would be heaped upon our heads like burning coals from the pit of Tartarus."

"Not if we come back with the proof we need to bring our concerns before the Pantheons," Apollo countered. "We could send scouts through each of the gateways."

"Who would we send?" Poseidon asked. "The demigods?" He laughed. "A human hero, perhaps?"

Apollo's visage changed as revelation struck. "No, Poseidon," he answered. "We send the Cyclopes."

II

I'd Rather be Fishing

Davad stood on the wooden pier with Triton, snapping out their cane poles to cast their fishing lines into the orange-tinted oceanus. His head overflowed with thoughts of his father. "I don't understand how two men can be so much the same and yet be so different."

Streaks of silver marked the temples of Triton's shoulder length, black hair granting an air of wisdom to the hard lines of his stoic face. "Men are not born," Triton told him. "They are shaped by circumstance." After re-baiting his hook, he cast again. "There comes a time in every man's life when a hard choice has to be made. That choice then defines him."

"I can see that, I guess," Davad said, rubbing his free hand over the ignis marks, thick slivers interlaced with shapes like cut diamonds in bold red and deep black, that traced through the tanned skin on his right arm. Triton's words chilled him.

"You guess?" Triton chuckled, his smile squinting his

onyx eyes. "When first we met in Catena Piscari, you were appalled by Jacob's actions, because you still viewed life as a boy. By the time you walked the gangplank and boarded my ship, your hard choice had been made. General Aquam bears the scars of it on his chest. That choice made you a man. It made you one of the Five. It made you a ruler of Pisces Stragulum.

"And you believe that Montilis's choice marked him a traitor?" Davad shook his head. "I don't see it, Triton. He was doing what any father should—what my father did. He was trying to save his daughter. How can a man be condemned for that?"

Triton cocked his head in Davad's direction. "I've wondered how long it would take before you were ready to finish our conversation." He set his cane pole aside, knelt by the edge of the pier, and cupped his left hand with his right. The aquis rose to meet it, until it cascaded over his dark-skinned palm and fingers like a child seeking its parents' touch. "General Aquam made a vow to the Regia Aquam Guard and to Palus Regia. The vows he freely spoke superseded all bonds of friendship or family. Every man and woman who ever served under his command was betrayed by his actions."

Davad shoved the end of his cane pole into a hole in one of the wooden planks and sat, turning sideways to face Triton. "And my father," he asked, "do you consider him a traitor for going after Shashara?"

"I like Shashara," Triton said. "The girl has grit."

"That doesn't answer my question," Davad replied.

"Do you believe in destiny? A fate that we cannot

change?"

"No." Davad scowled at the smile that wrinkled the old man's face and created lines that ran across his cheeks towards his double pointed ears. "I believe we forge our own destinies."

Though humored by Davad's intensity, Triton's visage took on a more serious cast. "Jacob's destiny, his quest, was to protect Tristan. In doing so he protected Superi. When Shashara was taken, your father lost sight of the bigger picture, and look at the result."

Slack jawed, Davad asked, "Are you saying he should have just left her in IA? He should have let her die?"

"To save the world?" Triton countered. "Yeah, boy, he should have let her die."

Davad trapped his bottom lip between his teeth and pressed down until the pink-tinted flesh turned white, as he fought back his anger in an attempt to understand. "My sister was not the only one rescued that day. If we hadn't gone into the tower for Shashara, Anliac would still be there. Malstar would have still transfused her. She would have still transcended, only she would have been alone and controlled by Calstar. The gateway would have still come open, and the god would have still come through. Superi would still be under the threat from the gods, only Tristan and Anliac would not be ready to challenge them. If I believed in destiny, or fate, I would say that perhaps my father fulfilled his, by giving his life, so that Anliac and Tristan could be brought together."

"And what of the General?" Triton asked. "What greater purpose did his betrayal serve?"

"And therein lies the difference between you and my father," Davad said. "We were told that Beth and Mathew gave their lives so that we could escape, so that we could live. My father gave his life so that Shashara could be saved. I could never fault Montilis for sacrificing everything to save his daughter." He pointed in the direction of the angeli-built dwellings where the others still slept within the white stone. "I would die for any one of them, because that's what you do for those you love."

"It is easy to give your life, Davad," Triton said. "The question is, can you sacrifice the life of one you love to save the lives of strangers?"

His breath faltered and he hesitated. "I don't know," Davad admitted.

"Well you'd better figure it out fast," Triton said, "because when the five of you gathered us all here, you gave oaths that supersede the bonds between you."

A bell tolled, and Davad's guard came rushing up.

"Sir," Nathin, a short, balding, rotund mortalis stood at attention in his silver-lined angeli uniform and waited for his charge to acknowledge him.

The suns were just beginning to rise. "It's too early for bad news, Nathin." Davad groaned as he stood, smoothing the seat of his brown trousers with calloused hands.

"I'm sorry, sir," Nathin said, "but we have riders approaching up the coast from the south."

"Are they wearing colors?" Triton asked, drying his hand on his pant leg.

"Yes, sir," Nathin said. "They're wearing the colors of the king. The scouts tell us they are all mortalis."

Davad's brows crawled up his forehead. "Well this should be interesting. Go and wake Set for me, would you?"

"Yes, sir," Nathin said. Stiffening, he asked, "Should I wake Tristan as well?"

"Anliac and Tristan share the same room now," Davad told him, "and Anliac is not a morning person. Better to let Set do it."

"Thank you, sir."

Davad and Triton chuckled at the relief on the guard's face as he took off to do Davad's bidding.

"Anliac has done better since their return from the Dura Mortis region," Triton said. "Why do you encourage fear?"

"Look around, Triton," Davad said. "People act differently when they know you can level a city. The gifts of homage paid have brought a level of wealth we never imagined. They bow down to Anliac and Tristan like they are gods themselves. Fear buys them a protection that strength of arms cannot. As long as the people fear what the angeli might do, the angeli have that much less on their consciences."

"You sound like Matthew." Triton laughed. "He was one of the best in our line of work, but his heart was never in it."

Davad fell silent as Triton's words settled. His father had said the same thing to him on many occasions, only he wasn't sure it was meant as a compliment.

"Just between us," Triton asked as Set approached, "who do you fear more?"

"Tristan," Davad replied without hesitation. "If any one were to try and use her, or worse, hurt her, there would be no reining Tristan in." He grimaced. "We see what the people do not," he said. "The violence, the deaths caused at their hands, it twists them up inside. Anliac has a harder shell than Tristan, because of the way she was raised, but Tristan's skin is thin. If Anliac is lost, Tristan will be as well. Besides…" His words trailed off as he shook his head.

Casting a sideways glance, Triton urged, "Besides, what?"

Davad sighed. "I think we've seen the extent of what Anliac can do, but Tristan"—he caught and held Triton's stare—"I think we've only scratched the surface of his power. Honestly, I'm a little scared of what he might be capable of."

Triton laid his hand on Davad's shoulder. "The five of you are too young to carry such a heavy burden."

"Hey." Davad grinned, though it did not reach his dark brown eyes. "I'm sixteen now," he said, "but it's still nice to know not everyone has forgotten that we are just a bunch of kids."

"Good morning, guys," Set said, walking up with a towel tossed over his shoulder and rubbing the sleep from his eyes. "I want to thank you both for the emotional overload that greeted my waking." Holding out a towel, he asked, "Which one of you needs this?"

Davad unfurled the fingers of his right hand as he reached for Set, igniting his fingertips in red and yellow flames. "That's okay." He grinned. "Just hold my hand until I feel better."

"Ha! No…" Set's grin bunched his cheeks, turning the blue teardrop marks on the left side of his face into waves that flowed. "Nathin tells me we have guests on their way."

"Yeah." Davad looked off towards the south. "Some of King Normis's men."

Shaking his head, Set said, "I don't know where the guy gets off calling himself a king. There are what, four, mortalis cities? What exactly is he supposed to be the king of?"

"We could start calling you King Set of Pisces Stragulum." Davad laughed. "Maybe then they would pay you homage like they do Anliac and Tristan."

"Uh, I think I'll pass," Set said. "What's already flowing into the treasury is embarrassing enough."

"There is no such thing as too much wealth." Triton scoffed. "Or too much power."

Davad and Set chuckled.

"Spoken like a true pirate," Set said. "Where is Tristan?"

"Still sleeping," Davad answered.

"Oh, absolutely not." Set turned away from the pier. "If the little brother has to be awake for this, then the big brother can drag his butt out of bed too."

As Set's voice trailed off, Davad asked, "Should we get back to fishing?"

Triton grinned, picking up his pole. "Absolutely."

***

Outside of the multileveled home made of white stone, two guards stood post in matching silver and black angeli uniforms. They held up their hands at Set's approach.

Micah, the nox assigned to Tristan, warned, "They're still asleep."

"And you know how Anliac is in the mornings," Lynette, Anliac's fulgo guard, pleaded. "We heard the bell, but are you sure you have to wake her?"

"Official business I'm afraid." Set grinned as he walked in. He stomped through the house and up the stairs, and then he pounded on their bedroom door.

"It's too early for so much freaking noise," he heard Anliac shout through the whitewashed wood.

"Ouch," Tristan grunted as a golden light swept beneath the doorway. "Stop pinching me. I'm up."

Set's lips pressed into thin lines as he suppressed his laughter. He didn't need to see the picture for the image to pop into his mind. The moans and groans that came with the two of them crawling out of bed was enough.

The door swung wide, and Anliac poked her head out. Glaring daggers with her golden eyes and wrapped in a blanket she'd pulled from the bed, she growled, "What do you want?"

"Sorry. I need my brother."

Tristan's head appeared over Anliac's shoulder. "Why?" he asked. "What's going on?"

"We've got riders coming," Set told him.

"Ugh," Anliac said as she disappeared further into the room. The bed frame squeaked.

Looking over his shoulder, Tristan asked, "What do you think you're doing?"

"What does it look like?" she snipped. "I'm going back to sleep."

"It looks like King Normis's men," Set said. "You should probably come too."

The house trembled.

"Or not." Set winced, backing away from the door with a

grin.

"You don't have to shout," she grumbled.

Large, taunt muscles played under Tristan's tight skin as he stepped into the hallway, tying his pants. With his shirt hung over his bare shoulder, he closed the door and chuckled. "You're a brave man to wake her."

"I wasn't shouting," Set told him.

"I know, little brother." Tristan's smile stretched from ear to ear. "Aren't heightened senses spectacular?"

Dubious, Set replied, "If you say so," as he followed Tristan downstairs.

The front room was sparsely furnished, leaving the spiraled circle of blue arcanite stone embedded in the floor to lay like a rug between the overstuffed couch and the rectangular table with maps spread atop it. A likeness of Tristan hung over the fireplace, and a bust of Anliac graced the mantle. As Set headed towards the door, he glanced at them and laughed.

"What's funny?" Tristan asked as he detoured through the dining room and into the kitchen.

"I thought you said those gifts from the mortalis village creeped you out." Set smirked.

"Huh?" He rolled his eyes. "Oh, you mean the likenesses of us. Yeah, well, we thought it would be rude not to display them."

"Of course," Set teased, "their display has nothing to do with your ever expanding ego."

Tristan shrugged off the jibe as tried to keep his golden eyes open to see his way to the counter. "It's still weird getting all of these gifts, but Anliac claims that to turn them away would be a great offense to our people."

"The greater offense," Set told him as he entered the dining room and took a seat at the table, "would be in making the King's men wait on your arrival. We really need to be going."

"I really need coffee," Tristan countered. "We were up all night talking."

"About what?" Set asked, shifting his chair towards the kitchen where he could see Tristan at the counter, filling the tin pot with water and grounds to put on to boil.

With a sheepish shrug, Tristan said, "About our feelings and…stuff."

"Gag me." Set rolled his eyes. "Between you and Davad, I'm the last man standing. Let us hope Normis's men bring a little trouble so that the two of you can redeem yourselves."

Glowing golden lines began to brighten beneath Tristan's pale white chest as his angeli markings revealed themselves. They spread over his arms and up his neck, wrapping around his torso from shoulders to waist to bathe the kitchen in a pale illumination.

Set leaned forward in his chair and laughed. "You can turn off the light show, brother. You don't scare me. I can drain your butt, remember? I might do it anyway," he teased. "I really want to find out if you're fast enough to run on water."

"I've told you," Tristan said, "I'll try it once the waves have calmed. The cold front blowing in has the oceanus choppy. I'd just trip, or sink, and I'm in no mood to be laughed at." Cursing under his breath, he said, "Where's Davad when I need him? This coffee is taking too long to boil."

Kicking his long legs out in front of him, Set asked, "And how does this make you feel?"

Sliding his brown linen shirt over his head, Tristan crossed his arms over his colossal chest and propped his hip against the counter. "We weren't talking about those kinds of feelings," he said. "We were talking about what we can physically feel. How we can hear all the way across town. I can hear more, but, you wouldn't believe the conversations we've overheard while lying in bed."

Set's face paled. "I hope you don't eavesdrop on me."

"Why?" Tristan teased. "Are you afraid that we over-heard your confession of love to Shashara the other night? Or the tears you both cried?"

"You son of goat herder."

"Hey! Watch it. We don't know for certain what my parents were. We've never met them. They just might have been sheep herders."

"Your parents were the same as mine. Way to take the sting out of good insult."

Tristan poured himself a cup of coffee and carried it with him to the table, then sat down. "This cold front, there's a"—he rotated his hand forward as he searched for the word—"pressure that moves before it. We can feel it in our bones, and when it rains, the pressure eases off." He took a sip and sighed as the caffeine rushed into his system. "Did you know that emotions, when they're strong enough, put off a scent?"

"Yeah, actually," Set said. "Fear smells like citrus. Hate smells like burning pitch."

"Exactly," Tristan said. "When I tried to tell Lan, he

laughed at me. Anyway"—he shook his head—"what do the riders want?"

"I've no idea. All I know is Davad sent Nathin to wake me up at the butt crack of dawn to tell me that the mortalis, self-proclaimed king, has sent an envoy to us. I don't even know how many there are." He paused. "What are you doing?" he asked when he noticed Tristan closing his eyes so tight that lines appeared in the corners.

"There are six horses," Tristan told him. "Two are carrying a heavier weight than the others, and one is carrying a woman"—his eyes came open—"or a very small man."

"Perhaps the king has come after all," Set said, as both of them laughed. "We really need to go, Tristan."

"Fine," Tristan grumbled, standing from his chair, "but try this." He darted to the kitchen, unfolded an animal skin, and picked up a handful of dried meat. Handing a long strip to Set, he said, "Lan brought it with him last night. He said it's made from some kind of small, flightless bird that lives in Dura Mortis."

Set tore off a piece as they moved through the front room. "It's delicious."

"I know, right?" Tristan said, gnawing on a piece himself. At the front door, he greeted the guards. "Morning, Micah."

"Good morning, sir." Micah nodded.

"Lynette," Tristan said, "Anliac is going to sleep in. Keep her safe for me."

"That's my job, boss." Lynette smiled.

As Tristan and Set made their way to the pier, Tristan asked, "Where's your guard, brother? You're not supposed to be alone."

Set rolled his shoulders. "I don't need a babysitter. I'm stronger than Davad and Shashara and not as important as you and Anliac, so…" He shrugged.

Eyes narrowing, Tristan said, "I don't like it."

"You don't have to," Set said, "but it's also not your call. It's mine."

Triton was gone by the time the brothers reached the pier where Davad and Nathin were waiting.

"Did you know that Tristan can hear conversations taking place on the other side of town?" Set blabbed to Davad.

"Seriously?" Davad questioned. "Talk about an invasion of privacy."

Wordlessly, and with a nervous swallow, Nathin nodded his agreement.

"If we're spilling secrets," Tristan retorted, "I overheard Set pouring out words of love and devotion to your sister a few nights ago. It was gag worthy." Tristan wiggled his eyebrows for Set's benefit.

The three men looked at Set and laughed.

"I caught Davad making out with Shorlynn last night," Set blurted.

"Hey!" Davad barked, half strangled. "I'm not the one revealing secrets here."

"Yeah, well, that's what you get for laughing at me."

"Shorlynn?" Tristan asked. "Really?"

Davad blushed. "Fulgo or not, don't act like she isn't one of the hottest females on Superi, and man can she kiss."

"Skylar is going to kill you." Tristan chuckled. "You know that, right?"

"What?" Davad asked, perplexed. "Why would she?"

Set laughed. "Are you really that dense?" At Davad's blank stare, he added, "They're a thing."

"No…" Davad gasped. His eyes grew round as he searched the dock for the feisty redhead, hoping she hadn't overheard.

The others threw their hands up in surrender.

"Would you take a look at that," Nathin said as six riders approached the docks. "Those are some big men."

To the right of a brown-haired youth sat a blond mortalis with grey eyes and the markings of an aer wielder. On his left was a blue-eyed man with a nasty scar that ran diagonally across his face from hairline to jaw. The three men who rode at the rear were drenched in weapons. Though their appearances varied, they looked battle worthy and hard as nails. The men kept a close watch on the fera guards in angeli uniforms and on the handful of pirates, who were acting as a security escort for Pisces Stragulum.

"You were right," Set said. "They have a nanus."

"A what?" Davad asked.

Tristan leaned in to whisper, "A little person. You know, someone who stopped growing before they should have."

Davad slugged Tristan on his shoulder. "It's a kid, not a freaking…What did you call it?"

"A nanus." Tristan grinned.

From his perch atop his mount, the slender youth sniffed as he lifted his chin with an arrogance that exuded from him. "Do you greet all dignitaries with this same level of insult?" he asked. Leaning forward in the saddle, he snarled, "I can hear you."

"Sorry about that," Tristan said, pulling on his double-pointed ear with his fingers.

"I am Sir Jorden Terra, son of Nathen Terra, of the High House of Terra. I have been sent to speak to the angeli. I demand an audience."

Tristan turned his head towards Set. "Is everyone from a mortalis city so formal?"

"Beats me," Set said. Cocking his head as he studied the boy, Set asked, "Do you think they act like this all the time, or, is it something they do only during their travels?"

"Do you think he could have crammed the word terra one more time into his introduction?" Davad chuckled, causing the others to laugh, including a number of Jorden's own contingents.

With a stiff spine, Jorden said, "I am about business far beyond the comprehension of you simple peasants. See to your duty. Summon the angeli." He kicked his leg over the side of his mount and slid to the ground. "And one of you see to the horses."

The five riders dropped to their feet, handing over their reins to a fera guard, before closing rank around their charge.

Tristan breathed deep as his shoulders hunched. His long, wavy black hair hid his pale white face, until he expelled his breath and unfurled. As his head rose, his arms spread wide, and Jorden found himself illuminated by the pulsating marks of an angeli. Tristan's bulging muscles swelled as his golden eyes flared.

Jorden backed away and would have fallen had it not been for the man at his back.

"The first rule of diplomacy, Terra, son of Terra, of the

High House of Terra," Tristan said, stepping forward, "is to know who it is you're speaking to before you let lose your arrogant demands. I," his voiced boomed—it rumbled, vibrating through the men's chests, causing their hearts to race—"am the angeli, and I would suggest you adjust your tone."

The five men who'd accompanied Jorden cast furtive glances at the angeli, and then at the guards of Pisces Stragulum, and knew the futility of putting up a fight. A collective sigh escaped them when Tristan's marks faded.

Jorden's mouth opened and closed as fear stole his words and scattered his thoughts.

"Where is Davimon?" Tristan asked the man standing to Jorden's right. "Should he not have forewarned us that Sir Jorden intended to grace us with his presence?"

"My apologies," Davimon said, as he and Lishous pushed their way through the crowd of men now gathered at Tristan's back. "I wasn't privy to Sir Jorden's plans."

III

Come and See

Lan breathed in the salty morning air through his beak. It helped burn away the fog of sleep in his mind. He tilted his bird like head to catch the conversation taking place at the other end of the dock. Surveying the newcomers through beady black eyes, he stopped beside Tristan. "Who's the kid?" he asked, adjusting the heavy silver chain, bearing the V symbol of the angeli, around his thick, white-feathered neck.

"The son of a High House in Regia Aquam," Davimon answered. "What brings you here, Sir Jorden?"

"I was sent to discuss terms with the angeli," Jorden replied.

Davimon's brow quirked. "That's my job."

Squaring his shoulders, Jorden told him, "You speak for the King. I speak for the Houses of Terra and Magnus."

"Is that so?" Davimon crossed his arms. "Without the authority of our King, your actions could be seen as treason, boy."

Shaken, Jorden pushed through. "I don't answer to you, sir, nor am I here to speak with you." He turned towards Tristan. "I am here for you."

"Well," Davad asked, handing Set the pole Triton had left behind, "since this is apparently an angeli problem and not a town problem, do you want to do some fishing?"

"Why yes, good sir." Set grinned. "I do believe I would."

"You guys suck," Tristan quipped as his family deserted him to deal with the stranger alone. "Hey," he said to Davimon and Lishous, "where are you two going?"

Davimon nailed Jorden with a cold stare. "To inform the King." He spun on his heels and headed back into town with Lishous at his side.

"Lan, put these men to work," Tristan said, waving towards those who'd come with Jorden.

"We are to stay with Sir Jorden," one of them objected.

"If you intend to eat today," Tristan told him, "you will work."

"Then we will go hungry," the man said, "but Sir Jorden will not be left alone in hostile territory."

"Do as he says," Jorden ordered.

"Sir?"

"Look around, Thomas," Jorden told the guard. "One of you, or all of you, if the angeli wanted to do me harm, there wouldn't be anything you could do about it." He asked Tristan, "Is there somewhere private we could speak?"

"Your arrival pulled me from my bed," Tristan told him, "and I'm starving. Walk with me."

Jorden swung his head back and forth as Tristan led him

from the docks and through the new marketplace. The bustle of activity made the town hum. "I learned of this place in my studies," Jorden said. "The abandoned city of ancient Superians. It's impressive what you've managed to do here in such a short time."

"Desperation is a great motivator," Tristan replied. "Housing was a problem, so we repaired the ones we could and built others. We had men who were injured and women and children with us." He pointed to Shashara's infirmary as they passed. "The dock, the storage buildings, the fields planted, the forge made, it was about need," he said. "These people, they've placed their trust in us. They've chosen to stand with us against the challenges Superi will soon face, and in doing so, they've become our responsibility."

Tristan stopped outside of a long, rectangular, wood framed building, where smoke puffed from several tin pipes in its roof. "This," he said, "is my favorite addition to Pisces Stragulum."

"What is it?" Jorden asked. Realizing what he'd said, he added, "If I may ask without offending."

Tristan opened the door. The scent of freshly baked bread rolled over them as Tristan grinned. "The mess hall."

Rows of long tables filled the floor space, occupied by people eating their breakfast before starting their days. Jorden paused inside the door, causing Tristan to turn back for him.

"What's wrong?" Tristan asked.

"In Regia Aquam," Jorden answered, "we recognize the need to deal with the nox and the fulgo, but outside of politics, we do not associate with them." His nose wrinkled.

"The fera are beneath us. We do not associate with them at all, much less share a meal."

"You will today," Tristan said. "Trust me, Sir Jorden, you don't want to talk to me on an empty stomach, especially if you're going to say things like that."

Jorden, his brows furrowing, followed.

Stopping to shake a few hands and pass out words of greeting, Tristan made his way to the back of the mess hall. "Grab a plate," he said, piling scrambled eggs and grilled meat onto his own, along with a huge piece of flat bread. "Thank you." He nodded to the fulgo, who handed him a glass of milk at the end of the line.

"I'm not hungry," Jorden said. "The peasants in here have cost me my appetite."

Hands full, Tristan's eyes flared. "Say that word again"— Tristan scowled—"and our time together will be at an end. I will personally throw you out of this building and send you on your way."

The mess hall fell quiet, as the people watched for orders from their leader. They didn't relax until Tristan turned from the food line and found an empty seat at a central table, where he sat down.

After glancing at the people sitting close, Jorden sat as well and then lowered his voice to say, "I've offended you but I'm unclear as to how, and I thought we were going somewhere we could speak in private."

"Your prejudices offend me," Tristan told him. "Such ignorant views are not tolerated here. If you have something to say, Jorden, say it."

"Surely you recognize the need to keep private matters of

rule. Knowledge can be dangerous, especially when one cannot differentiate between friend and foe. Anyone here could betray you."

Tristan swallowed the bite of egg in his mouth, chased it down with a drink, and then replied, "Matters of the heart, matters of family and friends, these are the things we speak of behind closed doors, but what you have come to discuss are matters of politics. Such things affect all of these people, and therefore they have a right to hear it. Be glad I do not call a gathering and force you to speak your mind before us all or go home unsatisfied."

Flustered, Jorden said, "That is just not the way things are done."

Tristan chuckled. "Men who fear the light and seek the shadows to whisper their words are either lying or about to lie. Behind closed doors, underhanded deals are made as those in power deceive and manipulate to gain favor...political or otherwise. Like prejudices," he added, "such things are not tolerated here."

"I'm afraid my training has left me ill equipped as to how to handle views such as those shared among the people of Pisces Stragulum," Jorden said, "but truly, I have no secrets to hide. It is the desire of the two Houses that I represent that you return with me to Regia Aquam."

"For what purpose?"

"They are interested in learning of your intent for Superi. Which cities will you take? Who are your allies? Who are your foes? Rumor says that you were born mortalis. Do you intend to over throw King Normis?"

Tristan choked on a piece of bacon. "Which cities will I

take?"

"These are valid questions. Strategically speaking, the taking of Pisces Stragulum was a good move. The city has been abandoned for generations, and therefore there was no one to dispute your claim, but unless you are immune to the chemical hazards of Rus Elisium, the next city you take will be occupied."

Men to either side of them chortled at the flabbergasted expression on Tristan's face.

"Are you serious?" Tristan asked.

Jorden shrugged. "Don't feel bad," he said. "They say that the alchemists that destroyed Rus Elisium mixed all manner of chemicals with the arcanite that set off the explosion. It doesn't devalue your position that you cannot take the city."

"In my opinion," Tristan said, "every scrap of spelled arcanite should be gathered and destroyed."

Jorden laughed. "Spelled? There's no such thing as magic." His grin broadened. "You cannot spell items, or enchant them. Such stories are for children."

He himself hated the patronization of being called a child, so he let the obvious joke slip past to ask instead, "If it is not spelled, then how does arcanite block abilities?

"It's simple," Jorden said. "Our abilities are a chemical reaction. Once the arcanite has been coated in an acidic epotose and placed on one with an ability, it neutralizes the chemicals we secrete. Arcanite placed on one without abilities would feel no adverse effect."

Nodding, Tristan said, "That information is of value to us. Thank you."

Jorden beamed. "You are most welcome," he said. "Now that we have established a friendship of sorts, will you answer my questions?"

"Ha." Tristan grinned. "My first inclination is to mess with your head and tell you I plan on taking over the planet, but I'm afraid you would take me seriously. We came to Pisces Stragulum because we had nowhere else to go. We have no militaristic or political agenda. Our only intent is to ensure that Superi survives the impending invasion of the earthling gods."

"Excuse me," Jorden asked. "Earthling?"

Tristan paused with a strip of bacon poised in front of his open mouth. "That's the problem, Jorden," he said. "There is too much that people don't know. Kings, rulers, lawyers, they are making decisions without the benefit of fact."

"So then share the facts with me."

Tristan sucked the grease off his fingers as he tossed the meat back onto the plate. "Do you know about what happened in Bealson's Grove a few months ago?"

Jorden nodded. "Yes. A gateway opened and a great monster was fought. The Imbellis Asylum suffered the loss of its infamous alchemist and many of its guards. They say that you saved Superi."

"It wasn't a monster. It was a god, and I did my part, but Anliac was the one who cast Apollo back through the gate."

"I'm sorry, who?" Jorden interrupted. "Apal..."

"A-pol-lo," Tristan corrected. "That is what he called himself before he attacked us. He claimed to be a god from Earth, as well as the god that beat us the last time—Superians, that is."

"By beating us, you're referring to the twin curses? You lay claim to having bested the one responsible for fracturing our bloodline and enfeebling our minds?"

"I told you, Anliac is the one who did most of the work, and no, I'm not saying he's the god who cast the curses. I'm saying he was one of the gods that chased us from Earth back to Superi in Nathon Bealson's day." He skewed his brows. "Tell me you at least know the history."

"The journeys of Nathon Bealson are a required study in Regia Aquam for those belonging to a High House, but the novel idea of monstrous gods ruling over the single-sunned planet is intriguing."

Tristan laughed. "You think I'm making this up?"

"I do not believe in gods," Jorden replied, "but I do believe in monsters."

Having finished his meal, Tristan said, "Come," with a shake of his head. "Let me show you what a world without prejudice looks like. See for yourself the power that coalesces when a people come together for survival without thought of personal gain. Let me show you what Superi needs if it is to defeat the monsters."

Across the marketplace, Shashara stepped out in front of the infirmary. "Tristan," she shouted, "if you see Swiney, tell him I need him please? We've a little girl with a fever, and the yarrow isn't bringing it down."

"Will do," Tristan shouted back.

"She's one of the Five," Jorden said in shock. "You would risk exposing her to illness?"

"Some battles are fought with abilities," Tristan said, "while others are fought with the mind. Shashara battles illness to protect the people. Her fight is an honorable one."

Jorden was forced into a jog as Tristan sprinted forward to help a dark-skinned nox woman with red, swirling ignis markings as she struggled to load a barrel into the back of a wagon cart.

"Ugh," the woman groaned as the weight was taken from her. "Thank you," she said, pushing her hair away from her face.

"Is this headed for storage?" Tristan asked.

"Yeah," she replied. Smiling, she added, "The crop is coming in nicely for having been planted so late, and the stores are filling up."

"That is good news indeed. I'm showing our friend Jorden around. He and I can take this out for you if you'd like."

"That would be great. Welcome to Pisces Stragulum, Jorden," she said, turning toward the forge where her ignis ability could be put to use.

Taking up the lead rope, Tristan urged the horse forward.

Falling in at his side, Jorden said, "One in your position is above manual labor. It seems your time would be better spent on matters of greater importance."

"We all have our roles to play," Tristan told him, "but none of us are of greater, or lesser, importance than any-one else. Without gatherers, what would we eat when the fields die, and the animals hide, and food grows scarce over the cold season? Without builders, how would we shelter ourselves? If left to freeze and starve, how long before our fighters' strength failed them? How long before the people start to die, and if that happens, what people will those who lead have to rule? We are all connected, Jorden, despite race or station."

The two came to the two large storage buildings, with the crop situated between them, on the outskirts of Pisces Stragulum. Jorden said, "Surely not all of these people agreed with you when first they came here." He looked around at the races working side by side. "How did you get them to set aside their differences?"

A large fera bounded up to take the wagon. He was covered in thick, brown fur and his black eyes gleamed. "Thank you, Tristan," he said. "Have you come to see the progress?"

"I have," Tristan replied, "and from the look of things, your men are doing a fine job. Do you need anything while I'm here?"

"No, sir. All is well in hand."

"Have you seen Swiney by chance?"

"Yes, sir." The fera pointed a clawed finger to the larger of the two barns. "He's sorting through our last shipment of supplies from Imbellis. He was grumbling something about the quality of herbs and whose head was going to roll for it." He chuckled.

"Will you let him know that Shashara is looking for him?"

"Will do,"

"Thanks." To Jorden, Tristan said, "We should be heading back."

They made it halfway before Jorden, pointing to the roof of one of the older stone houses, asked, "Is that my men?"

Shielding his eyes from the suns, Tristan looked and smiled. "Well would you look at that? Mortalis from Regia Aquam working hand in hand with feras." He slapped Jorden on the back. "There may be hope for Superi yet."

"I don't understand," Jorden said as his shoulders slumped. "I know those men. This morning they wouldn't have fought beside a fera if their lives had hung in the balance, and now they're working with them? That is not hope. That is an ambition born of the need to survive in hostile territory."

Chuckling, Tristan said, "Either you do not know your men as well as you think you do, or their actions reflect the will of their leaders; which in not necessarily their own. Given a choice, people, as a whole, seek peace. War is what is forced on them."

Drawing close to the dock, Jorden caught Tristan's arm, urging him to stop. "I would very much like to introduce you to the Houses of Terra and Magnum, but if our invitation is rejected, I would have you know the report I intend to deliver."

Tristan nodded, spreading his stance and clasping his hands in front of himself. "And I would very much like to know it."

"I will tell them that the angeli do not live above their subjects, but live among them, as one of them. I will tell them that the people of Pisces Stragulum are not a gathering of citizens, but that of an ever-growing family. Of utmost importance, I will tell them that the angeli perceive ambition as hope, and then they will know your greatest weakness." He held out his hand and said, "It is also what will make you a great king."

"You still think I intend to take over the world."

Tristan grinned, bypassing Jorden's hand to clasp forearms as friends would.

"No," Jorden said, starting forward towards the dock. "I believe that what you are doing here will spread, and as it does, Superi will fall at your feet."

Tristan threw back his head and laughed.

"Pay up, Triton," Davad said, seeing Tristan and Jorden's return.

Triton cursed under his breath, pulled a silver coin from his jeans, and slapped it into Davad's open palm.

"I told you Tristan didn't have it in him to toss the nanus out of town."

"Nah," Set told them, "something must have happened. The guy's different."

"I hear discrimination is frowned upon in Pisces Stragulum," Jorden said. "Is there an exception concerning the vertically challenged?"

Speechless, they stared back him, until Set grinned. "He thinks he's being funny…." He burst out laughing.

Tristan did too.

"Sir Jorden," Davad said with a chuckle, "you have a gambler's face. How about you and I find a game of cards before you leave?"

Delighted at being included, Jorden agreed. "It will have to be tonight. It is my hope"—the corners of his mouth twitched—"that Tristan will be leaving with me come morning."

"Absolutely not." Triton growled. "Tristan, you are not going off on your own."

"Right now your place is here," Davad said. "Pisces

Stragulum needs to see their leader, and you just got back."

Jorden perked up. "From where, if I might ask?"

Set smirked. "I see not all of your old ways can be changed in a morning. That is not your business. Brother"—he stepped in front of Tristan—"what are you thinking? Anliac would throw a fit. I'm sorry." He threw up his hands when Tristan opened his mouth to snap at him. "But it's true. Your daily lessons have been good for you both, but I think she's a long way off from being okay without you, and the both of you cannot leave again. Not to mention that you've taken over the training of the Angeli Guard. There is nothing more important than insuring that Pisces Stragulum is ready to face the threat of the gods."

"I agree," Tristan said. "That's why the two of you will be going in my place."

"What?" Davad squawked.

"Wait," Set said, backing away.

They looked at each other and then said at the same time, "We never agreed to that."

Jorden sighed. "There will be many who are disappointed, none more than I, but I do understand. If you say they speak for the angeli, then the Houses would find the arrangement agreeable."

"How did this happen?" Davad demanded.

"What are we supposed to say to them," Set asked, "and what are we going to do when King Normis finds about it?"

"I'm sure the King's questions will be close to those of the two Houses," Tristan said. "They want to know which cities we intend to conquer and who we intend to kill, and..."

"Uh," Set choked out. "Say again?"

It was Jorden's turn to laugh. "I think that joke was meant for me," he said.

"Yeah." Tristan nudged his shoulder into Jorden's. "But their faces were priceless."

"Oh." Jorden's eyes went round as Anliac joined them. As if drawn forward by an invisible force, he found his right hand rising. "How beautiful…"

Mesmerized, Jorden drank in the lean, feminine muscle caressed by the butter-soft breeches she wore. The sleeveless white blouse, cinched at her tiny waist with a tan rope, revealed rich, golden markings that flowed down the sides of her graceful neck and over smooth shoulders to pour down slender arms like a lover's touch. He licked his lips as if he could see what lay hidden beneath her attire, and his fingertips connected to the warm flesh of a transcended angeli.

Towering over the stranger by a good two feet, she peered over his head to Tristan and asked, "Why is this boy touching me?"

Jorden jerked. "I beg your pardon," he pleaded, bowing, as he backed away. "I don't know what came over me. Your beauty astounds and steals wit, beguiling a simple man to lose his senses."

"You flatter…" Anliac said with a smile.

"Sir Jorden Terra, of the House of Terra"—he bowed with his introduction—"from Regia Aquam."

"It is a pleasure to make your acquaintance, Sir Jorden," Anliac replied. "I am Anliac Aquam of the House of Angeli."

"Hey." Tristan took her hand and tugged her to his side.

"You're not allowed to swoon over words spoken by another guy."

"Then you'd better up your game." She grinned, leaning sideways to kiss his cheek.

"I'm glad you finally decided to drag your bottom out of bed," Davad grumbled. "Tristan's trying to ship me off to Regia Aquam."

"The Houses of Terra and Magnum have requested to see me, but," he told her just as her glare began to heat up, "I've been told I'm much too important to leave." He traced the side of her cheek with the backs of his fingers. "So I thought to send Davad."

"We should send Set with him," she said. "We are stronger in pairs, and having an empath to guide him will help Davad navigate the waters of unfamiliar territory."

"Crap," Set groaned.

Triton snorted. "Chumps," he said. "The angeli had you outmaneuvered before the game even started. Pack your bags, boys. You're going to see the King."

"Where are you going?" Shashara asked, wiping away tears from her big blue eyes with the sleeve of her blouse.

"Shashara." Set rushed to her, opened his arms, and pulled her close. "What's wrong?"

Her long, wavy chestnut hair was full of snarls and tangles. The sides of her soft brown tunic were wrinkled where she'd wrung the material in worried hands, and dirt stains marked where she'd been on her knees. Her eyes, swollen from an outpouring of tears, pierced their hearts as all but Jorden moved close.

She hiccupped as she swiped at her wet cheeks. "Swiney

said that the sickness formed a cyst on her..." She sniffled. "on her lung. When it burst, her lung collapsed..." She fell against Set's chest and sobbed. "I tried to help her."

"Your distress is for one of your subjects," Jorden said in awe. "You are the healer we saw in town."

Shashara looked up, devastated. "I am no healer." She turned and ignited her hands. "What does an ignis wielder know of healing?"

Dressed in blue with red stripes decorating his uniform, Davimon approached the group. The silver and yellow, four- and five-pointed stars that marked the left side of his face appeared to glow, as the pupil of his left eye pulsed with one vision while his other, as brown as his hair, saw the situation unfolding upon the docks.

Lishous, his companion and guard, stayed close. The fera's size daunted those who watched their approach, even as his beauty astounded them. His white fur was like snow, and he was the mountain it covered. His eyes, a startling blue, missed nothing.

"A true healer's ability," Davimon answered, having caught Shashara's question, "comes from their compassion, and you, dear lady, have it in abundance."

Shashara gave a pathetic smile, turned in Set's embrace, and leaned her back against him. She took his hands and made him wrap his arms around her waist. "Okay, Tristan." She sighed. "Where are you and Anliac sending my Set off too?"

"Regia Aquam," Tristan said, casting a glance at Davimon.

"Davad," she said, "you'll be going with him?"

"Apparently," he snipped.

"As will I," Davimon said. "The King eagerly awaits our arrival."

Anliac, head tilted, witnessed the silent, tense exchange between the Regia Aquam representatives. "Please tell your king," she said, "that the angeli find promise in young Sir Jorden Terra and would be most displeased if he were treated harshly for visiting us in Pisces Stragulum."

"I've no interest in political word play," Shashara said, "not right now." Pulling Set with her, she turned towards town. "If you are leaving tomorrow, then what is left of today belongs to me."

IV

Not Alone in Here

Shorlynn, her arms pumping in furious outrage, stormed towards the docks, her long legs eating up the distance as a grinning Skylar followed behind.

Set's eyes locked on the two beautiful fulgo women. He freed his hand from Shashara's grasp when they marched past him, and he turned back to follow them.

"What are you looking at?" Shorlynn sneered, bypassing the gawking, brown-haired boy to confront the others. "I am sick and tired of you five failing to keep me abreast of what's going on. Do you hear me? King Normis sends men to Pisces Stragulum and I'm kept out of the loop? That is unacceptable. Am I not the fulgo representative?"

"You tell them, babe." The red-haired fulgo laid her pale-skinned hand on top of Shorlynn's shoulder only to have it shrugged off.

Davad, seeing the territorial touch from Skylar, blanched, much to Tristan's amusement.

Leaning towards Triton, Lan said, "I thought the redhead

was the feisty one."

Triton grunted. "I guess you were never told, fera. Despite race, all women have claws."

"Shut up, Triton," Shorlynn snapped, "and one of you tell me what's going on."

"They waste time babbling back and forth about what should be done concerning Regia Aquam," Set said, his upper lip furling, "instead of acting against the mortalis king who dares to send a boy to Pisces Stragulum. They turn my stomach."

"Whoa." Anliac's stare hardened. "Excuse me? I make your stomach turn?"

"Oh…no." Shashara stepped between Anliac and Set. "He's not talking about you."

"Pfft, of course I am," Set retorted, waving a hand at Anliac. "She's as pathetic as the rest of the children playing at being rulers here. They are so blinded by their self-righteous morality that they cannot see the bigger picture."

The gathering of people fell silent, stunned by the unexpected outburst.

Tristan was the first to find his voice. "Hey," he asked, taking a step closer to his brother, "what is wrong with you?"

"What's wrong?" Set scoffed. "What's wrong? You muscle-bound, dimwitted oaf. We three are capable of snaring the entire world with our power. We can bring the rulers of Superi to their knees, and yet you stand here like a bunch of lawyers negotiating with these insects from Regia Aquam."

"Now hold on," Davimon started. "I mean no disrespect to any member of the Five, but you are on the verge of crossing a line."

Taking purposeful strides towards the mortalis representative, Set was stopped by Davad's hand against his chest. His words flowed nonetheless. "I say we open a portal to your city. I say we lay waste to it and then we demand your king's allegiance instead of asking for it. That is, of course, if I allow him to live."

Jorden trembled. "I don't understand," he said, wishing for the first time since his arrival that he'd not been separated from his guards.

Davimon's hand went for his sword, as Lishous, standing at his side, bared his claws and gave a warning growl.

Davad shoved Set back. "Are you trying to destroy everything we're doing here?"

"With Regia Aquam subdued, we'll have one less city to worry about," Set replied without hesitation.

Triton hooked his thumbs through the loops at the waist of his pants. "You have a point, boy," he said, "but it seems a bit drastic, don't you think?"

"Triton," Tristan grunted, "don't speak."

Tears welling, Shashara said, "Something is wrong."

"She's right," Tristan said. "Set, you don't sound like yourself. What's going on, little brother?"

Set's face contorted. "My little brother is dead!"

"What are you talking about?" Anliac said. "You don't have a little brother. You're not making any sense."

"I can't read your thoughts," Set said to the stunned group, "but your emotions read like writing on a scroll and they mirror my own. We loathe politics, so why try and play at it? And why are we standing on a dock? The view of the grove from my office would serve as a reminder of why we are here. I have all the maps and intelligence reports we'll need to come up with a strategic plan to bring each major city on Superi to heel. The towns and villages will naturally follow."

"Um, Set," Tristan said, "your office doesn't overlook a grove."

Shashara stepped in close and cupped Set's face in her palms. "You may not remember it right now," she told him, "but I made you a promise. I swore I wouldn't let you lose yourself. So… I'm so sorry." She reared back her hand and slapped him hard.

"Shashara!" Tristan shouted.

"Calstar!" she cried. "Get out of his head!" She slammed her balled fists against Set's chest. "Get out!"

Davad caught her around her waist and hauled her back.

Set shook his head, blinking rapidly, as he began backing away. "I, uh…" His wide-eyed gaze swept across all of those staring back at him. "I need some air." A collective gasp erupted from those gathered when he slammed his palms together and a portal opened behind him. Two guards to the left and right of the portal collapsed, but he was beyond noticing as each backward step carried him closer to his exit.

Tristan reached for him. "Whoa, little brother," he said, glancing beyond him through the opening of the portal where dawn had yet to break.

Set panicked. "Don't touch me," he said, "not right now. I might do something we'll both regret."

"Where are you going?" Tristan asked.

"Home." One more backward step and he was through.

V

Home Again?

Day returned to night as he stepped through the portal on the other side of Superi, on the outside of the northern wall of Exterius Antro. A dense fog hid the men walking the turret of the V-shaped wall, as well as those guarding the two gates. His skin felt afire and his blood boiled. The distance of the jump had been too great. He should not have been able to do it. The realization of how close he'd come to killing himself shook him to his core.

His stomach churned. His heart raced, and he found himself dropping to a dew-dampened ground and leaning against the trunk of one of the great trees of Turris as he struggled to find his animus hidden within that of Calstar's. His psyche was in shambles and threatened to shatter.

He heard the guards before he saw them walk up.

"I'm telling you, I saw a purple flash over here," a man said.

"The fog is heavy," another replied. "Perhaps what you

saw was one of the moons reflecting off of it. There are at least four purple ones out tonight."

"No," the first man objected. "It crackled."

Set stood still and waited for them to find him.

"Halt!" a third guard, a woman, shouted when she spotted him.

He shoved his hands into his front pockets. "I'm not moving."

"Where did you come from?" a guard asked.

"I live here," Set replied. "I was locked out."

It was the truth. Exterius Antro would always be his home, but since the night of Shashara's capture he'd been separated from it.

"Why are you sitting out here in the dark instead of announcing yourself at the gate?" the woman asked.

"I didn't want to cause trouble," Set told her. "I was going to wait until the gates were opened."

Misunderstanding, a male guard chortled. "I remember what it was like hiding my adventures from my parents at your age. Come on kid," he said. "Let's get you inside."

"Thanks." Set forced a smile as he walked with the three guards towards the postern gate.

The mortalis woman with blonde hair looked at him askance as he walked through. "You don't look as though you've spent half the night outside. Your clothes aren't even damp."

"It's true," one of the mortalis men said. "You're as dry as my wife's chicken."

"Ha!" the third guard, a feline fera, bursted. "Collibus Dolor isn't that dry."

"Watch it," the mortalis man retorted.

"You brought it up," the fera said. "Hey Scarlet," he asked, "do you remember the last time we were invited to dinner?"

Scarlet chuckled. "I remember."

"That chicken was so dry the slop pig wouldn't touch it." The guard snickered.

The other man threw a punch.

Scarlet ushered Set along as a brawl ensued.

"Are you just going to let them fight?" Set asked her.

Scarlet sighed. "It's like this all the time with those two. They are the best of friends with matching tempers." Reaching the inner wall, she said, "The main gates won't be opened until dawn, but you can enter here." She opened the door the guards used. "Make sure you're in the city before nightfall from now on. Okay?"

"Yes, ma'am. Thank you."

"No problem." As she turned away from him, he heard her shout, "Alright you two... knock it off," as the door was closed.

Memory washed over Set. The weight of it rooted him in place. The last time he'd gone through the wall, Jacob had still been alive. Life had changed so much since then. From where he stood, he couldn't see the oceanus, but he remembered watching as Anliac had pulled a wave of aquis from it. He remembered the rushing sound it had made as it flowed against gravity, up and over the wall, to wash down on their enemies waiting for them on the other side.

The city lay quiet as Set traversed the cobblestone streets. The only emotions bombarding him were produced by the dreams of those who yet slumbered and those conjured from within himself. He'd come here looking for peace, but every which way his head turned, memories threatened to steal it from him.

He thought of Clave's forge as he walked, and of the life Davad had wanted. Instead of becoming a blacksmith, he'd become the magistrate of Pisces Stragulum. Further on, he thought of Trennorson's inn in the middle of town. He'd been such a stupid kid. His infantile behavior had gotten Tristan hurt, had gotten them fired, had sent the guards chasing them through the streets. All so he could play with Tristan's abilities and impress a girl. Now, Shashara was the only girl he cared about, and Tristan was an angeli responsible for protecting the whole freaking planet.

With a heavy heart, he continued on. His feet carried him without conscious thought to the familiar street where his old home was waiting. Reaching it, he wiggled the metal door lever and was crushed with despair when it would not turn. Leaning his forehead against the whitewashed door, he felt a presence inside the house, but before he could decipher the intruder's intent, a voice came from behind him.

"It's against the law to break into someone's house."

Set recognized the boorish-featured city guard leaning against a lantern post across the street. "I didn't feel you come up."

Sizon's head kicked sideways. "You mean you didn't see me?"

"Yeah, whatever," Set replied. "I'm not breaking in. This is my home, remember?"

"Where are the other two…and the girls?" Sizon asked.

"You mean the other three and the girl, right?" Set answered with a question of his own.

Sizon grunted as he crossed the street. "I know about the mercenary's death, boy," he said. "He was good man, and I'm truly sorry for your loss." Handing Set a key, he said, "I've kept the house from being taken in case any of you needed a place to go."

Set was perplexed as he took the key. "Thank you," he said, "but why would you do that? We weren't exactly your favorite people."

"I know about the three guards that were killed the night you all disappeared," Sizon told him, "the two at the wall and the one found out by the coast."

Set's fingers twitched as he readied himself to wipe the memories from the guard's mind.

"Don't worry," Sizon said. "The two at the wall were bribable and have since been replaced with more trustworthy watchmen, and my old partner was scum. I was grateful to have been relieved of his company." He gave a pause. "So, are you going to tell me where the others are?"

Set gave the first name that popped into his head. "Rus Elisium."

"Liar. Thank Superi the poison of that city doesn't travel by air, but had you been there you wouldn't be standing before me now. You'd be dead, as would your family."

"Why do you want to know? Why do you care?"

"I was on duty the day of the ambush. We'd been given orders that had come out of Antro to wait in the marketplace for a portal to open. We'd been told that a great threat to Superi was coming through, and that those who emerged were monsters. Our orders were to take you all out."

"I see." Set sighed. "You were the ones chasing us."

"No you don't see. You boys were a constant thorn in my side, but none of you were a real danger. I knew of the ambush from Imbellis that waited on the other side of the northern wall, so I gathered the city guards loyal to me, and a riot ensued as we kept those inside from falling in at your backs. We did what we could to help."

"Oh, wow," Set said, running his fingers through his hair. "We wondered why the guards from inside Exterius Antro hadn't joined the fray. Two of us were taken, but without your action it could have easily have been all of us. Thank you for that."

Sizon scratched at the coarse twirl of brown hair sticking up between his pointed ears. "I'm not sure what that yellow-eyed brother of yours is, and I'm aware that the marks on your face have changed. I can guess at what that makes you, but you are all children, including the nox girl that was that with you that day. I have a family of my own, Set. I couldn't be a part of your deaths."

"How did you know I'd be here?"

Sizon chuckled. "A crazy fulgo arrived in the city two days ago. He created quite a stir when he revealed his ability to the gate watchers. The magistrate wasn't sure what to make of him, especially when he requested to see me."

Trepidation crept up Set's spine. "Who is he?"

Sizon grinned. "I have no idea. I was told to be here tonight, so here I am."

"Come inside with me," Set said, turning to slip the key in the lock. "Maybe we can figure it out." As he lifted the lever he asked over his shoulder, "What was the fulgo's ability?"

"He's an oracle."

A great smile split Set's face. Opening the door, he called out, "Socmoon?"

Socmoon's tall, lanky frame overflowed Jacob's rocking chair. His long, wild, white hair further paled the transparent skin that his colorful robe did not cover. His one yellow eye reflected the light from the fire burning in the hearth, but his right was a milky covered with his pupil was a small as a needle head.

"The future revealed has become the past, and you lived to tell the tale. Grateful I am, young Set, to see you doing well."

Having entered the house behind Set, Sizon smirked. "What did I tell you? Crazy, right?"

"He's not crazy. It's just the way he talks," Set told him, taking a seat on the sofa situated against the far wall of living room, while Sizon hung back by the door. "You have no idea how good it is to see you, Socmoon, but why are you here?"

"A vow I gave on the day we did part," Socmoon reminded him.

"I remember." Set nodded. "You said you would be where I needed you to be."

"Indeed." Socmoon smiled.

"Well," Sizon said, "I'll leave you two to catch up."

"Captain Nitron," Socmoon said, "do not yet depart. You too must hear of the war to start."

"What war?" Sizon asked.

It was Set who answered. "The war between Superi and the gods of Earth."

"Now you're the one who sounds crazy." Sizon snorted. "What on Superi are gods?"

"Gods do not dwell on Superian soil," Socmoon told him. "Their vile ambitions upon Earth they toil. Yet now that the gateway has crackled again, soon through the rift five monsters they will send."

"I'm just a city guard," Sizon said. "If you really believe Superi is going to be invaded by another world, you should be telling all of this to those of higher rank."

"There are but two who rank higher than him," Socmoon pointed to Set. "The angeli are in Pisces Stragulum. They as well have much to learn, much to see, such as the letters I carry with me. Yet for the moment, I am here for you, to set your path for what you must do."

"Which is?"

Socmoon rose from his seat to tower over the fera. "Rally your guards to the angeli's cause, for if they fail, Superi will fall."

"What cause?" Sizon questioned, his voice deepening with frustration. "Who are the angeli? And how do they even exist after so long? The curses were cast forever ago."

Set stood as well, with guilt pinching his visage. "Tristan was the first angeli to be reborn, or, recreated. The nox girl with us the day of the ambush…she was the second. The Imbellis Asylum wanted to use them to reopen a gateway to Earth, but they failed. Instead, a god from that planet opened the way from his side and came through. He killed a lot of people before Anliac and Tristan were able to shove him back onto his side. The god, Apollo, vowed to return with others like him."

"It will not be the gods we see," Socmoon said touching the center of his forehead, "but monstrous beasts. Through single orbs they seek our secrets, and though they live or die, it is their presence here that does the war incite."

Sizon's gut twisted. "How am I supposed to rally my men to fight against monsters no one here believes exists, to fight for the cause of angeli who Superi thinks are extinct in order to prepare for a war against beings called gods, from a planet only a handful of people have heard of?" He dragged in air after his rant was over and then he added, "This is insanity."

"Insanity dances were chaos reigns, and the coming storm brews change," Socmoon told him. "The only question that yet remains, is will you rally or run? For nothing will be the same when the battle is settled and done."

Sizon's large shoulders squared. "I don't run," he said.

Set and Sizon watched as Socmoon's tiny pupil dilated until the entirety of white was blacked out. "And so it begins."

"What does?" Set asked.

The oracle blinked. "Now, epoto. To Pisces Stragulum we must go. Pull strength from me if you must, if you find your strength is not enough." He clasped Set's left hand with his own.

"Epoto?" Sizon gulped.

"Stand back," Set told him. "I'll open a portal."

"You're a gate maker?" Sizon questioned further.

Distracted, Set replied, "I am whatever I need to be."

As the suns crested the horizon over Exterius Antro, they

left Sizon with an impossible task as they emerged from the portal in Pisces Stragulum, where the scent of food being prepared for lunch greeted them, as did the angeli guard who rushed forward.

"Sir," the guard said, "allow me to escort you and your guest back to the others."

"Thank you," Set said. "We've much to discuss."

Socmoon shook his long, slender finger. "Not we," he said, "but me. You must leave before long to travel to Regia Aquam."

"I can't be trusted," Set told him as they followed along behind their escort. "I'm no longer alone in my head."

"I know better than most the pieces of the puzzled minds that work as ours," Socmoon replied. "It is the cost of our power."

"So then tell me, Socmoon," Set pleaded, "what do I do?"

"You hold to the course," Socmoon said. "You see it through."

VI

Reunion

The tall fulgo, Socmoon, wore his hooded patchwork robe with the pride of a great storyteller. Its pattern of plum purple and dark green, sewn in silver thread, caught the eyes of all. Yet it was his presence and what he stood for that brought smiles to their faces. With his long, wild, grey hair whipping about and tangling with the bushy beard that lifted from his chest to fly over his broad, boney shoulders, he seemed oblivious to the attention as he and Set walked through the town.

"Why are you smiling, boy?" Socmoon asked. "There's nothing funny so far as I can see, and your glib grin reads a travesty."

Set's grin broadened. "In the darkest of hours we must still see the light, lest our lives become small and trite."

Socmoon grunted as he came to a stop. "Do you prepare to take my gift, or curse, as it may be? Or do you dare to mock me?"

"I'm just glad you're here." Set smiled and then clutched his chest as pain lanced through it. He rubbed at his sternum as a burning heat blossomed there like a rose with thorns, bittersweet and filled with agony. "Something…" he said, "is wrong."

Set recognized Shashara and Anliac's guards standing post outside his office. He left Socmoon to catch up as he took off at a dead run. The guards came to attention at his approach, but it was Nathin who had the foresight to throw open the door and to move aside, because Set would have crashed right through it. Set could feel someone's pain, her pain.

Shashara leaned sideways in her chair, her head buried against Anliac's stomach, as she clutched at the arms that held her together. Her sun-kissed skin was pale, deepening the color of the purple scar that marred her smooth cheek. When she turned to him, her blue eyes were piercing daggers in pools of brilliant red.

Tears glassed his eyes as he crossed the floor to kneel at her side, ignoring for now the animosity directed at him from the others. "Shashara," he whispered, "forgive me?"

She crumbled and reached for him.

Set wrapped his arms around her and buried his face in the hollow at her neck. Without loosening his hold on her, he told the others, "Socmoon is outside." The announcement had the desired effect as they all headed towards the door.

Word of Set's return had spread. Davimon and Lishous converged with Lan and Triton, and as a unit, they joined those stepping outside of the office building to greet their visitor.

"Socmoon." Davad clasped forearms with the oracle. "Welcome to Pisces Stragulum."

"It's good to have you here." Tristan dipped his head. "Allow me to introduce to you, Anliac Aquam."

Anliac gave a slight bow. "You honor us with your presence, oracle. Welcome."

Lishous, unsure of his place, bowed at the waist, as Davimon stretched out his hand and stared in awe at the dark blue sunburst markings that covered the entire left side of the man's face.

"It's a pleasure to meet you," Davimon said. "You're the first level three I've encountered."

Socmoon clasped the proffered hand and gave a crooked grin as Davimon became overwhelmed by the current of aether that surged and cycled through him at Socmoon's whim.

Tightening his grip to prevent Davimon from pulling free, Socmoon said, "Lesson one, young seer, offer not your hand to me, unless your secrets you wish me to see."

"I've got a lesson prepared for you as well, oracle," Lishous growled, "if you don't let him go."

Davimon inhaled when released and shook his head to clear it. Every vision he'd ever had was replayed in his mind without his summons. Socmoon had seen it all and yet try as he might, he'd been unable to turn the tide of aether to take anything from the oracle's more powerful psyche.

To Lishous, Socmoon said, "For now you follow your master, but in truth and time thou wilt see, that when the next path is chosen, he will instead follow thee."

Seeing Davimon and Lishous so taken aback, Triton

chuckled. "He's a pain in the arse, but his words are true. The problem is in trying to understand them." He clasped forearms with Socmoon. "It's good to see you, old friend. You've been missed, but you know I have to ask. Why are you here?"

"We must wait for those who are absent," Socmoon replied, "and here is not the place, though urgency I would suggest if we are to prepare the Superian race."

With Shashara's hand trapped in Set's own, they emerged.

"Oh, sweet Shashara." Socmoon enfolded her in his arms. "Such a soft heart have you," he said as he cupped her cheek before backing away.

Wide-eyed and still sniffing, Shashara replied, "Uhh… thank you? Set has told me some of what you've done for him." Her voice broke. "I can't express my gratitude."

The space around the oracle widened as the pupil of his left eye dilated, leaving Davimon alone to creep forward against Lishous's tug on the back collar of his jacket. In anticipation, those gathered waited to hear his words, but they did not come. His lips pressed thin and he swayed beneath the burden of his gift.

"We need to get him somewhere he can rest," Set said. "I drained him pretty good to get us back."

Coming out of his trance, Socmoon sagged. "Indeed, young Set, I do agree." His eyes ricocheted from face to face until at last he looked at the ground. "I'm exhausted by all I see."

"Sir," Nathin offered to Tristan, "I do believe the angeli dwelling located directly behind the one you and Mistress

Anliac share is still empty."

"Thank you, Nathin," Tristan replied and indicated with his hand which way Socmoon should head.

Socmoon pitched his voice for Tristian alone, though when Anliac tensed he knew her hearing was heightened as well. "What I have to say is for the Five and other ears abound. Privacy we will need or I'll not issue a single sound. No offense do I intend, but on dangerous ground we tread, and once the knowledge is released panic is sure to spread."

"I'll take care of it," Anliac said. "You guys go ahead."

Triton never slowed his pace. Fifteen years gave him the right to follow.

The personal guards for the Five kept pace as well.

Turning, Anliac faced those not of the Five and held out a hand to halt their progress, making note that Shorlynn and Riker had joined their number. "The House of Angeli respects each of the positions you hold, and your friendships are of great value," she said, "but the oracle is here to speak to the Five."

"Since when is Triton one of the Five?" Davimon scowled.

"So then, we are to be shut out of the conversation?" Riker rolled his shoulders to loosen the tension her words created.

Lan's beady, black eyes were unblinking. "The Alphas will not be pleased."

Anliac was not the only one surprised when Shorlynn moved to stand beside her.

"Enough," Shorlynn said, planting dainty fists on slender hips. "We are representatives of other regions and have sworn no oaths of loyalty to the House of Angeli. So unless you are willing to denounce your current rulers and kneel…" She let her words play out.

When the men stood silent, Anliac squeezed her shoulder. "Thank you," she said, and then her image blurred, rustling leaves and stirring dust. Her cloak sucked up around her like a cocoon as she shoved against an inertial force to stop in front of the angeli dwelling, where Socmoon had been taken. She walked past the posted guards and said as she entered, "No one comes in."

The guards straightened their backs and nodded.

Davad was using his element to bring water to boil at the stove, and Shashara and Set had the table prepared for tea. The cups sat upon porcelain saucers with strings dangling from their sides. Tristan sat at one end with Socmoon at the other, while Triton leaned against the nearest wall. Set and Shashara sat together on one side, and so Anliac took the empty seat on Tristan's right, as they waited for Davad to join them.

Once the water was poured and Davad seated, Socmoon eased an aged scroll from a pocket deep in the folds of his robe, and with equal care, unrolled it. "You must see the past if the future is to be clear." He handed the parchment to Shashara. "Lend your voice, if you will, my dear."

"Of course," Shashara replied. She placed the scrolls on the table and then smoothed them gently. She read aloud:

"Who are the Superians? Really? What are they teaching children these days? I don't expect them to know the history of earth mind you, but I expect them to know their own. Ignorance could mean their death.

"Who are Superians? Please…We are! Or at least we once were. We were the superior life form, meant to rule the pathetic humans that cower beneath the pretentious rule of the so-called gods that terrorize their world out of cruelty and spite and for their own personal gain.

"Tyrants, monsters, and the humans call them gods because of the power they wield.

Our power was greater. Our number was greater. We were born perfect in both beauty and form, and then we made the mistake of following the likes of Nathon Bealson through the gateway, because he believed Earth needed saving. Ignorance!

"We did not go to Earth to conquer, but the humans begged to be ruled. They begged us to take command away from the gods who demanded the highest sacrifices in return for mere survival. Like sheep they searched for a shepherd strong enough to face their suppressors, and we were.

"Or we thought we were. We could have been, had we known, but the temples to us were buildings that signified wealth and opulence, and the gods did not hold the monopoly on greed. Had we known, perhaps our choices would have been different. Had I known, I would not have smashed the statue of Poseidon, who defiled the doorway of the temple I desired for my own. Ignorance! For it was Poseidon that arose from the churning waters to punish my actions, and he did not come alone to deliver retribution to those who'd overstepped.

"Our children should be taught the lesson their forefathers learned through blood that was shed. The battle that erupted was catastrophic. The god, surrounded by his element, was indestructible, but our aquis wielders gave as good as they got. We sank one of Poseidon's precious cities into the bottomless pit of the oceanus he ruled. Had it been him alone we faced we would have triumphed, but such was not the case. From the apex of a mountain, from every far-reaching corner of earth, the gods rushed forth to Poseidon's aid and in defense of the rule they claimed. They converged against us on the coast where the gateway stood open.

"Our arrogance became our undoing. The humans, caught between the angeli and the gods, died by the thousands. The gods, immortal on their own planet, could not be killed, and we were dying. Pride gave way to survival, and we were forced to tuck our tails between our legs and run like cowards.

"If only it had ended there, but the Egyptian god had other plans. He cursed our bodies, splintering our perfect race into four that were incapable of rising against them again. Perhaps it was no more than we deserved, but what the Greek god did next ensured that we would be back. He cursed our minds. The ignorance he gave birth to dampened our fear, and without its hindrance, we will stop at nothing to avenge what was destroyed. The gods are without honor and therein lies their weakness.

"There are those who whine and complain about what was done to them. They resent the pain and turmoil introduced with the curses into their lives, but not all. Some of us remember that there were those left behind. *Not all made it back through the gate. Not all were accounted for. No one intended on leaving them behind, but we realized too late that we couldn't return. So, on earth and on Superi, we bide our time until our circumstances change.*

"I am the last oracle on Superi. The hope of all lies in the lineage of my line. Should another be born, heed my words. The recreation of the angeli race will come to pass. Aid them! Find the one that can reopen the gateway. Face the gods! Here is what you must know to win: We were not ruined. We were but broken. Prepare the damage by placing the pieces together again and we will be assured of victory.

"And as for the children, teach them well, for they will one day lead us to war."

Finished, Shashara leaned back in her chair and the scroll rolled closed, but the words hung between them.

Anliac, the first to recover, asked, "Who wrote it?"

"He was of my line," Socmoon told her, "and his prophecy was passed to me. I buried it deep and bid my time until the boys I met at sea. Race I did to recover the words as soon as I disembarked, but I am too late, and the war did start."

"I don't understand," Davad said. "As far as we know, the gateway has remained closed."

"Ugh," Set growled. "I'm an idiot."

"Why?" Tristan asked.

"Not that we don't completely agree," Davad teased.

Set shook his head in sorrowful regret. "When I copied the information from Calstar's mind, there was so much to take in. My mind filed it away. There is a lot I don't know that I know"—he shrugged—"until I need to know."

"And no one will blame you for it," Shashara said, spreading a warning glare amongst them all, but mostly at her brother. "What is it you've remembered?"

"The, umm…" Set's eyes squinted as if he was reading small font. "The gateway in Bealson's Grove, it was made by Superians. Chances are Apollo saw Malstar trying to open it, and that's how he found it to open it himself. But there are other gateway sites, and according the journals, they are anchored by the gods."

"What does that mean?" Anliac asked.

"It means that we've been watching the wrong place. The gods won't attack from Imbellis. They'll attack through the gateways they control."

Tristan stiffened. "Do we know where their gateway sites are?"

Triton, who still stood leaning against the wall, spoke up. "The better question would be, what did he mean by placing the pieces together? Without going to Earth, we can't break the curse, so how then is that the key to winning the war that is to be waged here?"

"One question before another," Socmoon said, "and no answer do I have for the first. We must look to the epoto to quench our ignorant thirst."

"In Exterius Antro, you said it had begun," Set said. "You talked about one-eyed beasts coming through a rift. Do you not know where?"

Socmoon shook his head.

"Are the names of the sites listed in one of the journals?" Davad asked.

"If they are I can't remember." Set rubbed at his temples. "We'll have to ask Calstar."

"And what of the key?" Triton asked again. "What did

your ancestor mean?"

Socmoon's shoulders slumped. "For truth I cannot see. I might as well be blind. For each time I seek, the answers elude, and more clouded becomes my mind."

"Whatever it means," Shashara said, "we don't dare ignore it. The last line proves the ancient oracle's visions were true."

"I agree," Anliac added, "but while we try and figure it out we need to unite the regions. If Socmoon is right, we are out of time."

Davad worked at a kink in the back of his neck. "King Normis has requested a visit from the House of Angeli. Set and I can meet him in Regia Aquam. The city is old. Perhaps while we're there, we can discover where the sites are located."

"And Socmoon told me in Exterius Antro that I was to leave for Regia Aquam," Set informed them. "So I guess that is that."

Tristan nodded. "The two of you can handle this. We trust you both."

"We'll do our best." Set breathed in and held it for a long moment before he let it go. "I just hope that when we arrive it is me, and not Calstar, who is introduced to the king."

"Socmoon," Tristan asked, "can you help him separate his psyche from those he absorbs?"

Set went rigid, but answered in Socmoon's stead. "There is a cost to my gift, and it is myself."

Beneath the table, Shashara took his hand.

"The cost is greater than you know," Triton said.

Set spread his glance amongst those gathered. "What is

that supposed to mean?" he asked.

Shashara squeezed his hand a little tighter. "You kind of drained everyone around you when you opened the portal," she told him.

Set went pale. "But," he said, "I didn't touch anyone."

"Yeah, well," Davad said, "you dropped three people and withered the grass you were standing on until all that was left was dust."

"That's impossible." Set panicked. "I didn't touch anyone. I know I didn't."

"Breathe, little brother," Tristan said. "We'll figure it out."

To no one in particular, Socmoon said, "Further than you think is the epoto's reach when his connection with Superi is complete."

Anliac stiffened. "Are you suggesting that Set drained those people because they were standing too close?"

When Socmoon didn't answer, fear struck home.

VII

Into the Depths

Billowing, white clouds darkened to grey, stealing the sunlight as Poseidon stared in disbelief and said, "You would have me use my children."

"Let us not forget that it was a Cyclops who forged the lightning bolt that killed Asklepious. The Cyclopes are not your progeny," Apollo stated. "They are your creation."

"If you had ever breathed life into more than your ego, you would know there is little difference. And to be clear, it was one of Gaia's Cyclopes that created the weapon leading to your son's temporary demise."

"Let us leave such words to the past. No good will come from giving them new birth. Will you use the Cyclops? Or do you refuse?" Apollo held his breath as he awaited answer.

"No," Poseidon replied. "I will send them." Fat, sloppy drops of rain plummeted down on them as he said, "But I do so with a heavy heart."

"The Cyclopes are brutes," Apollo chortled, "with dim-witted minds. They're good for little beyond the craft for which they were created." When the rain turned to hail, Apollo held up his hands. "Okay. All right. I'm sorry." Shoving his drenched, blond hair out of his face, he said, "Look at it this way, Poseidon. The ones you send will become legend among their kind. What greater aspiration could a father have for his children?"

"There is even less belief in them than what remains of us. I've not the strength to summon them."

"Nor I the will to battle the humans of this age if they were to lay eyes on them." Apollo laughed.

A ray of sunlight speared through the clouds as Poseidon grinned. "Agreed," he said. "So then we must travel to them."

Crossing his arms over his chest, Apollo's pectoral muscles jumped in anticipation of a long-awaited answer. "Where have you hidden them away all these centuries?"

"Somewhere that will buy us a day," Poseidon replied, "before we are discovered by the others."

"Lead the…" Apollo's hands flew to his throat. His eyes widened when his lungs rejected the air and he could not breathe. Flaps of cartilage opened on either side of his neck. He could feel them beneath his fingers. His mouth moved, but words were beyond him.

"Cyclopes were made to dwell in volcanoes," Poseidon told him, "but I could not very well leave them on the surface to be discovered by the humans."

A giant wave rose and bowed off of the coast to wash inland, collapsing on top of them and carrying them out to sea. Annoyed, Apollo drew in his first breath of salt water, emitting bubbles from his new gills as the now-useless oxygen was expelled. Not as fast as the sunbeams he rode upon, but fast enough, the current Poseidon placed them in sucked them downward. So deep they traveled that the blue waters turned to grey and then to black. If not for the turbulence left in Poseidon's wake, Apollo would have been lost. He cursed, though no sound was made when his head cracked against stone.

Poseidon snatched hold of the brown leather strap of Apollo's quiver running across his chest and dragged him into the opening of a cave.

Apollo needed no urging to travel towards the light, nor to seek the heat it offered after the biting cold of the waters, but upon reaching an enter chamber his instincts held him back.

Poseidon swam behind him, and with a foot against his backside, kicked him through.

Gills flapping, Apollo once again found himself unable to breathe. His bow appeared in his hand as his quiver refilled with conjured arrows. Angry, Apollo strung a golden projectile and aimed it at the sea god.

"Relax," Poseidon chortled as he returned Apollo to his natural state.

He dropped the bow and arrow, which disappeared before they hit the ground as Apollo bent at the waist, gasping. "Zeus as my witness," Apollo snarled, "if you ever do that again I will find a way to kill your immortal hide. We could have used a portal to get here."

"That would have left a trail in the aether for the others to follow," Poseidon told him. "Besides, I owed you for the way you were talking about my children."

Standing upright, Apollo took in his surroundings. "Where are we?"

"In an outer cave that connects to an underground volcano," Poseidon replied.

Apollo's nostrils flared. "That explains the stench of sulfur." He walked over to a wall and slid his fingers down it, then looked at the black soot coating them. A deep rumble had him turning towards Poseidon as he wiped his hand clean on a pant leg that showed no stain. "What is that?"

"My children have sensed my return," Poseidon told him, as the booming of heavy footsteps drew near. "It has been too long."

"How many are here?" Apollo asked as he found a boulder upon which to perch to avoid the chaos of what approached.

"Volcanoes litter the ocean floor," Poseidon replied. "There are perhaps a dozen here."

Chunks of obsidian dropped loose from the cavernous ceiling, revealing raw pockets of diamonds and other jewels that reflected the light of the smoldering, molten fire from the stone corridor off the chamber where they stood.

"That many, huh?"

Poseidon laughed. "Not all of them will be joining us. Only those I've summoned for the task."

"Father!" voices of varying depths cried out as the chamber's closed space was filled with five hulking, one-eyed giants. Meaty hands reached for Poseidon with awed respect.

Growing to match the height of the thirteen-foot-tall Cyclopes, Poseidon reached to caress the bald heads that were bowed to him, as he tugged fondly at the bony horns protruding from there. "Yes, yes," he cooed. "I've missed you all as well. Listen to me now. I have a very important task for you all," he said to focus them. "Do you remember the Great War of Heaven?"

The largest of the Cyclopes crooked his head and scratched the top of it, as he said, "No, father."

"In the Great War of Heaven, there were beings called angels that wanted to take Earth from us," Poseidon said.

Wide mouths full of jagged teeth opened to howl as if the ancient war had only just begun.

Gesturing to Apollo, he said, "They destroyed his temple. They sank my beloved Atlantis. They wanted to hurt us. We won the War of Heaven, but, I fear they have grown strong with the passing of the ages, while we, my children, have lost power."

The Cyclopes slammed their closed fists together, creating a concussion of sound that rattled the chamber. "We strong, Father. We protect you. What they look like? We kill them," they vowed, speaking over each other in their desire to please their god.

Apollo jumped free of his perch as the boulder broke loose from the ceiling, startling the nearest giant, whose club-like arm swung wide. With a grunt, he was slammed into a wall before his feet could touch the ground.

"Sorry," the Cyclops said, his one eye blinking while drool dribbled from the corner of his mouth.

Using the wall to gain his feet, Apollo moaned. "Don't worry about it," he muttered, cracking his spine back into place. "They are a cursed race," he told them. "Some have bodies twisted between that of man and beast, but even those who reflect the image of a human have warped minds that threaten us. They need to die."

"That is not what this is about, Apollo," Poseidon said, his voice deepening in warning. To the gathering of Cyclopes, he said, "There are five points of entry between Earth and Heaven. Apollo and I will open them. My children, your quest will be to journey through them. I need each of you to be my eye, to scout the layout of their land, to gather information on their numbers, their strengths and weaknesses. It will be dangerous, but I know that you will not fail me."

"No, Father," many voices said as one.

With sadness, Poseidon said, "Out of love, I have chosen the five of you for greatness. You will step through the gateway forgers of godly weapons, but when you return you will be like unto the gods themselves." He glanced at Apollo and then said, "You will become legend. Come to me, Polyphemus. You will lead the way."

"How I get back?" Polyphemus questioned as he came forward to do his father's bidding.

"Heaven has two great suns," Poseidon told him. "When they have reached their zenith the gateway will reopen. Should you encounter opposition, Polyphemus, I want you to remind these Superians of why they have feared us for centuries, but do not lose sight of your goal. Gather information for me, my child, and return."

"Father?" Polyphemus asked.

"Yes, my son?" Poseidon smiled to encourage his query.

"What opposition mean?" Polyphemus asked. From the vacuous eyes of his brothers, they didn't know the word either.

"It means that if anyone, or anything, tries to stop you from getting back to me, or from gathering information for me, you are to kill it. Do you understand?" Poseidon asked.

The Cyclopes all nodded. Their smiles grew once they knew Poseidon's orders would be easy to follow.

A cavern opened behind the Cyclopes, and Poseidon motioned for them all to enter the large, rectangular room, etched with carvings on the walls that mimicked the shape of doors. Standing before one such carving, he brought his hands together in a concussive boom, and the door receded into the stone. "Polyphemus," he said, gesturing the Cyclops forward, as a glowing red and purple gateway appeared in the door carving.

The giant, lifting to his foot to avoid the sharp edge of the gateway, stepped through. When he emerged on Heaven, a wave of nausea assaulted him. Stretching wide his long arms, he caught himself on the brown, outer wooden walls of single-storied buildings that straddled the narrow alley in which he stood.

At one end, he spotted two human men standing at the entrance of yet another wooden building. He became confused and tilted his head. He squinted his large eye as brass buttons on blood red uniforms, with blue stripes of rank on their chests, reflected the strange suns' light in a painful ray. Rocks jumped loose of the cobblestone that cracked beneath the pressure of his steps as he started forward for a closer look.

"You human?" the Cyclops asked.

The quake of the ground and the deep bass of a male

voice turned the two mortalis around. Chunks of terra ripped free of the street, hovering before the man on the left, as flames burst like torches set from the hands of the man on the right.

Polyphemus's single eye narrowed as his wide mouth opened to growl, "You not human. Humans no make fire. You…monsters!" Raising his melon-sized hands over his head like a nanus swordsman taking the high guard, he charged.

The terra wielder let fly the chunks of ground he held at the ready.

"Hee, hee," Polyphemus chortled as a right hook sent the first piece crashing through the wall of one of the buildings, while the second, larger mound put a pothole in the cobble-stone street. "I like games," he said, leaping over it. "This one fun."

"Yeah," the ignis wielder snarled. "Let's see if you like to play with fire."

The terra wielder jumped to the side. He watched as his partner took off at run. As soon as the ignis wielder's knees bent, he shoved with his terra ability, and the street became a ramp that projected his partner towards the giant's head.

The Cyclops swung his head from side to side when the man grabbed hold of his horn with one hand and covered his eye with the other.

"I've got you," the ignis wielder proclaimed.

"Hahaha," Polyphemus laughed.

"Burn, fera!" the man shouted…and then he began to scream.

"Hahaha!" Polyphemus's hands went around the man's

waist, his fingertips touching behind the man's back, and yanked. Tossing the bottom half of the wielder's body to the side, he said, "Fire no hurt me," as he shook his head again to loosen the dead man's grip. Torso and head thudded to the ground.

Yanking a cord around his neck, the terra wielder pulled a silver whistle from beneath his uniform's collar and blew like his life depended on it.

"Agh!" Polyphemus covered his ears. "I don't like this game." Shoving off the ground, he leapt into the air and pounced on the man who was hurting his ears. He brought his fist down on the man's head, following through until he hit the ground through a puddle of broken bones and blood. "Ugh…" Air gushed from his lungs as something cold, and big, slammed into his back with such force that he broke through an exterior wall of the building on his right and face-planted on a tavern floor.

As tables overturned and chairs tumbled, the patrons made quite a racket as they scrambled out the door to witness the Cyclops reemerging through the hole in the side of the wall. They watched as he tugged at two support beams, breaking them loose as he advanced on the two dozen city guards standing in a narrow formation, six deep, to take down the threat to Media Forum.

A fera solider, singled out by his dark blue uniform with vertical red lines on his sleeves that marked his rank as Captain, saw the disadvantage of fighting such a beast in the close quarters of the alley. His thin black lips pulled off his protruding snout as he growled, "Fall back."

As a unit, they retreated into the marketplace.

"Regroup," the captain shouted, his russet fur quivering in anticipation of battle as his men fell into a wide formation, two deep.

Polyphemus, support beams held in his meaty grasp, followed. He stood tall as the cobblestone path led him out into an oval opening. Wooden buildings, with little space between them, enclosed it, and a fountain worthy of the gods dominated the heart of it.

"You've killed some of my men," their captain said. "For that you will die." Polyphemus cracked the two beams together. "For Father." He grinned and advanced. Swinging the beams wide, he crushed the nearest two human-looking guards. He dropped one of the beams and slid his hold on the second until he could swing it with a hard uppercut that sent a beast man flipping head over feet.

The guards gave room but did not retreat. Instead, a voice shouted, "Set that wood to flame!" A semicircle formed around the giant as the beam in his hand ignited.

"Hey!" Polyphemus scowled as he let the charred remains fall. "Bad wolf," he chided their captain.

"Aquis wielders!" the captain shouted, drawing out the words to be heard over the cacophony of noise created by the fight and gathering crowd.

Rain barrels located under the buildings' eaves exploded. Their contents turned into whips that lashed against Polyphemus's thick skin from every angle. He growled when the water began to freeze around his feet and ankles.

"Go for his eye!" the captain shouted.

The water formed frozen hammers. Polyphemus threw up one arm to protect his face as he dropped low to smash the ice holding him in place. Rolling forward, he came to his feet and lunged for the closest man. He snatched the man up by the feet and tossed him through a window. Grabbing a black fur-covered guard, Polyphemus pivoted in a circle, swinging the beast man's upper body into the curved line of men, sending them flying as he followed through until the beast man slammed into the side of a wall. Polyphemus dropped the dead weight.

From behind, an aquis wielder dove between the legs of the monster and grabbed hold of Polyphemus's wrists upon rising. Using his element, he encased the monster's hands in chunks of ice.

"Agh!" Polyphemus roared at the unfamiliar pain of burning. Yanking his hands apart, he slammed them together with the man's head caught in between. The ice shattered along with the man's skull.

An ice spike flew straight for his head. He dodged to the side, snarled, and threw his weight behind his shoulder to break through the wall of a tavern, as volleys of spikes were loosed.

"Aqua Guard," the captain said, "get a perimeter up."

Gathering around the central fountain, the guards took up position and levitated the water over the surrounding buildings, drenching their roofs and walls with protection as their captain shouted, "Ignis wielders….torch it," and like dry tinder, the tavern ignited as four more guards joined the battle.

The inferno raged, evaporating the wood to ash, and from within it they heard the monster scream. Celebratory back slaps and smiles accompanied the sound of their short-lived victory.

Polyphemus began to laugh, a great, boisterous rumble that continued as a large beam of burning wood crashed through the weakened front wall. Taking it in hand as a weapon, he hefted it onto to his shoulder and emerged, throwing it like a spear.

He followed behind the beam's trajectory as it knocked two human-like men aside only to impale a third. Ducking his head, and holding his arms straight out in front of him, he crashed through one shell of a wall, stirring soot and ash as he made his exit through the other side and back into the oval area. The building tumbled sideways into the building across the next alleyway, spreading the flames.

"Wielders, get that fire out," the captain barked from behind the line of guards. "Arms! Prepare to attack!"

While their formation split, Polyphemus gained time to find his next target. With a backhanded swing, he smacked a would-be hero to the cobblestone and crushed his head beneath his heel.

The remaining mortalis guards hefted shields from their backs, as they bared steel, while their fera comrades extended their claws. Their sharp teeth were exposed as their lips pulled back in aggression. Four men across and two men deep, they waited for their captain's orders.

Advancing to the fore with his pike in hand, the wolfish captain growled, "Now you'll deal with me."

"Hoorah!" his men shouted.

Using his speed ability to his advantage, the Captain blurred forward, taking a gouge out of the monster's thigh with his pike, before veering to the right. As the beast turned to snatch for him, two of his men came in from the left, maneuvering to slice the backs of both of the invader's calves.

Throwing back his head, Polyphemus roared, but the two guards escaped back into formation.

The captain smiled. Blurring forward again and building up speed, he dropped backwards as the giant raised his club-like fists to hammer down on him. He slid between the monster's legs, raking the pike's blades against the inside of the monster's thighs, and popped up on the other side.

Bent over, the sides of his fists hammering into the ground, Polyphemus had left the back of his neck exposed. Two of the guards took quick advantage. He howled as a bear-like man ripped into his flesh with sharp, pointed claws and then retreated before he could be captured. The second, a scaled beast with fangs as large as ivory husks, went for the thick vein pulsing at the side of his neck. Polyphemus lifted him by the front of his uniform and slammed him into the ground, crushing his chest.

A swordsman stepped forward to replace the downed fera, as their Captain threw his pike, lodging it in the back of the giant's left shoulder. With a grunt, the Cyclops pulled it free and speared one of the guards.

The captain, full of fury, appeared mere feet before the beast. "Stop killing my men!" he said, pulling short blades from sheaths on his back while he advanced, one held high and the other at a low guard.

Polyphemus was caught up in a whirlpool of blades. Each slice of steel delivered a gaping, bleeding wound that drained his strength. The slower he became, the faster the injuries appeared. Fortune alone connected his backhanded swing with a glancing blow to the side of the captain's head that sent him flying sideways and skidding across the cobblestones.

At the sight of their motionless captain, the remaining six guards issued a war cry and attacked full out.

The men hacked with swords and raked with claws while the wielders tried to keep the Cyclops down. A spike of ice as thick as a man's wrist impaled the creature's single eye, as a swordsman's blade sliced through the beast's neck below his bulbous chin. A feline fera pounced on the monster, claws raking across his face and ripping through his torso.

"Retreat!"

The call of their captain had the fera shoving off, as he and the others closed rank around their wounded leader, who stood holding his right shoulder with his arm dangling uselessly at his side.

Swaying on his feet, bloody and blind, Polyphemus cried out through a frothing throat, "Father! Help me!"

"Archers," the captain shouted. A slew of angry bowmen, dressed in matching red and blue uniforms, appeared on every rooftop around the oval area. Steel-tipped arrows were nocked and aimed at the intruder. "Fire!" he bellowed, and the arrows were loosed.

Polyphemus, the first of Poseidon's creations, fell dead.

VIII

What are you?

Centered before another etched doorway, Apollo laid his palms flush against it and shoved. The door slid inward and the gateway opened.

Apollo crossed his arms over his chest and cocked his head to the side. "Was there not a city here once? Now there is naught but a bog." A buzzing before his face brought his hands together. "Ugh," he groaned as he wiped the squashed insect that had flown through the portal onto his pant leg.

"There," Poseidon said, pointing. "They've shrouded their city by fog, but their homes are built upon high ground. Their suns have betrayed them. It reflects off their roofs. Euryalus," Poseidon summoned the next Cyclops forward. "Look," he said.

A solitary, human-like man in a multicolored uniform of browns and greens had turned to gape at them.

"A gift?" Euryalus asked, grinning with glee.

"Of course, my child." Poseidon patted the back of his

shoulder. "Feel free to play with him a bit, but then hurry to the city that lies beyond the fog. Remember, you must return to the gateway when the suns are directly overhead."

"Yes, Father," Euryalus replied as he rubbed his hands together and stepped through.

As the gateway collapsed, the nox soldier levitated on a wave of murky water and added distance between them until his mind could grasp what it was he stared at.

Twelve feet tall with shoulders half as broad, the monster stood on legs as thick as tree trunks. The drab grey linen he wore as pants was marred with burn holes and covered in soot. The long, muscle-bound arms dangling from the sleeves reached past his knees, but it was his face that in- spired fear. A horn protruded from his bald, knobby head. Beneath his forehead was one great red eye perched above a broad, flat nose that dripped green ooze into his wide, teeth- filled maw.

"Come, monster," Euryalus stated. "We play."

"Who are you calling a monster, you freak?" the nox sol- dier replied, as his thirty comrades came to attention atop a raised, grass-covered levy behind the Cyclops and prepared to defend Palus Regia.

"State your business," the nox said.

Turning sideways to protect his rear flank from the lone man, Euryalus glared at the slew of dark-skinned Superians armed with weapons of war.

"Submit," said the soldier standing at the fore of those upon the levy, "and you will be escorted from our territory without being harmed. Refuse, beast, and you will surely die."

Euryalus growled.

"Very well then," the nox replied. "Let it begin."

With his right arm he sent ten of his soldiers surfing down the bank of the levy to glide into position behind the invader. With a forward flick of his wrist, ten more split their rank and flanked the beast's sides. Three men to the right side, with three more at his back, the strongest wielders raised their arms. As they did, elemental warriors, conjured of water, rose from the surface of the swamp and closed in on their enemy.

When the Cyclops's eye turned in the direction of the city, the soldiers readied, placing bows to cheek, hefting spears, and whirling swords into offensive positions.

Targeting those on the perimeter, Euryalus didn't see the elementals that liquefied only to resurface in his path. He dodged the first, but tucked his shoulder and slammed into the second without slowing his pace.

"This sack of dung is fast," a soldier said. "Prepare!" he shouted for those on his side of the line to hear.

A moment before collision, an elemental yanked the Cyclops back, melted, and then reformed into an icy cage with bars a foot in diameter. The long spears of several soldiers found their way between them to press at five points into the giant's neck.

"Last chance, fera," the lead nox shouted from his position.

"That is no fera," the man next to him said.

Ignoring the comment, the lead nox asked, "Why have you come? Tell us what you want."

Again the Cyclops refused to answer. Instead, he reacted, moving with much greater speed than anticipated as he became unhinged. A swipe at the spears with his right hand snapped three of the shafts. Turning, he grabbed the remaining two, ramming the end of the first through its owner's gut, before drawing the second one in along with the one holding it. He released the shaft and reached between the bars and grabbed the soldier's head, slamming it in quick succession against the cage. The ice shattered, the Cyclops broke free, and the nox fell dead.

The conjured elementals dropped back into the swamp and reemerged in closer proximity to the monster. At their wielders' command, they attacked. With fists hard as hammers and claws sharp as blades, the elementals struck again…and again.

Unable to defend against the assault, Euryalus barreled his way through them. They broke apart upon impact, falling in great plops into the swamp from which they came, but a heartbeat later they reanimated in front of him with conjured swords in hand.

Euryalus pivoted in a circle with his arms thrown wide, using his mass to scatter the threat. The meat on the inside of his bicep was flayed and a great gash had opened along the side of his face. He grabbed two elementals and smashed them together, shattering them. Reaching for another, his hand passed through without impediment as the remaining three liquefied, denying him retribution.

Running towards the line blocking his path into the fog-covered city, Euryalus snapped the shaft of an arrow that impaled his shoulder and then dodged a spear thrown at his head. He watched the eyes of the armed guards widen. When a smaller of version of the elementals he'd faced rose, he pivoted around it to reach his target. He wrapped his hand around the man's throat and twisted his grip. The man's neck snapped and his body crumbled. Euryalus hesitated when the small elemental lost form as well.

For a moment the soldiers thought he was going to submit. The Cyclops's muscles relaxed as he stood drawing in ragged breaths, his expression slack. His eye blinked and then a laugh began to build in his chest. It burst forth as the beast changed course, abandoning the path into the city for one that would carry him to the levy.

The rear-positioned soldiers gave chase, but the Cyclops was faster. The wielders tried to freeze his feet, but his giant legs were too strong. Like a boulder rolling downhill, their enemy gained momentum. He was coming.

One after another, the wielders threw up ice walls to no avail. The Cyclops busted right through them. They combined their efforts, conjuring a high wall five feet thick.

With a bellow, Euryalus leapt over it and continued on.

Rods of ice speared up from the swamp, each exploding into a dozen spikes that stuck into the Cyclops's flesh as he passed. Most did no fatal harm, but one found payday as its tip buried into the artery on the inside of his upper thigh.

Euryalus wrapped his hand around the wrist-thick projectile and pulled it free, howling at the pain of it. Slowed, but topping the levy, he swung the rod with both hands and sent the closest wielder flying towards the city. Five more elementals dissolved. With blood gushing from his wound in violent pumps, he roared and faced the monsters threatening Earth.

The elementals flowed onto land, as with the wielders and soldiers, they attacked from all angles as a unit.

Too far outnumbered to defend himself, and too weak to charge through them in an attempt to escape, Euryalus was beaten into submission. His growl became a cry. "Father!" he bellowed. "Come to me!"

"Who is your father?" the lead nox asked, grabbing the giant by the scruff of his shirt. Even kneeling, the hulking creature was on eye level with him.

"Poseidon," Euryalus said, "Lord of the Sea." Tears leaked over the bottom lid of his eye to coast around his nose and off his chin. "Father…" His head dropped forward on his shoulders.

Sensing the beast's slow mind, the nox said, "One does not enter war without being prepared to die. As a warrior, you know this, but you have faced us in battle with honor and great prowess. In reward, I will grant you a swift death."

"I die now?" Euryalus asked, lifting his head.

"Yes." The nox held his sword high and to the side. "Go in peace, brother."

Euryalus grinned. "You die first." Punching his arm straight out, his hand broke through bone to grab hold of the nox's heart, even as the man's sword separated his head from his shoulders.

Their blood mingled, their bodies entangling, they both prepared to embrace death.

The remaining soldiers converged around their dying brother and the monster as their general came at a run.

"Move out of my way," Montilis said as he dropped to his knees and cupped the soldier's head with one hand.

"Hang in there brother," he said, as the man coughed a fountain of blood. "Truhur," he shouted, searching among his men for the medic's face. "Where is the healer?"

"He is on rotation, sir," a soldier answered, "but we've sent for him."

The dying man's eyes bulged as breath was denied him. Groping, he clutched his general's hand, fear evident in his stare.

"None of that, soldier," Montilis's order was also a plea. "You hold on. Do you understand? You're not dying today."

The soldier nodded in compliance but the life flowed out of him.

"You," Montilis barked at the closest pike man, "make sure that thing is dead."

"With pleasure, sir," the pike man replied. He flipped his pike around and aimed the point at the monsters throat. "Auhhhh!!" he shouted as he drove it through the monster's flesh into the dirt beneath it.

The Cyclops didn't move.

A guard came at a run, dragging the healer along with him.

"Sir," Truhur said, "I am here."

"And you're too late," Montilis growled as he closed the dead soldier's eyes. "This is why a healer is with every patrol! This man's death is on your captain's head. Where is he?" He spread his glare among the men as he came to his feet.

"Captain Huysen was the first to attack the beast, sir." A soldier pointed towards the swamp where their captain lay, his uniform standing out against the muck. "He is there."

"I see." Montilis took a deep breath to stem his ire before taking it out on men who were undeserving of it. "Get your brothers and sisters out of the water. I want a death count and a full report on what happened here before the day is out." Before the soldiers scattered, he searched the surrounding forest and asked, "Was this the only one of them?"

"As far as we know, sir. Do you want a patrol sent out?"

"Yes," Montilis replied and then called another man's name. "Beals."

Beals moved from behind his general and came to attention before him. "Sir." He saluted.

"Summon squads four through twelve. I want a full sweep of the forest, and someone tell the magistrate that I am assuming command of the city." Before his words were finished, his men were moving to do his bidding.

A whining, nasal voice called from the bottom of the levy. "You're assuming what?"

Montilis looked down at the man responsible for the question and waited until they stood face to face. "I am putting the city on war alert, and until I see the threat is gone, you are relieved of your duties as per the law."

Rayner's black eyes rounded as his dark nox complexion paled by three shades. "You can't do that without just cause."

Montilis stormed forward, closing the slight distance between them. Inches from the magistrate's face, he snarled, "Just cause?"

Rayner stepped back from the fury lighting Montilis's eyes.

"Are you so desperate for authority that you would deny

the obvious truth?" With his hands clenched in tight fists, Montilis continued, "The angeli have been reborn. An earthling god has made his way to Superi, and now, a monster like none have ever seen has attacked my men! I invoke the authority to put the city under military rule until the threat has been alleviated. Stand...down."

Rayner's chin lifted. "I will not. I..." Rayner began.

"Seize him!" Montilis ordered.

Rayner's private guards grabbed him, binding his hands, while kicking the backs of his knees to force him to kneel.

"Montilis, I will not stand for this," Rayner said as he took note of those involved. "I'll remember all of you...I'll see you all pay."

"Gag him, and then throw him in the private prison of Riker's home where I was held."

"Traitors!" Rayner thrashed his head from side to side. Despite his effort, his jaw was forced open and a loose rag shoved in. Another, tied around his head, held it in place.

As Rayner was dragged off, and soldiers worked to gather the dead, one of Montilis's private guard asked, "What is next, sir?"

"You"—he pointed at a nox female solider on his left— "call a meeting of the Heads of the Houses." Catching the eyes of another of his guards, he said, "Prepare the war room. Have the body of beast laid out upon the table when they enter."

"Sir." The guard placed hand to heart. "I'll see it done."

Taking up his mount's reins, Montilis launched himself into the saddle. He heeled the horse's sides and made for the city. When he reached his house, he slid from the saddle and took the steps leading up to the door two at a time. "Yongur," he shouted. "Get out here."

From the office chamber, Yongur stepped into the hall and found his way to the open living space. "You bellowed?"

"Rayner has been arrested."

Yongur's eyes popped wide. "On whose authority?"

"Mine. The city is now under military rule. An entity of Earth has invaded Superi, and I can't image he was alone."

Panic brought a sheen of sweat to Yongur's flesh. "You can't afford to leave now. Sinpine has not given up. He sews seeds of discourse and mistrust among the Houses. He means to convince them to take your seal."

Montilis poured drinks for the two of them, handed Yongur his, and then raised his own glass. "You and I are going to ensure that doesn't happen."

"How? If you leave Palus Regia with the army to aid the angeli it will be seen as an act of treason. Your actions will give credence to Sinpine's words and then there will be no changing the Houses' minds."

Montilis lifted the leather strap that held the signet of his House from around his neck and held it out for Yongur to take.

"What is this? I do not want your House."

Montilis laughed. "Nor am I offering it." He dropped his arm. "The Houses will soon see the wisdom in standing with the angeli. Of that I have no doubt, but you're right about Sinpine. A man of his ambition, denied his desire, would see this House burn. As Regent of the House of Aquam, you will have the power to stop him." He held out the signet again.

This time Yongur took it. "I'm not of your line." He shook his head in slight movements. "I'm not even an aquis wielder." He held up his forearm, bearing his aer markings. "Why would you trust me with this?"

Bracing himself against the vulnerability he intended to show, Montilis refused to lower his eyes. "In my darkest moment…with enemies seen and not seen crouching at my door…you were there and you have been by my side ever since. I have done nothing to warrant your loyalty, and you've asked nothing in return, and so this is how I chose to show my gratitude."

Tying the signet around his neck, Yongur grinned. "In all this time you've never asked after my reason. Out of respect for the honor you've shown me, I'll tell you."

Montilis tensed but did not speak.

"Not long after your shackled return to Palus Regia, an aged oracle stole into my house in the dead of night and roused me from my bed with a bucket of cold water."

Montilis fought back a grin…and failed.

Yongur's right brow arched at his friend's humored expression. "He spoke of being in the bilge of ship docked at Catena Piscari, where a mercenary's mistake would lead to the waking of prophecy. Oh." It was his turn to grin as Montilis's visage fell. "Do I now have your attention? Good," he said as Montilis scowled. "This is what the oracle said to me: 'The one named Betrayer has been betrayed and the traitor has changed the course of his fate. Yet destiny is not so easily denied. It will first break him so he then can rise. Military rule must be declared, the army dispatched. Beware. War cometh.'"

After a moment of stunned silence, Montilis asked, "Why did you not tell me?"

"In truth, it sounded like rubbish, but then I heard of your return and your imprisonment. When Inabeth's betrayal was made known, I began searching for answers. That is how I learned of Sinpine's intentions. Locked away I could not reach you, and when you were finally released you were at the bottom of a bottle. I had come to believe in the words of the oracle, but feared you would not heed his warning, and so I did what I could to draw you out of your despair."

Montilis laid a hand upon his shoulder. "You are a good friend, Yongur, and you were right to heed the oracle's words."

"It's hard not to," Yongur said.

"Did he say what would happen after I placed city under military rule?" Montilis poured out the glass instead of drinking it and turned to sit it down as he waited for Yongur's reply.

"Only that the army must be dispatched. Where are you going?" he asked as Montilis nodded and headed for the front door.

Mid-step, Montilis paused and turned back to meet Yongur's searching gaze. "I go to meet with the Houses," he said, "and then I go to war. Should I not return, I entrust my House to your care. See to it that it is kept whole, for with my passing the House of Aquam will be led by an angeli."

After exiting his home, Montilis remounted and headed for the gathering of Houses. Word had spread of the attack in the swamp. The citizens were on edge, and the city guard had been doubled. Heavily armed soldiers patrolled the borders. The atmosphere of Palus Regia was tense. *Good*, he thought. Fear would help the Houses make the right decision.

"This is an outrage!"

Montilis heard the shouts of fury and disbelief coming from beyond the door of the war room. He nodded in gratitude towards the servant who opened it.

"General Aquam," Sarif shouted as he came to his feet, "you have some serious explaining to do."

"What is the meaning of this?" another asked, gesturing towards the dead monster laid out before them.

"What manner of creature is this," asked a third man, "and where did it come from?"

"Take your seats, gentlemen," Montilis told them, "and we will begin."

"We will have answers!"

Montilis slammed his fist into the tabletop. His eyes were narrowed, and his jaw clenched, as he glared at each of the men in turn. "I left Palus Regia to rescue my daughter from the Imbellis Asylum. You are each responsible for my failure. As a result, the alchemist, Malstar, forced two children to meddle in things they did not understand. You were told of the god that emerged in Bealson's Grove and of his threat, and still you tied my hands. This"—he gestured to the one-eyed beast that had appeared in the swamps of Palus Regia—"was Earth's next move. Tell me, what do you believe will follow?"

Those who ruled over the Houses sat back in their seats, having had their bluster stolen. Sarif was the one to speak.

"You believe there will be more of the beasts to come?"

"I believe he was sent to test our defenses," Montilis said, "and though I have not had time to confirm it, I do not believe we were the only ones attacked. This creature had the strength of an angeli. He had an angeli's speed. He was slow of mind, yet his determination to see his task to completion was steadfast. In my opinion, this was the first wave of war and the weakest opposition from Earth we will face."

"We did not hear you before," Sarif said, "but we are listening now. What do you suggest we do, General?" He cast a quick glance to those gathered. "The Houses will stand with you."

Montilis stood in stoic silence as he loomed over the others, exuding an aura of disgust and disdain towards those who'd caused such unnecessary obstacles. "I will send word to the House of Angeli. I will tell my daughter that at last Palus Regia has found its spine and that we stand with them. When they call upon us, the Nox go to war."

IX

The Pero

"What in hades, Trachius," Apollo asked, "you're taking a club?"

"I make. I take." Trachius growled.

"Whatever, man," Apollo chortled as Poseidon receded the stone and opened the third gateway. "You might need it."

The vision inside the gateway was a garden that even Zeus would envy. A high stone wall with the images of winged angels ran the perimeter. The shorter walls that meandered throughout were covered with wisteria vines. The bases of the grey fountains were surrounded by multicolored stones, and flora of all kinds dotted the serene setting with brilliant colors. The fresh, clean scent wafting into the dark chamber was sweet.

Six large pillars with jasmine growing between them held aloft a canopy that sheltered a small circular table and chairs. Torches set every five feet lined the walls of the garden, lighting the area as if the suns were up. A man with pale skin and yellow eyes, tall and slender and dressed in royal blue robes, stepped from beneath the shade.

"Well, mortalis," the yellow-eyed man said, lifting his voice so as to be heard from across the expanse of the main garden, "do you intend to come through, or do you prefer to hide in the hole you're in?" His jaw went slack and his eyes widened when Poseidon stepped aside and Trachius took his place before the opening.

"Father no mortal," Trachius replied too low for the taunting Superian to hear. "He a god!"

That, the man in blue heard just fine.

One long stride carried him through and the gateway closed. Forty feet behind him was a black wrought iron gate, and nearly one hundred feet separated him and the one he faced. With high stone walls to both sides of him, Trachius didn't see another exit.

He hefted his club as yellow-eyed men with strange pointed ears appeared from the nooks and crannies of the garden's maze-like walls. Two rushed in from his right. He rose his weapon, and their chests collapsed beneath the blunt force before they were heaved into the nearest wall, where their skulls cracked and their bodies rebounded onto the ground, dead.

Two more attacked from behind. The thudding of their boots betrayed their location. Pivoting around, he tossed his club into the air and struck out with closed fists. Their facial bones crushed as the impact threw them backwards.

Trachius snatched his club on its descent and then howled as a spear pierced the heavy muscle in his back. Without pause, he turned on the coward who'd attacked from the rear and smashed his club into the man's gut. Twice the man's length and girth, the club's end folded him in half.

A braver man came forward…spear in hand. With a practiced lunge, the point found its mark in Trachius's right thigh before it was pulled loose by its wielder. A second man, as blond as Apollo with Hades's dark scowl, whirled his blade as a master swordsman and advanced.

The swordsman gave a surprised shout as Trachius closed in on him faster than anticipated. He attempted a crouch but wasn't fast enough.

Stepping inside the man's reach, Trachius grabbed him by the throat and groaned. He lifted him from the ground in one fluid motion and impaled him on the other guard's spear.

"No!" the spearman roared as he skittered across the ground to his fallen comrade. He looked up in time to see the giant's foot smashing down and then he saw no more.

The man in blue stood beside another in a black uniform as Trachius returned his attention to them.

"Nutrine," the man said, drawing his short swords from the scabbards hanging on his lean hips, "you need to run."

"Nonsense," Trachius heard the man in blue reply, "call in the Pero."

"I can't leave you here alone," the guard said.

"Do as I say," Nutrine growled.

The guard backed away, his eyes trained on the Cyclops. Entering a pocket of pruned shrubs, the man disappeared through a hidden hole in the ground.

"Hehehe," Trachius chortled, starting forward. "Now it just you and me."

"Ahhhhh," a battle cry sounded as a solitary man shot

forward at an angle to intercept him.

Planting his left foot, Trachius leaned back his weight and kicked straight out with his right leg. The powerful blow launched the man across the length of the garden. Nutrine held steady as the body flew, head over feet, missing him by mere inches to crack a pillar behind him.

"Your brute strength and swift agility are attributes to be admired," Nutrine said as the giant began to advance. "You claim your master is an Earth god."

Trachius continued on in slow, even steps.

"I'm as close to a god as Superi has. Kneel before me, and I will grant you your life."

With half the distance crossed, Trachius paused when a purple portal opened to Nutrine's left and five men stepped through it. As tall as the others, they bore a heavier weight on their frames, laden with the long, thick, corded muscles of agile warriors. Armored in light, black chainmail overlaid with uniforms of fine, red silk, they measured their enemy. One, with a golden rope running the length of his left arm, stood out from the others.

"From the looks of you, giant, your master cares little for your wellbeing. I offer you a place here and an advance in your station," Nutrine told him. "I do not make such offers lightly, nor do I make them often, so consider your next step carefully, Earthling."

Trachius's single eye narrowed as his nostrils flared. "You talk too much."

Nutrine pinched the bridge of his sharp, angled, nose. "Insolence." He pressed his lips thin. "Your choice is made." To his guards, he said, "I'd see him hurt before I saw him dead."

One of the five, who bore red, swirling marks over the right side of his face, brought his hands together. When they parted, a black hole tore through the aether. The man wearing the golden rope disappeared through it.

A moment later, Trachius felt a heated blow to the back of his head. Twisting his hulking torso around, he snarled at the fire wielder who stood before the wrought iron gate.

A fire ball shot out of the gold rope-wearer's hands and hit Trachius in the head, engulfing his face.

"Exoculo!" the man shouted his order.

Three of the pointed-eared, human-like men placed themselves in a bowing curve, with the red-marked man standing in the concave before the one called Nutrine. It was the last thing Trachius saw before the strange world went dark.

The gate maker of the five opened a portal before their aquis wielder, who stood at point.

Pulling his element out of the closest fountain, he whipped cords of it through the portal, where they exited through two more conjured behind the Cyclops. The beast was knocked forward as the blasts of water hit the back of his head, peeling flesh from bone.

Though he could not see, Trachius turned towards the threat, covering his face.

A spear levitated from the ground by their telekinetic's hand. A flick of his wrist sent it flying.

Trachius howled as the sharp projectile entered the top of his right thigh and didn't stop until its head had punctured through.

A fourth portal was opened, completing a circular pattern around the Cyclops's head, and the aquis wielder did his worst. From the safety of his place at the other end of the garden, he conjured a steady flow of water from several fountains and then pummeled the giant with it.

Trachius was lost to the whim of the telepath, disoriented by the darkness. The warmth of his blood mingled with the ice-laced water being beaten into his head and face. Reaching out, he screamed when his hand was severed from his wrist, courtesy of a portal's edge he could not see.

Needing a heavier tool, the telekinetic began to lift a stone statue that teetered on its foundation.

Nutrine scowled. "You are replaceable," he said. "It is not."

His fun spoiled, but refusing to be left out the fight, the telekinetic lifted a dead guard instead and hurled the corpse at the back of the Cyclops's knees. They buckled, and the beast fell to his back.

"Finish this," their golden rope-wearing leader bellowed, his voice growing louder as he approached.

The three small portals combined into a gaping black hole, with a purple edge flowing with energy, hovering parallel to the downed giant.

The grass at the aquis wielder's feet shriveled as he pulled the moisture from the ground. Nearby basins went dry, and the fountain he'd used cracked as he stole the last of its substance. So great was the ice spike he formed that when he cast it through the portal, its edges were sheared off. The backsplash drenched Nutrine and all four wielders.

The ignis wielder was doused when the ice spike made its exit. He jumped back with a curse on his lips, blood sprayed from the Cyclops's chest and mouth as his body was severed in two.

The portals vanished as the men walked with Nutrine over to their leader and the now-dead body.

"It would appear you're losing your touch, Maltris," Nutrine said. "You didn't faze him, and you"—he turned to the aquis wielder—"will pay for the damage to my garden."

The man's throat bobbed and he bowed deep.

"I don't understand it," Maltris said. "It's as if he is fire resistant."

"Nonsense. Only ignis wielders are resistant, and feras do not possess elemental abilities." At Maltris's dubious expression, Nutrine added, "Do you think he would not have used it if he were able?"

The others backed away as Maltris conjured a fire ball in his right hand. Kneeling, he pressed the rolling flames against the giant. The grey linen the giant wore turned to ash, but the flesh beneath remained whole.

"I don't think this a fera," Maltris told him, "and neither do you."

"You're right," Nutrine said. "I do not."

"What are our orders, sir?" the gate maker asked.

Maltris looked to Nutrine for answer.

"Travel to Pisces Stragulum," Nutrine said. "Find Shorlynn. It is time your betrothed came home, and then we prepare for war."

X

Bigger than ME!

"I was beginning to think Superi knew no snow," Apollo said after the next gateway had been opened, "but this place is covered in it."

"I no like cold." Acamas crossed his arms to ward off the biting chill blowing into the cavernous chamber.

"Do not worry, Acamas," Poseidon said, "you'll not be here long. Remember, when their twin suns reach their zenith, the gateway will reopen, and you will return a legend."

"It is dark on this side of the planet," Apollo said to Acamas. "Only their moons are out, so do not travel so far that you cannot find your way back."

Acamas acknowledged Apollo's warning with a nod and then said, "For you, Father," as he stepped through and turned to watch as the gateway was closed.

His large eye squinted to catch the dim light cast by moons of Superi over the vast, white landscape of nothingness. The harsh wind blew against him, chattering his jagged teeth. He prayed to Poseidon as he made his way forward that his tracks would not be covered over, or he would be lost.

Topping a rise, he peered down into a valley where domed mud huts where clustered in an outward growing circle. The largest, nearly twenty feet tall, sat at the center. He squatted, hunching against the relentless chill of the wind, and waited for the denizens of Superi to reveal themselves.

From behind came the gasp of a female. Acamas pivoted round as he stood to his full height to gape back.

Brown-furred with long whiskers and protruding bucked teeth, the female fera held a wrapped bundle in her arms that squirmed and cried out at its mother's tightening hold. The growl of her mate was that of a wolf as he cast off the hide blanket from his shoulders, his black and white fur rising along the ridge of his spine. He dropped to all fours and bared his sharp teeth as he prepared to defend his mate and young.

"Monster!" Acamas bellowed as he charged the couple.

"Run!" the male shouted as together they raced towards the safety of the village. "Incoming!" The wolf howled to give warning of impeding danger as they slipped and tumbled down the edge of the rise.

Acamas, sinking to his kneecaps into the snow, was slowed, but having been discovered he trudged on. Entering the village between two huts located on the perimeter, he grunted as a heavy weight crashed against him from both sides.

Sharp claws ripped through his flesh as he lifted an arm to ward off one attack, while clenching his fist to bring it down upon the second. The human-faced woman's neck snapped under the pressure. Her orange fur, dotted with black spots, contrasted with the snow as she fell dead upon it.

Acamas had no time to relish in his first victory as teeth clashed against the bone in his forearm. With a vicious shake, he dislodged the teeth in his flesh and sent the bearer sailing through the air and through the wall of the nearest hut.

Within the house, a fire burned, wooden and cloth toys were scattered about the dry earthen floor, and a family of monsters with their cubs between them peered back at him with terrified eyes.

He watched as the villagers spilled from their homes on the verge of flight, but one stood still.

Fury pulled back the thin, black lips surrounding its protruding muzzle as its triangular ears twitched. Lean, agile muscles tensed beneath its red fur as it goaded, "Chase me, giant, and I will lead you to your death."

"Hehehe," Acamas chortled. Stepping from the loose, powdered snow onto the harder, packed ground inside the village, he gave chase.

The red-furred monster's tail bushed as he tucked it and ran towards the heart of the clustered huts, howling, "Belua! Defend us!"

Nearly upon his enemy, Acamas opened his arms wide to capture his foe in a deadly embrace, but a monster of epic portion emerged from the largest hut to block his path. Rising to his full height, he prepared to face the new threat, but fear rippled up his spine when the monster rose as well to tower over him.

No animal he'd ever seen matched that of the one before him. The head of a hyena, with the neck of a boar, sat upon shoulders twice the length of an axe handle. It shrugged off the grey fur mantle it wore, and Acamas found further reason to fear. Bulging muscle prevented the monster's arms from resting at its sides. Its barrel chest narrowed to more slender hips, but the legs upon which the monster stood could have as easily been oaks.

Afraid that he'd encountered a god, Acamas hesitated.

The monster did not.

The ground shook as it came at him with the promise of retribution in its pale blue eyes.

Acamas roared and braced for initial impact as one powerful arm shot out, palm open, to smash into his face. He felt himself falling and reached back to catch himself. His single eye grew wide as the monster hefted a spiked club the size of a tree from its back.

"No!" Acamas cried, covering his head with both arms, but his plea fell on deaf ears.

With a mighty heave of a single overhanded blow, Acamas met his end as his skull cracked, spilling his brain and staining the snow.

The villagers spilled from their hiding places and gathered round their guardian, bowing in gratitude.

Acknowledging the accolades without basking in them, Belua asked in a deep, resonating voice, "Are there more of his kind?"

"No, Belua," the red-furred fera replied, "but we'll send scouts to make certain."

"Good," Belua said. "Sera." He gestured over to a slight female with slick silver fur who dipped her head in difference. "Homes have been damaged. See their inhabitants are placed in another until repairs can be made." Glancing overhead, he added, "A storm moves in, and I'll not have our people suffer the cold."

"Of course, Belua," she said and then turned to the task.

"Move…move…move, move," came a rushed, flustered order, rising in pitch, as a tall, grey-feathered fera fought his way from the back of the crowd. His useless, speckled wings broadened his lanky frame beneath his long, hooded cloak from which emerged two spindly arms. "Bring me my tools," he insisted, dropping to his knees beside the strange creature who'd invaded their home. "I want to open him up. I want to know what he is."

"The Alphas will as well," Belua stated. "Find me the answer."

Retracing the steps of the monster, Belua's long legs carried him to the top of the rise. A place of slush marked where a gateway had been opened. There were no trees for an enemy to hide behind, but with care he studied each mound of snow, each dip in the landscape, lest his eyes be tricked. It had been a long time since someone dared attack Dura Mortis, and he would not be caught unaware twice.

Seeing nothing of note, he returned and found Kershna elbow-deep in the monster's flayed chest, its skull sawed from the top of its head.

"What is it?" Belua asked.

"For truth, guardian," Kershna replied, "I do not know. It has a heart the same as we do, but its brain is of diminutive

size. There is evidence in the tissue of an ignis ability, or"—
he shook his head—"at least a resistance to the element.
The creature is one of brawn, not of brain, and that tells us
that he did not act of his own accord. He was released upon
Superi as a hand of destruction."

"I would find the arm responsible for wielding it," Belua
said, "and see it severed from the whole along with the life
that gave it direction."

"As would I," came a gruff voice, thick with emotion.

Belua turned towards the black-scaled man in thick robes
who held one of their dead, his mate, cradled in his arms.
Her orange fur stood in contrast against his dark chest.

"The ground is frozen solid," the man's voice broke, "and
there is no wood for a pyre."

"Brother." Belua approached, relieving the man of his
burden. "Come with me."

Together they entered the largest center hut, and Belua
laid her upon his own padded bedding. Crossing the earthen
floor, he knelt before the burning hearth and entreated Huron
to do the same.

"Let us focus on our Alpha," Belua said, "and summon
her awareness so that we may tell her of what has transpired.
We will implore her to send an ignis wielder that will prepare your mate's body for her next life."

Kneeling with the guardian, Huron said with clenched
teeth, "And we will seek war in retribution."

"Indeed."

Focus became their intent until Luna's voice entered their
minds, relaxing their tense muscles, as she took control.

"*Huron, your grief is tangible,*" she said. "*What weighs*

so heavily upon your heart?"

"The death of my beloved," Huron spoke aloud though the conversation was one of the mind.

"By what means was her life taken?"

It was Belua who answered. "A gateway was opened, Alpha," he said, "and a monster was belched from its maw and descended upon our village. Its appearance was not that of the human image you implanted in my mind, nor did it wield power beyond its own strength. It viewed our world through a singular eye, but lacked the intelligence to comprehend the encompassing danger it was in. Brutish as it was, I felt as if I struck down a child. Regardless, Nomi's life was lost. We seek direction, Luna, and your will."

"Make preparation and see the village secured. Sole and I will journey to Dura Mortis. We would see Nomi set to rest. Afterward, we will lay eyes upon this son of Earth and speak of war reignited."

"Thank you, Luna," Huron said in breathless relief. "I seek blood for blood."

"And soon, it will flow in abundance."

"Will my sister accompany you?" Belua asked, feeling the connection between them beginning to weaken.

"Torren would have it no other way."

Once the connection was severed, Huron's knees cracked as he gained his footing. Turned in the direction of his beloved, he kept his gaze lowered. Tears dropped into the hard-packed terra at his feet.

"She was the smallest of our warriors," Huron said, "yet her bravery was unparalleled. Her beauty like no other. Her smile…" His words trailed off into a heart wrenching intake of air.

"Your sorrow is my greatest fear," Belua said, speaking as softly as his deep voice allowed. "She was my smallest warrior. Her sacrifice for Dura Mortis placed her name among those who will be exulted for all time. It is my pride in her that is unparalleled, and though she has been absent from the world for but a moment, I miss that smile as well." He squared his shoulders. "I seek no mate, for you are a stronger man than I. The sorrow you bear would be the end of me."

When Huron turned to face his guardian, the life had left his eyes as surely as it had left his beloved's body, and what remained was vengeance incarnate. "I will join her in death as quickly as I am able, but first," he said, "Earth will pay."

"Indeed it will," Sole said, as he parted the leather flaps covering Belua's door.

Luna followed after.

It was a tossup as to whose knees hit the ground first as both warrior and guardian bowed before their Alphas.

XI

Time Difference?

"Ugh." Apollo held open the gateway, but turned his head from the vile stench wafting through the opening. "Hurry up, Elatreus," he said. "This is one gate I am anxious to see closed."

Elatreus retreated from the dead city his Father urged him towards, nearly knocking Poseidon over when he backed into him. "This bad place," he said. "Death walks here."

"The city seems abandoned, my child," Poseidon stated, "and you know better than to fear spirits."

Apollo chuckled and then gagged at the intake of rancid air. "I know a few I fear," he said. "Thankfully their souls are bound in Tartarus."

"Tartarus"—Elatreus pointed through the gateway—"is there."

"Nonetheless," Poseidon said, "you will enter because it is my will."

"Father," Elatreus pleaded, "no make me go."

"I will return for you." Poseidon pulled a wave from an underwater chamber that washed the Cyclops through.

Elatreus scrambled to return to Earth, but Apollo closed the gate and sealed him out. He took off his shirt and tied it around his mouth and nose, blinking rapidly as his eye began to burn. Fear carried him forwards as he began to search for an exit.

Not a single blade of grass cushioned his bare feet upon the dusty streets. The trees, grey and lifeless, spread their bare limbs like fingers of death over homes held together by rotted wood.

The absence of life, even that of insects, made the silence surrounding him all the more terrifying as he approached the inner city. Buildings made of rock and mortar sat side by side, with only narrow alleyways in between, facing forward from four directions towards the communal well. Parched, he made his way to it, but bitter bile rose in his throat at the putrid skim overlaying the water.

Feeling faint, he continued onward towards the high surrounding wall of the city, but stumbled to a stop when a giant hole barred his path. Black, scorched earth bled outward from the crater, creeping like the plague. Runes were carved in the ground around it lined in a blue metal he'd never seen.

He began to cough and then choked as the linen wrapped around his head grew moist. Yanking the material loose, he panicked at the sight of blood. Wiping his nose with the back of his hand, it too was slicked with the scarlet fluid.

Too weak to run, dizzy and nauseous, he forced his dragging feet to carry him around the sore in the earth. The closer he came to his freedom, brown, twisted, snarled vines began to appear running up the walls of both houses and buildings. Even the might of the high stone wall was no match for the destructive vegetation. Everything the vines touched crumbled and was pulled down.

Nearing the exit, desperate to reach the huge healthy trees that lay beyond, he was afforded a closer look. A yellow pus oozed from cracks in the vines' crusted shell, the source of the foul odor permeating the air.

Stumbling from the city, he went as far as his strength would carry him and then collapsed as he rolled to his back beneath the shade of healthy trees to breathe in fresh air. His vision cleared, and he found himself entranced by the orange haze in the Superian sky. Its two great suns burned a fiery red, but despite their light a multitude of colored moons hung in the background.

The need for water soon outweighed his need for rest. Using a tree trunk to support his wavering weight, he waited until he was steady and then pushed off. The further he traveled the better he felt, though his skin was raw, and his lungs burned with each intake of breath.

Keeping close watch on the positions of the suns and dreading the hour he would have to return to the damned city, he found himself before another stone wall. This one was higher than the other with a wide turret atop it and was built in a V shape that reminded him of an arrow's head.

Heavily guarded on both sides by human-like men and warped beasts that spoke with words he could understand, he listened, gleaning what information he could for his father. One voice was lifted above the others.

"He's been spotted," a man said.

"Was he alone?" another asked.

"The scouts saw only him, but they run in packs," the first man replied. "Exterius is sending guards to replace us. Gather your weapons. We are going hunting."

Elatreus had seen no one and was confounded by his discovery. Not knowing what else to do, he turned and fled. His head twisted towards the dead city, but he ran past. He ran until he reached the edge of the wood and a plain of wheat-colored grass that rolled out before him.

Head and shoulders above the height of it, and with no other way to hide, he traversed deeper into the field in a crouch. He fell forward, his weight braced on his feet and fingertips, and encountered a creature that blended so well into the surrounding environs that it was at first invisible. It was the rapid clicking issued from the back of the beast's throat that first alerted him to its presence.

"What are you?" the creature, clothed in light brown linen overlaid with medium leather armor asked, his drooping, grey eyes focused.

"What you?" Elatreus retorted.

"If you are fera," the creature said, "I've no quarrel with you. From what region do you come?"

Like a great ape perched on three limbs, Elatreus scratched at his bald, horned head. "Earth?"

The creature's rumbled growl was echoed by companions hiding in the grass. Sharp, dagger-like claws dangling from overlong arms dropped to the ground. With a slow buildup of speed, the creature said, "You should not be here," and then he lunged.

With a backhanded swipe, Elatreus knocked the creature

from the air. The creature rolled and came back to his feet with a nasty gash on his forehead. An orange feline hissed, baring teeth and claws; she attacked, climbing her way up the Cyclops's back, slicing his flesh with every inch gained. He threw himself backward to smash her flat.

Shoving off his back, she flipped and landed on all fours. "Nice try, you big oaf," she quipped. Tail lashing, she prepared to pounce again.

The earth gained a heartbeat as a bull-like creature with twin horns protruding from the sides of his head stomped his feet. His cylindrical snout crinkled as hot breath blew from flared nostrils. Pulling a staff from his back, he drew the female up short.

"Back off, Luce," he said. "He's mine."

Circling, her gaze momentarily distracted as she checked on their wounded leader, she replied, "He hurt Rupert. You'll have to fight me for him."

Sickened from the city and bleeding profusely, Elatreus feared his demise. Salvation came in the form of the hunting party, a squad of Superians dressed in white and green tunics and drenched in weapons, some already aimed at his would-be executioners. They froze when their eyes fell upon him.

"Well don't just stand there," Rupert shouted. "He's an Earthling! Kill him!"

"What in tarnation is an Earthling?" one from the hunting party asked another.

Having no answer, the one who'd issued commands at the wall replied to Rupert instead, "We're not here for him. We're here for you. The magistrate of Exterius Antro wishes to speak to your tribal alpha and he's willing to bet your capture will bring her to him."

"That's not going to happen," Rupert snarled. "Luce," he said, and the feline creature moved to his side. "Dunhold," he added, "do not let that thing escape."

Hearing the order, and daunted by the strength exuded from the creature while he was so weakened, Elatreus fled in the only direction offered to him. His longer, more powerful strides gained him distance from his pursuer, but his stamina was waning, and the suns had reached their zenith without his notice.

Reaching the toppling outer wall of the dead city, he fell against the edge of the stone entry and howled as a vine's pus spread beneath his palm. Grabbing his wrist, he suffered as the flesh on his hand turned black and peeled outward as if to escape. His wide-eyed stare, however, was on the creature who'd come to a stop some distance away with his back against the trunk of a tree and his arms crossed.

"The death you have chosen I would not thrust upon my worst enemy, but I'll stay until it has claimed you."

A fevered chill swept over him at the creature's words. The blackness was spreading down his fingers, running up his arm in thick lines edging their way over his shoulder. His chest began to hurt as he turned his back on the creature and prayed to his father that the way would be open when he arrived.

The dry, dusty streets cutting lines through the city all appeared the same. Tears coursed from his eye, both from pain and fear, when at last he reached the dark crater. From there he was lost. Just as panic seized him, streaks of lightning showed him the way. The bright flashes of purple and white cut through his impending blindness, offering him direction.

"Elatreus."

He heard his father's voice.

"What did they do to him?" Apollo asked. "Watch out!"

In his haste to cross over, Elatreus failed to raise his step and was cut off at the ankles as he spilled through. "Father," he cried, "I dead."

"No." Poseidon bent on one knee beside his creation. "You have returned."

Apollo, amidst disgruntled complaints, stemmed the flow of blood gushing from both of Elatreus's lower limbs and asked, "What happened?"

Elatreus grasped for Poseidon's hand with the one he could still lift. "They monsters. Dead city a trap. Walls everywhere. Grass hides. Beasts." He began to cough, spewing blood. "Talk."

"What curse did they put upon you, my child?" Poseidon asked as the rot continued to spread across Elatreus's flesh. "I vow to deliver one far worse."

The Cyclops opened his mouth to reply, but his engorged tongue burst on his jagged teeth, and his words were lost as he drowned in his own contaminated blood.

Poseidon gathered his son into his arms, holding him through his last gurgling breaths as his body quaked with a father's rage. "Open the gates," he demanded.

Apollo laid a hand on Poseidon's shoulder. "I know you're angry, but we've been here long past the appointed time, and I've opened them every four hours." Removing his hand, he stared down at Elatreus's decomposing corpse. "Poseidon," he said, "I don't believe your sons are going to make it back. The other gods need to know how dire the situation is."

With salty tears coursing down his face, Poseidon rocked Elatreus, though the creature was beyond comfort. "The Superians do not deserve curses. They deserve far worse. I'm going to rip the heads off of every angel I find."

Apollo grew concerned as the chamber began to fill with water.

Standing, as Elatreus's body began to float, Poseidon turned to Apollo. "Call your summit. Make sure that all gods are there, not only our Pantheon. We are going to rip their planet apart this time."

Elatreus's corpse drifted towards the cavern from which Poseidon's sons had first appeared. "Leave me," Poseidon said. "I'll rejoin you."

With the water level now at his waist, Apollo asked, "What are you going to do?"

"I'm going to bury my son."

XII

Ship? What Ship?

Having said their goodbyes over breakfast, Set and Davad rode out of Pisces Stragulum to the south. They came to a stop by a sparse cropping of trees that stood just beyond sight of the city's wall. From beneath the shade of the biggest trees with heavy, green boughs and bold splashes of color, the two ogled the flamboyant white carriage with cushioned seats of crushed red velvet and curtains of silken gold that were tied back from its windows. Lacquered wooden luggage with silver fasteners was piled atop it and strapped down with rope. Four white horses with r ed harnesses pranced in eager anticipation of being off.

"Is this yours?" Set asked Jorden as he watched the younger boy dismount and hand his reins over to one of his men.

"My advisors cautioned against arriving by carriage," Jorden explained. "They warned the Five were a simple people and may find such a grandiose entrance ostentatious." He

---

125

shrugged. "I needed you to see me as one of you." Grinning, he added, "I'm glad I listened to them. As it was, you guys were hard enough on me. You were actually kind of mean."

"We weren't mean," Davad countered. "We save that for people we like."

Set laughed at Jorden's confusion and slid from his saddle for a closer look at the carriage.

"You aren't seriously going to ride in that thing are you?" Davad questioned.

"Well, yeah…" Set replied. "Have you ever seen a ride this nice? I haven't." He peeked through the open door.

"No, but"—he twisted in his saddle to search for witnesses before turning back around— "someone might see. We'd never live it down."

"I won't tell a soul, sir," Nathin said, a grin teasing the corners of his mouth. "As your guard, your secret will be safe with me."

"See," Set said, "he won't tell, and we're leaving the rest of these guys in Regia Aquam."

"You might enjoy it, sir," Nathin added when Davad eyed the carriage askance.

"That's what I'm afraid of," Davad said. "I think I'll stick to the saddle."

"Suit yourself." Set grinned as he used the step mounted beneath the carriage to duck through the door behind Jorden. "Ahhh," he sighed, falling into a seat and wiggling his rear deeper into the plush cushion. "You were right not to try this, Davad."

Maneuvering his horse, Davad peered in through the window.

"Once you've felt this kind of comfort there is no unfeeling it," Set said. "I wonder if saddle seats could be fashioned with cushions."

Davad heard Jorden reply, "This is the only way to travel across land," before he tuned them out.

As the driver took up the reins, and the coachman climbed into his position, Jorden's guards scattered to cover all sides of the carriage. Nathin rooted himself at Davad's left flank just as Jorden's knuckles rapped against the carriage's ceiling. A sharp snap of the reins and the wheels jerked into motion.

They rode in silence for a time, allowing the plains of vibrant green to roll past as they traveled alongside the sea bluff. The oceanus was turbulent with choppy, white waves frothing at the shore. Gusts of chilled morning air rushed inland, whipping Davad's hood from his head. He turned his face into the wind to blow away the hair that blinded him. A guard was staring, not at him, but at his sword.

"Forgive me," the guard said, bowing from his saddle. "I do not mean to stare."

"No worries," Davad said. "I understand it is a bit much for me to carry." His hand went to the hilt of the dracon sword at his waist. He could feel the blade against his outer thigh. "My father was a master swordsman. When my skill matches what his were, I will be worthy of it."

"I've seen you at practice," the guard told him. "You are not without natural ability." He nodded. "You'll find your aim in time."

Pulling his hood into place, Davad wrapped the edges of his father's cloak tighter around his shoulders. "Can I ask you a question?"

"Of course, sir."

"You have come with Sir Jorden to undermine the authority of the king, whose colors you wear." Davad looked over. "Is that what Regia Aquam considers loyalty?"

The guard stiffened.

"I mean no offense, but we are soon to meet your king and we know precious little about your ways or culture. Ignorance is not something we can afford."

"There is but one king on Superi, and that is Normis. He attained his power, as did his predecessors, by strength of body and wit. He usurped his king, and it is inevitable that he will be usurped by one Ruling House or another. It is how we ensure that the most fit rules. It keeps us strong against outside enemies. I obey the king, but my loyalty is to the House of Terra. I wear the king's colors"—he tugged on a thin length of brown leather tied about his neck and held out the silver signet of stacked squares dangling from its end—"but I am bound to Mitable Terra."

"What, then, would you do if your king asked you to turn against your House, or what if your House asked you to act against your king? How is Sir Jorden's visit not looked upon by Normis as treason?"

The guard grinned with half his mouth. "In Regia Aquam, a man can only be prosecuted if caught with physical proof of wrong doing."

Davad shook his head.

"You do not approve?"

"No," Davad answered. "I do not."

The stiff tension and lack of conversation was manageable, and it allowed Davad's mind time to race ahead.

Davad let Set sleep until the city of Caterva Concentio appeared on the horizon. "Stop the carriage. Set," he said, reining his mount close to its window, "it's time to wake up."

With a languid stretch, Set blinked several times before climbing out. "Best sleep I've ever had," he said as his horse was untied from behind the carriage and brought to him. "Thank you," he said to the guard as he pulled himself into the saddle.

Davad barely heard him. "I hate this place." His eyes narrowed. "If ever a city needed razing, it would be the one that delivered Shashara and Anliac from the oceanus and into the grip of the Asylum."

"I know," Set said. "Of all the scars Shashara carries, it's the one on her temple, from the rock that little girl threw, that haunts her the most. Shashara told me that she pitied the people of Caterva Concentio more than any other. Pities them." He shook his head. "Can you believe that? Your sister's heart is too big to hate, so I hate this city enough for the both of us."

"From what I hear, we're not much going to like Regia Aquam either."

Jorden's head popped out the window. "Wait...what?" he asked. "Why would you say that?"

"Normis is a dictator," Davad said, "a tyrant who gained his power by betraying his king, and the Ruling Houses are circling, waiting to pounce and prove that they've learned well the tactics of their leader."

"No." Jorden paled. "It's true King Normis is powerful,

but he is also just. He places the needs of his people before his own, keeping always the greater good at the forefront of his mind. He sees and rewards ambition. He is a good man."

"Isn't your House trying take his throne?" Set asked.

"That's what I asked." Davad rolled his eyes. "And I was told that the king expects nothing less from his subjects than stiff competition for his rule. It is their way."

Set's brows crawled up his forehead. "What kind of loyalty is that?"

Davad's arm rose dramatically and his hand smacked his leg on its descent. "That's what I said."

"Wait until you've met him," Jorden pleaded, "before you judge him."

"Tell us about him then," Set said.

Jorden's brows drew down. "I don't understand. I just did."

"No," Davad countered. "You spit out a piece of rehearsed drivel prepared by one who has not likely ever met the king."

Jorden swallowed.

"I'm guessing neither have you," Set said in response to the sheen of sweat that broke across Jorden's forehead.

"I've seen him," Jorden blurted, and in a more sedated tone added, "from a distance. He's a large man, heavy with muscle. His hair is black and he has a goatee…"

"What's his ability?" Davad asked. "What level is he?"

Jorden's head dropped, his chin touching his chest, as he sat back in his seat to disappear from their view.

Set and Davad exchanged a smirking glance, as they entered the city on a long dirt road that ran alongside the dock.

Caterva Concentio was set up in sections separated by narrow streets. A mercantile sat on their left next to the Town Council, both buildings made of wood, and then they came to two inns sitting side by side. A trading post with crates of vegetables and barrels of potatoes was located further down, but it was the slave stage at the end of the road that drew their gaze over and over again. The long, wooden platform stood before a rectangular building where cages held the prisoners brought into the city by the slavers.

They knew, of course, that Shashara had never been held there, but they hated what it represented. When Jorden rapped his knuckles on the ceiling, and the carriage rolled to a stop before the first inn, they drew rein and dismounted.

"Nathin," Davad said, "see the horses taken to the stables." He withdrew a few coins from his pocket. "Make sure they are wiped down and well fed."

"Yes, sir." Nathin gave a sharp nod and, gathering their reins with his, led the beasts down a narrow alley to the back of the inns where a communal stable stood.

A conglomeration of people of differing races crowded the street, and the presence of Jorden's carriage created a stir. Those passing bowed, and Jorden's chin lifted with arrogance.

Two of his guards took up position on either side of the inn door, while the others stood unobtrusively waiting for orders.

"Return the carriage," Jorden told the driver, "and offer my gratitude to Sir Ridrick for its use."

"Yes, sir," the driver replied, snapping the reins and ambling down the road.

Stepping from the dirt onto the covered boardwalk, Jorden tracked Davad and Set's stare to the slave station and said, "The slave trade is an essential part of the city's economic stability."

"There is no excuse for imprisoning innocent people," Davad snarled. "It's a deplorable act that the Angeli intend to put a stop to when this war is over."

Jorden chuckled. "Good luck with that." The menacing glares he received had him clearing his throat and continuing, "Caterva Concentio used to belong to the fulgo, but became neutral ground after the last war. A sect of mortalis thought to claim it as their own without the authority of the king. That"—he grinned—"did not go over well. Now it is run by a council consisting of representatives chosen by the people." He shook his head. "It's ridiculous. Commoners know nothing of what it means to rule."

"Is that so?" Set retorted. "In that case, Pisces Stragulum is in trouble."

Jorden's eyes rounded as he realized what he'd said. "Forgive me. I didn't mean to imply…"

"So what is the plan?" Davad cut him off.

"We will stay here for the night," Jorden answered, "while we wait on my ship to be readied."

"What ship?" Set paled. "You never…" He looked to Davad. "No one said anything about a ship." He shook his head in slow turns. "I am not doing it."

Davad chuckled. "Calm yourself, Set." To Jorden, he said, "You don't have a gate maker we can use?"

Perplexed, Jorden replied, "The gate makers of Regia Aquam are employed by the king. I came by ship. The journey will only take a few weeks, and I assure you that your accommodations will make the time pass quickly."

Set gagged and was forced to swallow the bile that spilled into his mouth to keep from embarrassing himself in front of Jorden and his men.

Jorden's eyes darted between his two companions. "Is there a problem?"

"Uh, yeah," Set snapped.

"Set doesn't do well over water," Davad explained.

"Set...isn't going out on the water," Set stated. "It's a deal breaker."

"We gave our word," Davad reminded him. "Anliac and Tristan are counting on us. So, unless you intend on pulling the information from Jorden's head to make a portal, I don't see where we have an option."

Set's head continued to shake. "It's not going to happen. I don't care if it's a ship, a boat, a canoe, a stinking piece of rotted driftwood, I'm not getting on it."

"I miss the open oceanus."

"You can grow flipping fins and live in it if that's what you want, but my feet aren't leaving shore."

Jorden perched on the edge of panic. "You will each have a private cabin and a full staff of servants."

"I can jump us to Exterius Antro," Set said as though Jorden hadn't spoken, "and then extract enough information from our boy here to get us the rest of the way."

"If he's willing," Davad pointed out as he opened the door to the inn.

"He will be," Set replied, stepping past Davad to enter the foyer, "if he wants me to go with him."

"What?" Jorden gulped.

Davad smacked him on the back, urging him inside. "Don't worry. It doesn't hurt…much." He entered the inn himself.

The innkeeper, a rotund mortalis with a perpetual blush to his bulbous cheeks, skittered across the room to greet them. "Welcome," he said. "We've been expecting your arrival."

Nathin came in from outside and moved to stand behind Davad and Set.

"How did you know we were coming?" Davad demanded.

His tone had Nathin's spine stiffening as he prepared to defend his charge.

"Thanks for waiting for us this morning."

They all turned toward the sound of the gruff voice to find Davimon and Lishous, arms crossed, filling the entryway between the foyer and common room. Four others stood at their backs. Their uniforms, which had been those of the Angeli Guard, had been replaced with those of the mortalis king.

"Why did you sneak out of Pisces Stragulum?" Davimon questioned.

"First off," Set said, "we don't answer to you. Secondly, we didn't think you'd be traveling with us."

"I can offer you what this boy cannot. We have a gate maker waiting to jump us to Effugere Aquam. From there another will take us to Antro, and then another will portal us to Regia Aquam. If your bodies can handle the traveling."

"Yes!" Set bellowed, startling the others. "Yes," he said

again. "That sounds like a reasonable plan."

Lishous chortled. "I'd heard rumors that one of the Five was scared of water."

Set squared his shoulders. "I'm not afraid of it, but it is my enemy. It has tried to kill me too many times to consider it otherwise."

Davimon grunted as he and Lishous were shoved apart by a mortalis woman who was nearly as wide as she was tall. The bright blue dress she wore was two sizes too small and her curves threatened to spill from both the top and bottom. Red spirals of hair sprang from her head to bounce as her tiny feet carried her forward.

She took Set by the hand. "Don't you worry, honey child. Hyntra is here now." She smiled. "I'll get you to Effugere Aquam without you having to board a ship. Yes I will."

"Um…" Set fought the urge to laugh. "Thank you, ma'am."

Davimon cleared his throat. "Allow me to introduce Hyntra. She's a level one gate maker in service of King Normis."

"A level one," Set said. "That's an awful big jump. Are you sure you can handle it?" he asked her.

Her green eyes crinkled at the corners. "I can't hold it for long, and the portal will be small, but if you and your companions don't hesitate to cross, all will be fine."

"No offense, Hyntra," Set said, "you seem like a very nice lady, but I think it would be better if I opened the portal to Effugere Aquam."

"Suit yourself, love," she replied, peeking at the innkeeper, whose face blotched with scarlet color. "I wasn't quite ready to leave anyway."

"You're forgetting that you can't portal to Antro," Davad pointed out.

"No," Set countered, "but I can get us to Exterius Antro."

"If you can get us to Effugere Aquam," Davimon said, "there is a gate maker of the king's that can get us to Antro."

"I'm concerned about going through more than one portal in a day," Jorden grimaced. "They say the side effects can be…unpleasant. Would it not be better to spend the night in Effugere Aquam and travel on to Antro from there in the morning?"

"No," Davad and Set spoke as one.

"We will not stay in Effugere Aquam any longer than absolutely necessary," Davad added.

Lishous's head cocked to the side. "Is there something we should know?"

"No," they said, but as the pupil of Davimon's white eye dilated, they knew they'd been caught in the lie.

Jorden's shoulders slumped. "We're going to be so… sick."

"Davad and I have gone through more than one portal in a day," Set said. "We were never adversely affected."

"Nor were we." Davimon grinned, nudging Lishous's shoulder when a deep rumble issued from his chest.

"Right," Lishous said. "It's not bad at all."

Set shook his head. They were lying, but if it prevented him having to board a ship, he didn't care. Remembering the damage he'd caused to the inn in Catena Piscari, he turned to the innkeeper. "Can I open a portal in the street," he asked, "or is there a place designated for it?"

"The back alley would suffice," the man offered. "Just

watch the edges, and keep out of line with the horses. No good would come from spooking them."

"Hyntra"—Set bowed and kissed the back of her hand—"it has been a pleasure to meet you, and we thank you for your willingness to serve."

"My, my." She fanned her face with her free hand. "You do know how to make a woman feel special. You boys hurry on now while I introduce myself to this handsome gentleman."

The innkeeper, flustered by the bodacious gate maker, bent his arm as her hand wrapped around it. "Can I interest you in a cup of coffee and a sweet cake?"

As Hyntra followed the man into the common room, the others laughed at her reply.

"Oh honey," she cooed, "you are speaking my language."

Around back, Set took in the sight of the fifteen men waiting on him to get them to Effugere Aquam and sighed. This would be the biggest portal he'd had to open yet.

Davad leaned close to whisper, "You've got this, Set. Just…focus on the dock, okay? The last thing we need is spill out into my mother's front yard."

"Get behind me," Set told the gathered men, "and once the portal is stable, pass through as quickly as you can."

He closed his eyes, focused, and mentally brought forth an image of the dock as he pressed his palms together. As he slowly spread them apart, the portal began to form, but something was wrong. His breathing changed to short, shallow pants as the required bend in the aether fought against him to hold its natural line. His strength drained from him faster than he'd expected and he panicked.

Suddenly the air crackled around him. He felt the hair on his head begin to float and his skin set fire with tingles. His psyche expanded, searching for energy. It was there. He knew it was there. He could sense it…feel it. So when he found it, he took it, gulping it in as fast as he could. A smile started on his face.

His footing grew unsteady as the terra trembled beneath them. He looked down as energy surged from the ground and up through his soles, up his legs, to land like a heavy meal in his gut. Like a lock snapped in place, the purple lightning subsided as the portal stabilized. Its edges smoothed and its corners rounded, creating an egress that offered a wooden dock and a beautiful orange skyline on the other side. Set breathed deep and let it out on a relieved sigh.

"It's done," he said.

One by one the others filed through with Davad holding to the rear. Set was so weak with relief that he nearly let the portal collapse before going through himself. The mild concussion of energy as the points separated shoved him forward several steps before he steadied.

"Cutting it a little close there," Davad said with a pointed look.

"Tell me about it," Set replied, shaken and a little pale.

People darted out of Jorden's way as he rushed for the dock's edge to vomit violently over its side. The locals laughed. Lishous looked as if he might join him, much to Davimon's amusement, while the rest tried not to jest at Jorden's expense.

"I feel bad for him," Set said out of the corner of his mouth.

"Bad enough to take a ship from here?" Davad quipped.

"Ha, no," Set said without hesitation.

As Jorden, groaning, stumbled to where they stood, Davimon suggested, "Our number is great enough to cause concern to the city's guards. It might be better to wait at an inn until I can find our gate maker."

"We'll take our chances," Set said.

Davad added, "We're not leaving the docks."

Davimon's jawbones worked overtime, but he didn't bother arguing. "Lishous, stay with them."

"No," was the fera's quick reply.

Davimon bowed up, his chest inflating with air, but instead of yelling, he exhaled in a heavy gush and turned to the other four guards he had with him. "Do not," he ordered, "let anything happen to them."

"Yes, sir," they replied in unison.

Set and Davad grinned at each other as Davimon and Lishous took off at a steady trot. It was the first time they'd seen Davimon get told no.

Davimon was right. The dock workers' labors had ceased as they stared. The citizens walking past found reason to tarry, their eyes wandering in the group's direction. Davad nudged Set. "Are you seeing this?"

"They're just curious," Set replied. "I'm tracking their emotions. If there's a spike, I'll let you know."

Enough time passed that they were no longer the spectacle to watch but still they stood at the ready.

"What is it about this place you two hate so much?" Jorden asked, holding his tender stomach. "I can understand about Caterva Concentio with what happened to Ms. Shashara and Ms. Anliac, but…" His brows pulled down.

Davad made a sudden study of his boots.

"That's not your concern," Nathin snapped, turning to face Jorden as he came to Davad's defense.

"Watch your tone," one of Jorden's guards warned. "Sir Jorden is of a Ruling House and deserves respect from those in lesser standing."

"The rankings of your king mean nothing to me," Nathin retorted.

"Enough," Set said, then sighed. "Thank Superi." He spotted Davimon and Lishous on the road, headed back from the main square with a mortalis woman they recognized.

"Is that…" Davad squinted.

"It looks like it," Set replied, reaching out his hand when the distance had been cleared and the three stepped onto the wooden planks.

"It's a pleasure to see you again," the woman said as she took it, flinging her thick braid of long, blonde hair back over her shoulder. She smiled, the corners of her grey eyes wrinkling, transforming her plain face into one of unique beauty. "Especially since you both appear to be doing well."

"You know each other?" Lishous asked, drawing a stern look from the woman.

"We are not in Regia Aquam, Norween," Davimon stated. "Answer my friend's question."

"I do not answer to your king, Davimon." Her smile was now tight lipped and forced. "I am doing him a favor by helping you, seeing as how his own gate maker is occupied with sleeping off a hangover."

"We've been here before," Set explained before Norween

let slip details they'd rather keep quiet, "under very different circumstances. It was before I became a gate maker. She uhh…opened a portal for us."

"I'm assuming you're the one that brought this group to our city," Norween said, examining the teardrops she remembered now caught within a fine webbing on the left side of Set's face.

"It was a larger portal then I'm used to," he admitted. "Usually I only have to hold them open for a couple of people."

"Indeed," she said, "and I'm guessing you've told Davimon you refuse to stay here long enough to recuperate your power."

Set and Davad stood rigid.

"Where do you want to go?" she asked, letting them off the hook.

"Antro," Davimon answered for them.

Only after Set and Davad confirmed their destination did Norween open the portal. Her stare bid them to wait for the others to go first. When only they remained, through teeth gritted in exertion, she said, "Davimon is loyal to the king for saving his life and taking him in. Be wary of his intent for it will always be to the king's gain."

"Thank you." Davad nodded, almost in a bow. "I think," he said, squeezing her shoulder, "Pisces Stragulum would be a good fit for you."

"Is that an invitation to join the Angeli I've heard so much about?" She grinned.

"It is," Set assured her. Noting the strain in her voice, Set urged Davad to go. "Thank you again," he said, and then followed.

The suns were directly overhead as the two emerged in Antro and found themselves in a walled-off, roofless structure that was in the main square. Citizens passing peeked to find the source of the nauseating sounds coming from within.

Jorden was miserable. Balanced on his hands and knees, his head hung from his shoulders, he emptied his stomach of yellow bile. "I hate all of you," he groaned, gagged, and vomited some more.

"Help him up," Davimon barked at Jorden's guards, who rushed to comply.

"Where's the closest inn?" Davad asked since Set was too busy swallowing down his own nausea to speak.

"Two blocks in from the main square," Lishous told them, swallowing convulsively as he turned to lead the way.

When they entered the wooden building, they checked in with the front counter to secure rooms and then started for the common room, where they could regroup. Jorden caught one whiff of the braised chicken and steamed apples wafting from the kitchen and did an about face.

"I'm not hungry," he groaned. "I'm going to bed." Turning from the wooden tables and chairs littering the common room floor, he ignored Davad's mockery as he returned to the foyer, escorted by his guards.

"Bed?" Davad snorted. "But it's still early." When Jorden glared over his shoulder at him, Davad's grin turned wicked.

Mounting the staircase on the other side of the foyer, Jorden and his men disappeared.

Davad and Set chuckled. Nathin rubbed the tip of his

nose with a crooked finger to hide his amusement.

"Take shifts," Davimon told his four men as he scanned the common room for a table. Finding one against the far wall, he wound his way through the others, saying, "I want two guards posted outside; one in front and one in back. You other two get some rest while you can." Taking a seat at a square, wooden table as the others did the same, he rubbed his growling stomach. "Is anyone else hungry? I'm starving."

"I feel like Tristan right now," Set said, his stomach rumbling like a beast.

When Nathin took up position against the wall behind their table, Davad asked, "You're not hungry?"

Nathin's stomach gave his answer.

"Take a seat, Nathin," Set said. "Eat with us."

"If it is permitted," Nathin answered, "I would very much enjoy that."

Davad chuckled without humor and ran his fingers backward through his hair in frustration. "You're the guy who has my back. Of course you can eat with us."

In the chair next to Davad, Nathin leaned in and dropped his voice. "Have I offended you?"

"If we can't get those of Pisces Stragulum to understand what we stand for, how are we supposed to change the thinking of the rest of Superi?" Davad asked. "Though somehow I've been titled the Magistrate of Pisces Stragulum, you are my guard. You are not less than me, nor are you greater. We are equal men who serve the angeli in different capacities."

"We believe the value of lives are equal," Set added, "and the spending of each a great cost."

"The Five are very idealistic." Davimon grinned.

Whether Davimon knew it or not, it was patronizing, and Set's temper sparked. His shoulders squared and his frown was obvious.

Davimon noticed and raised his hands to signal peace. "The lives of those like the king, and of the angeli, are far more important than the lives of those who serve them. To suggest that a baker holds equal value to a soldier is suspect."

"Without the bakers, the soldiers would starve," Davad countered. "Without the soldiers, the angeli would not be able to focus on the true threat to Superi. If a baker and an angeli stood before an executioner and one had to die, the angeli would sacrifice themselves to save the other, as the baker would do for the angeli. It is that equality that strengthens the loyalty between the House of Angeli and its people."

"To lead is to serve," Nathin quoted the mantra of the angeli, "and to serve is to lead."

A wide grin stretched across Davad's face. "Exactly," he said, relaxing as his point was made. He waved his hand to bring over the waiter talking to one of Jorden's guards, who'd returned from upstairs to fill his belly.

They ate in relative silence, focusing on their meal to avoid further conversation. When they were finished, Lishous and Davimon bid the other three a goodnight and left the common room.

"Do you really think you can change them, sirs?" Nathin asked them both.

"I don't know, Nathin," Set answered as they too went in

search of their beds, "but we are going to try nonetheless."

The room Set and Davad were to share, though not large, was spacious enough. The hardwood floor was polished to a high shine, and the chest of drawers was free of scuffs. The white water basin and pitcher were trimmed in blue and boasted vibrant yellow flowers on their sides that matched the drapery over the window, and the quilts covering the two beds positioned against opposite walls.

With Nathin standing guard outside, they stripped down to their small clothes and stretched out across the beds to stare up at the white ceiling.

"Can I ask you something?" Set asked without looking over.

"Mmhmm," Davad murmured from the edge of sleep.

"Earlier, you announced that the Five intend to abolish slavery from Superi after the war with the gods is over. I thought when the war was over, we were going home."

Davad leaned up on one elbow. "That's not a question, but I'll answer you anyway." There was a pause as he gathered his thoughts. "There is no going home, Set, not to Exterius Antro and not to the children we were when we lived there. Do you remember what my dad used to say about a man who stood for nothing?"

"A man who stands for nothing is worth nothing, and therefore should not call himself a man," Set mimicked the inflection that had always been carried in Jacob's tone when he spoke of cowards.

"Saving Superi from the gods of Earth is pointless," Davad said, dropping back to the lumpy mattress, "if we're going to let it destroy itself. Maybe I shouldn't have spoken for the Five, but if I live through this war, I'm going to make sure every innocent slave is freed and that every slaver and slave handler is given a taste of what they've done to others."

"I've seen into Calstar's mind. The segregation of not only race, but of rank and the discriminations that stem from it, Davad…" He groaned in frustration as his fists clenched. "The depths of it is beyond comprehension. It's thousands of years in the making. The only hope we have of seeing it end would be in ending the curse that caused the division."

"Then we will make sure the curse is ended, or die trying."

XIII

Unfair Advantages

Set opened the door to their room and Davad followed him out into the hall.

"Good morning, sirs," Nathin greeted.

Eye's narrowing in concern, Set asked, ""Nathin, do you ever sleep?"

"I thank you for your concern." He dipped his head in respect. "I sleep enough to keep me sane and you safe." Nathin's smile reached his eyes, making them shine. "Where would you two like to go while we wait?"

"Wait?" Davad asked.

"According to Sir Jorden's guards," Nathin said, "the young master has yet to rise and isn't likely to do so before midday."

Nudging Davad's shoulder, Set snorted. "Well that must be nice. Can you imagine what your dad would have done to one of us if we'd tried to sleep the morning away?"

Laughing, they walked with Nathin down the staircase

and into the foyer of the inn.

"Should we take a walk to wake ourselves," Nathin asked, "or would you prefer I wake the kitchen to prepare breakfast?"

Davad glanced through the front windows. "It's not even dawn. I say we go for a walk."

"I wouldn't recommend it," a feminine voice said from the direction of the bar inside the common room, "unless you want to end up in the lock tanks."

Their heads turned and their feet followed the path of their eyes towards the gorgeous, tan-skinned mortalis woman grinning at them. Flinging her wavy blonde hair over her shoulder, she reached for three pewter mugs and lined them up on the polished wooden bar. Sapphire blue eyes twinkling, she said, "You boys have a seat."

"Why would we be arrested?" Set asked, sliding onto a stool beneath the overhang of the bar.

"I gather you're not from Antro." She chuckled as Davad and Nathin took their seats next to Set.

"Actually," Davad replied, "we lived in Exterius Antro for years."

"Well," she said, reaching for a carafe of coffee, "just because they touch doesn't make them the same place." She poured their coffee. "The fulgos are the dominant race in Antro, so they make the rules, and they say no one goes out before dawn. Unless, of course"—she slid the cups to them—"you are of a Ruling House."

The skin between Davad's eyes furrowed. "What is their reasoning?"

"They say it is a public service. A well-rested citizen

makes for a happy, productive city." With a smirk, she added, "In truth, it allows the entitled an advantageous opportunity to make deals with the merchants and ship captains that come in the night."

"The fulgo," Set asked, "or the Ruling Houses?"

"Yes and yes," she replied, "and in that order. The Ruling Houses pay the fulgo and they in turn allow the Houses to steal advantage from the merchants."

Davad's upper lip curled. "By forbidding them to go out, they ensure they have no competition."

"And since all the Ruling Houses here are fulgo," Set added, "their race gets richer, while the other races merely get by."

"Pretty much." She smiled, tight-lipped. "They wrote it into law years ago when the fulgo finally agreed to let the mortalis and fera settle here. It's a good way to keep us in our place." Her chin lifted in indignation. "Or at least that's what we're told."

Set's eyes widened. "That's why there are only small fishing docks on Exterius. The fulgo keep the actual docks all on Antro. That way," he said, "they control both the import and export of goods. Making profits coming and going."

"Exactly," she said, waving her dainty hands in a large circle. "The fulgo want it all."

"Ignorant men," Davimon grumbled, drawing their attention and causing them to turn. "They shouldn't make their tactics so obvious."

"They shouldn't use such tactics at all," Set countered.

Davimon took the stool at the end of the bar beside Set. "Every city has its way of keeping the segregation of race and power. Most just do it without making a great issue of it. Coffee, please," he said to the barmaid. He then continued, "For example, Rus Elisium was dominated by mortalis before the catastrophe that left it abandoned. They forced both the fulgo and nox citizens to account for all their income through a written ledger, but"—he reached for his full cup and nodded his thanks—"the Mortalis were exempt."

"Wait," Davad said, his head kicking sideways. "Wouldn't you want to keep a ledger of what you'd sold?"

"Not when you are only taxed on what is recorded," Lishous said, joining the group and taking a seat at a table behind them.

Davimon explained. "If you are only taxed on what is recorded in the ledger, and only certain groups are forced to keep it…"

"Ugh." Davad shook his head. "Then those not required to keep a ledger pay far less taxes and therefore profit far above the others."

"Exactly," Davimon said.

Crestfallen, Davad slumped in his seat. "So much needs to change."

"The injustices of politics are so engrained in the people of Superi," the barmaid said, propping her hip against the edge of the bar, "that I doubt many of them even realize that they are part of the very system they hate. And the ones who've figured it out"—her tightlipped smile returned—"they've learned to take advantage of it."

"Ahem." Someone cleared their throat.

They turned to see one of Jorden's guards standing rigid in the entryway between foyer and common room.

"Hey," Set asked, "is he up?"

"Sir Jorden would like the group to know that he will be down to resume the trip once he is feeling better." The guard turned to go.

Davimon called out, "That's not really a time of day." The guard did not stop.

The barmaid, chuckling, grabbed a deck of cards from behind the bar and put them down in front of Davad. "Looks like you're going to need something to keep you busy."

XIV

Regia Aquam

"Feeling better?" Davimon asked as Jorden met them at the site where they'd come through the portal the day before.

"No," he grumped, "but I can't get back to my ship and I don't want to get stuck here when you guys leave. So"—he scowled—"here I am."

A grey-haired mortalis man, who looked put out by his morning's chore, walked up from the direction opposite of the way Jorden had come. Three yellow crescent moons marked his leathered brown skin; one ran from temple to temple across his forehead, one masked his hazel eyes, and the other bridged his nose.

"Who are you?" Set questioned him as he joined the throng of men.

"I'm your portal to Regia Aquam," the man replied without offering his name. Raising his voice, he said, "If you would all move to one side, I'll begin. I do have other places to be this morning."

With grumbled complaints, their number moved to one side of the roofless stone structure as the gate maker clapped his hands together with force. His markings began to move, not changing shape as was the norm, but collapsing into one solid image. The purple lightning that crackled to life as the portal grew was typical enough, however.

The men eyed the wobbling edges of the portal with trepidation, flinching as the occasional tip of a lightning bolt breeched the inner circle through which they had to pass.

"Off with you, then," the gate maker snapped. "I haven't got all day."

Single-file, they entered and exited the portal. Jorden was puking again, but the sound was drowned out as Set's and Davad's hearts began to pound. Turning in a slow circle, they noted the high, thick stone walls that allowed for a turret to run along their slopped tops, where posted men pointed arrows down on their heads.

"Davimon," Davad growled, shaking his hands in an attempt to keep flames from igniting, "do you want to explain this?"

Before the sentence was complete, the guards recognized their citizens and lowered their weapons.

"Sorry about that," Davimon said, scratching his whiskered chin. "In hindsight, a warning was probably in order."

"You think?" Set snipped. Twisting his torso, he measured the expanse of the large, square room of stone and mortar. Artistic symbols etched in arcanite covered the walls and floor. "What is this place?"

"One of the city's defenses against gate makers," Davimon answered, leading them towards the room's only egress.

He continued his explanation as they walked through the large, double-winged, metal-reinforced wooden gates. "The tops of the mountains north of Parva Forum are covered in nutris trees. Their sap is extremely acidic, and it was discovered that when mixed with arcanite, it has potent drawing properties in relation to the aether."

"Meaning," Set said, fascinated, "when a portal tries to open in Regia Aquam, it is redirected to that killing room." Set's eyes danced. "That's...well, that's brilliant."

Davad looked at Set askance.

"Strategically speaking, Davad," Set responded, "it's brilliant."

"As a warning," Lishous said, "you should not attempt to open a portal anywhere in Regia Aquam except within that room—and even there, act quickly, else the arcanite will draw the energy from the gate maker himself. None survive that."

"Ha," Set's outburst was not one of humor. "Thanks for letting me know. That would have sucked."

Davad laughed outright at the awful pun, leaving the others to their self-control.

"Pretty good, huh?" Set asked.

The others broke and began to laugh as well.

As they passed through the door and into the throng of bustling citizens going about their days, a young man dressed in blue and gold silk caught Davad's attention. He found himself staring at startling green eyes, and that was when he realized the man was focused on the room they'd just exited.

"Hey, uh"—Davad glanced over his shoulder, as he

picked up his pace to catch up—"is that room new?"

"Why do you ask?" Davimon queried. "Oh." The corner of his mouth twitched. "You mean him."

"Who is he?"

"One of the king's messengers," Davimon told him. "There are usually three or four of them available at any given time. Portals are a quick way to send letters across the planet. Even level one gate makers can accomplish such a small task."

Set's steps faltered until he came to a stop.

The others stopped with him.

"That's how you've kept your king so well informed from Pisces Stragulum," Set said. "We haven't made one move that Normis doesn't already know about…"

Davimon grinned.

Crowding into Davimon's side as they started forward again, Set changed the subject. "The ingenuity of using arcanite to funnel portal energy to a designated location is awesome. How did they figure out how to make it work?"

Davimon looked down at the eager young man at his side. "The same way most things are discovered: through a great mistake." He paused. "During the first water war, the city's alchemists were experimenting in the room on large pieces of arcanite, melting and mixing the metal with all types of concoctions."

"Thinking they understood what they'd created," Lishous said, "they ordered symbols to be carved into the walls and ground and then to have them filled with the laced arcanite. When the metal had cooled and set, the troops were allowed access. They opened a portal to exit the city, as they had done every day since the start of the war."

"Only this time, things went wrong. The portal was held open too long, and the arcanite drained the gate maker's power and used it against those trapped inside the room. It was a terrible day. Stone and flesh melded as one as they were sucked into the ground and walls…the screams of agony from those whose faces were spared the stone…the kicking feet and clawed fingers of those whose words were silenced…" He shook his head. "They could not be freed in time. They all died, and the room was repurposed to capture those who'd dare enter by portal against the will of the king."

"It was renamed Hutnip Terra, in memory of the alchemist who discovered the nutris sap."

Davad wore a pensive visage. "I'm not sure such weapons of destruction should be allowed to stand."

"Your father taught us," Set said, "that the cost of knowledge is great, because of the power to be gained from it. I thought once to put a man to sleep, but in ignorance, I severed his mind from his animus and he died. I gained the knowledge of how to kill, but the cost was a man's life and my innocence."

Having crossed an open area laden with cobblestone, they stopped before an imposing fortress of grey rock, ground flat to prevent grab holds. Small, rectangular slits, covered like deadlights over portholes, allowed for the fortress's defenses without worry of a breach. Higher up there were windows, but the guards standing at the tops of four towers watched over every side.

"What's your point?" Davad asked.

Set opened his mouth to say, *don't you get it? I have the potential to destroy us all*, but said instead, "You sound like those who hunted down the epotos of old and slaughtered them out of fear. The price of knowledge has already been paid. To hide that knowledge away makes the cost of lives spent worthless."

Davad's face went slack at the accusation.

Clearing his throat to break the tension, Davimon informed them, "This is the home of King Normis. I will make sure to let his advisors know that you are here, but it may take some time to arrange a meeting. First"—he gestured towards the door, opening his arm—"allow me to show you to your rooms."

"If King Normis is housing them," Jorden grumbled, hollow-eyed and green, "I'm going home. I want a healer and a bed…hot soup might be nice." More or less talking to himself, he did not pause to say goodbye as he trailed off in another direction with his guards in tow.

"I guess the kid was right," Davimon teased. "There are some who should not portal." He laughed when Lishous's right upper lip pulled away from his teeth.

Feeling Davad's unease, Set said, "I think the three of us would be more comfortable staying at an inn. No offense to your king's hospitality, but we're not here on his coin and accepting would put us in his debt."

Set and Davad watched as the pupil of Davimon's marked eye dilated, but the emotion he shoved off was stifled before Set could read its meaning.

"I cannot say the king will be pleased," Davimon replied, "but I doubt he can argue your logic. Come. It is easy to get lost in the city. I'll escort you to a suitable establishment for your stay."

The area around the king's fortress was full of the upper class.

"It is a wonder they don't trip," Davad quipped, "with the way they hold up their noses. And just look at them all. I've never seen such bold fabrics as to rival the jewels they're drenched in."

Nathin chuckled and then, abashed, dipped his chin and kept his eyes down.

"Forget about the people," Set stated. "Look at all the angeli dwellings. There are dozens of them." To Davimon, he said, "I'm surprised Normis didn't commandeer one of them for his house."

"They are not as easily defendable as the king's fortress," Lishous replied, "nor do they have direct access to the..." He paused. "What did you call it?"

"The killing room," Davimon supplied with a smirk.

"Right." Lishous nodded. "So, the king bestows these dwellings to the Ruling Houses of Regia Aquam—and to others who have gained his favor."

"I guess that's one way of keeping your enemies close," Davad quipped, surprised when Davimon and Lishous laughed.

The noise brought them attention and most of it was not good. Upper lips furled, and nostrils flared and wrinkled, as if their little group carried with them a sour scent.

"What's that all about?" Davad asked.

"Do not take offense, young master," Lishous said as he fell a step behind to walk beside Nathin. "It was my presence at Master Davimon's side that drew their ire and disdain. Forgive me. For a moment I forgot that we've returned home, and in that moment I overstepped my place."

"That's absurd," Set said as he began to turn towards Lishous.

Davimon prevented it by taking hold of his upper arm.

Set's right brow arched as his head tilted to the side.

"I know the risk in laying hands on an epoto," Davimon whispered in a rush of sharp words, "but by defending Lishous, you only endanger him. I beg you to let it go."

"I don't like it," Set snapped and yanked his arm free, but he kept his feet moving forward.

"And that is to your credit," Davimon replied, leading them across a wide street to a two-story inn.

The lower floor was made of grey stone. Stained glass windows offered its patrons privacy while allowing the suns' light to do their work. The upper floor was constructed of wood and painted a dark blue, with balconies spreading before every window. A sign dangled from the first eave that read, Riders' Rest in gold lettering, with an image of a horse plopped on its haunches out beside it.

As Nathin darted ahead to open the door, a lady and her escort exited. The pale brunette touched the white lace at her throat as if startled. Dropping her hand to catch the long gathering of soft blue cotton, she tugged her skirt and stepped closer to the man in stiff, formal black trousers and a white linen button down shirt overlaid with a crisp, black cloak.

Lishous bent at the waist and didn't come back up.

Nathin, feeling Lishous's tug on the hem of his coarse

linen tunic, bowed as well.

The man captured his mustache between his thumb and first finger and greeted, "Davimon," as he slid his fingers off one pointed end of his facial hair.

"Master Porter," Davimon said, "allow me to introduce Davad Jacobson, Magistrate of Pisces Stragulum, and Set Matthewson, head advisor to the House of Angeli."

Porter smirked. "The king sent you for the angeli, and you come back with children. Surely you and your pet will lose favor with the king now."

"It would be to your king's loss," Set assured him, "and very much to our gain. Let us hope he is that stupid."

Lishous's shock at Set's boldness was great enough to stand him upright.

Porter's spine went ramrod straight. His mouth opened and closed, but no words came forth. Wrapping his arm around the woman's shoulders, he stormed off in a huff.

"The king will hear of that, I assure you," Davimon said as he waited for Nathin to reopen the door and then walked through.

"I sure hope so." Davad said out-loud for everyone to hear.

"Master Davimon." The innkeeper rushed from behind the counter, hesitating as his eyes fell on Lishous. "It is always a pleasure," he gushed, regaining his bluster. "And how wonderful. You've brought company. Should I prepare a room…for you," he stressed and then added, "and for your guests?"

"I'll wait outside, Master Davimon." Lishous gave a slight bow and then retreated through the door.

Davimon's countenance darkened. His words were clipped when he said, "I am to return to the king's fortress. Two adjoining rooms will suffice."

"As you wish, my lord." With a wave of Davimon's hand, the innkeeper bowed as he was dismissed.

Davimon's mood lightened when a young man in simple white robes entered. His short-cropped blond hair made his bright green eyes jump out of his tanned face as he approached them.

"Michael," Davimon said, "I'm glad you picked up my message. Set Matthewson, Davad Jacobson, meet Michael."

"Good to meet you," the two said in turn.

"Likewise," Michael replied, his nerves unsettled when they offered their hands.

"He is a level one telepath," Davimon informed them, "and has been assigned to you for the duration of your stay. He will know when I've returned from speaking to the king, so while I am gone, feel free to explore the city."

"It is my pleasure to serve." Michael bowed at the waist.

"If you want to hang out with us, Michael," Davad said, "you're not allowed to bow again."

"Excuse me, sir?"

Davimon groaned. "I'll leave you to it then," he said, pivoting to head back the way they'd come.

Lishous fell into step behind him as he exited the door.

"Come on, Michael." Davad grinned. "We passed a leather shop on the way here. Set mentioned wanting to talk to a leather worker about cushioning his saddle seat."

"Sir?"

Davad and Nathin laughed as they left the inn and headed in the opposite direction from the way they'd entered the city to see what else it had to offer.

Set barely heard their conversation as he fell further and further behind. The hairs at his nape were standing on end. His skin crawled as someone's disdain of them washed over him like a river. The last time he'd felt such animosity, they'd been dodging bounty hunters in Exsulto, while trying to escape the reach of the Imbellis Asylum.

Without noticing, Set dropped behind, until his head turned to look down an alley. A hooded man with dark green eyes stared back at him. Dressed in fine black silk with gold buttons and fasteners, he pressed a finger across his lips to warn silence, while with his other hand he beckoned Set forward.

Set, having little to fear from one man, took the turn and entered the alley that ran between two tall buildings. As an epoto, distance was his enemy, so he closed the space between them and waited for the other man to speak.

"I was wondering if your power was great enough to feel my pull," the man said.

"Yeah, well, you have my attention," Set replied. "Why don't you tell me what you want?"

"I have a proposition for you."

Set crossed his arms over his chest. "Apparently this city is ripe with them."

A wave of wary tension exuded from the man in black, and his voice took on a cautious edge. "Are you interested in hearing it?"

"I'm standing here, aren't I?"

"I know you're here to speak with the King." The man

paused.

"And still you waste my time by asking no question." Set dropped his arms. "If you wish to keep this private, I would suggest you ask me now, before my companions come in search of me."

The expression of the man in black went flaccid. "I hate children."

"I don't much care for adults these days either, but that's still not a question."

"I'll make this simple," the man hissed. "I have a journal that you want, but before I give to you, there is something I need you to do for me."

Set's lips pressed thin. "Is it black?" he asked.

"Yes," the man said, taken off guard by the knowledge he hadn't expected the boy to have. "It is invaluable to you personally."

"What do you want for it?" Set asked, growing tired of the word play.

"The King has brought you here to discuss terms on behalf of the angeli."

"There are no terms to discuss. He will stand with the angeli against the gods of Earth or his city will go unprotected."

"Yes." The man's green eyes grew intense. "Say only that when you stand before the king. Agree to none of his demands, and I will give you what you seek."

"Master Set," Michael called from the opening of the alleyway. "I feared I'd lost you."

"Sorry," Set said, "I was just talking to…" He turned back to the man in black, but found him already gone. He forced a smile. "Never mind. I think we should head back to the inn."

"Of course, sir." Michael started to bow, caught himself, and grinned cheekily instead.

When Set exited the alley, Davad stopped him. "Why did you dart off?"

"Not now," Set cautioned.

"Set...Davad..." Jorden waved at them from atop his horse, looking refreshed and renewed. Cantering over, he said, "I'm so glad I found you. My father wishes an audience."

"What do you think, Michael?" Davad asked their guide.

"No member of a Ruling House would dare bring harm to an invited guest of the king," he assured them both, "and I am attuned to Master Davimon. He will receive message of where we are."

"How?" Set asked.

"If you hadn't disappeared when you did, you'd know the answer," Davad said. "According to Michael, Regia Aquam is full of level one telepaths."

Set's eyes dropped to see the proof for himself. Green, vine-like markings encircled the first joint and knuckles of Michael's right hand.

Davad never paused in his explanation. "The king has cast them out like a net over the entire city. Each one is linked to another, who is linked to yet another until nothing happens here that good King Normis doesn't know about."

"Mitable Terra may not be the king," Jorden stated, "but he's also not one to be kept waiting. Please, will you meet him? I brought horses for the two of you."

Set's head cocked. "But there are four of us."

Jorden sighed. "In Regia Aquam, body servants do not ride. They walk beside their master's horse."

"Then we will walk," Davad said, "as will you, if you wish for us to accompany you back to the House of Terra."

Jorden flung his leg over the horse and slid from the saddle. "Man." He sulked, shoulders drooping. "You guys must really like me."

Davad, Set, and Nathin were still laughing when they reached the ancient angeli house. The white stone crawling with dark green vines had yellowed with age, dating it older than the angeli dwellings in Pisces Stragulum, but the domed red roof marked it for what it was. There was no fence or gate to bar their way down the stone mosaic path through an estate where colorful flora abounded. There were a half dozen white stone bowls scooped into the terra. They held clear blue water upon which green-leafed pads floated. Shade trees dominated the property, and beneath most of them were benches or chairs.

Davad looked over at Set and then did a double take. "Are you all right?"

Set flinched. "Yeah," he said a touch too quickly.

"Then why were you grinning like one touched by the curse of the Cruxen Clav?"

"Man, look at this place. It feels like home. One day"— he covered his mouth with the side of his closed fist and cleared his throat—"I want to give your sister a home like this."

Davad grinned and punched him in the side of his arm. "This is why you are the better choice."

The massive, aged, wooden door opened before they reached it. An elderly mortalis with drooping jowls, long ears, and no hair to speak of stood on the other side. "Gentlemen," he said, bowing at the waist with one arm folded across it, "welcome to the House of Terra. Sir Jorden"—he bowed again, his head bobbling as he gave each word his slow, undivided attention—"welcome home, young master. Your father requests that you confine yourself to your rooms until after his appointment with his guests."

Jorden turned red and then purple. He clenched his jaw as tightly as he did his fists and stormed into the house. A stairway carried him from view.

"If you would please follow me," the servant said as he turned.

Michael closed the door behind them.

Painted canvases of breathtaking landscapes decorated the beige-colored walls. Flowers from outside had been gathered and sat in stunning arrangements in colored glass vases or clear crystal with jewels coating the bottoms.

They were taken into a sitting room, awash with natural colors, with a fireplace at each end of the open, square space. Overstuffed sofas and chairs sat in random clusters on top of woven rugs. Shelves that were full of books lined one wall, interrupted only by the large double window in the center made of stained glass.

"If you would please wait here," the servant told them, "Master Terra will be with you shortly."

"Thank you, sir," Davad and Set replied.

Michael and Nathin lowered their eyes and dipped their chins.

"I can't get over how beautiful this place is," Set mused.

"Master Terra is known for his passion for beautiful things," Michael told them. "He told me once it was to hide the memories of horror left in the wake of the wars."

Thundering boot steps from the hall had them turning towards the egress before they'd had a chance to choose a seat. The man who filled the opening exuded danger. He had flames bursting from Davad's fingertips and Set's wrists turning out in preparation to lay hands on him.

His fine green silk shirt contrasted with the hard lines on the man's stoic face from which cold, ice-blue eyes scrutinized them. Sinister did not begin to describe him, and six feet seven inches of huge, bulking muscle was enough to put them on the defensive. Dark as a nox, with coal black hair, the deep bass of his voice did little to ease their concern.

"Put those flames out, boy, before I decide to take offense," Mitable said. "I am the Master of this House."

The flames pulsed hotter. Leaning towards Set, Davad whispered, "Uh, might need a little help," and then grunted, as Set touched his forearm and temporarily severed the connection between his animus and his ability.

"Now," Mitable said, "we can talk. Michael"—he nodded and gave a genuine smile—"it is always a pleasure to have you beneath my roof. Have you decided to come work for me yet?"

Michael grinned and then bowed. "You honor me, sir," he said, but did not give an answer. "Allow me to introduce Davad Jacobson, Magistrate of Pisces Stragulum, and Set Matthewson, head advisor to the House of Angeli."

Mitable's smile disappeared. His jaw clenched as his

countenance darkened. Crossing the floor to a long, rectan-, gular table laden with fine liquors and delicate glassware, he poured himself a shot of rum and tossed it down his throat.

"Do you think because I offered you welcome that you can forget your station and jest in such a manner with me?" Mitable roared.

"Sir," Michael replied, "I do not jest, nor would I dare to do so."

Much faster than one would credit a man Mitable's size, in long, powerful strides, he moved against Michael, striking him across the cheek with a backhanded slap. As Michael landed on his tailbone, Nathin moved, sword in hand, to guard Davad and Set.

"Whoa," Davad shouted. "There's no cause for that." Nudging Nathin so that their guard stayed between Set and the furious Mitable, he said, "He's telling the truth. We come from Pisces Stragulum, as members of the Five and of the House of Angeli, to speak on their behalf."

"To speak to whom is the question," Mitable said, turning his ire on Davad. "I sent my son to bring back the angeli, and instead he returns with children, and to add insult to his offense, he allows them to be escorted into the city with Da-vimon…" The last came out a snarl. "There is talk of your impending meeting with the king. What authority could you possibly have?"

"You've been given our titles, Master Terra," Davad stated, "and we're not much for having to repeat ourselves. Refer to us as children again and it will be the last civil conversation we have." He pointed to Michael. "Strike him again and you will be marked as an enemy of the House of

Angeli. How is that for authority?"

Mitable's chest swelled as his eyes narrowed. "I could snap you like a twig."

"There is a reason I am here," Set spoke in calm monotone. Pushing Nathin back towards Davad, he added, "Threaten us with violence again and I'll reduce you to a drooling cripple."

"You." Mitable pivoted towards Michael. "Find Davimon, and get my son down here. I want answers! Now!"

Michael bowed low. "Forgive me, Master Terra, but I cannot. I am sworn solely to Master Set and Master Davad for the duration of their stay."

Mitable turned purple and his eyes bulged.

"It matters not," Davimon said, walking into the room with his shoulders back and a smirk dancing at the corners of his mouth, "for I am here. The king has sent me with a message."

Mitable's chest deflated as uncertainty replaced hostility within his heated stare. "It is not treason to seek advantage when a new political or militaristic power rises."

"Interesting." Davimon grinned. "I will inform the King of your intent. However, the message is not for you."

"Why you manipulative cur," Mitable cursed.

Eyes twinkling, Davimon turned to Set and Davad. "The king will see you now."

Jorden entered in time to hear his father bellow, "Get out! All of you!"

"Not you." Mitable pointed to his son when he would have skittered away.

Set laid a hand on Jorden's shoulder in passing as they

made their way down the hall to the front foyer and then out the door. Lishous, who'd waited outside, fell into step.

"Are all those of rank so disrespectful to you?" Set asked Michael.

Lishous snorted.

"We are servants, young masters," Michael replied. "It matters not what House we serve. We are answerable to any above our station. The only citizens of lower rank are those indentured or enslaved. It is our way."

"Well, your way sucks," Davad piped in. "I'm sorry for what happened back there, Nathin."

Nathin's mouth pressed into a line. "I'll admit it is not easy to guard one's charges when footing is lost to constant shifting of shoving hands."

Set laughed. "Apologies, but our focus was on the pompous oaf standing beyond you."

When an errant chuckle parted his lips, Michael put his hand over his mouth and begged pardon with his eyes, as he said, "Forgive me, sirs, but…I've never refused an order before. Master Terra's expression was…" He cleared his throat. "Let me just say it was worth being struck."

"You would love Pisces Stragulum," Set told him. "No one speaks to anyone the way he just spoke to you in there."

"It sounds utopian." Michael smiled, but doubt was written all over his face.

"It's true," Lishous told him. "In Pisces Stragulum, I am just a man guarding the back of his closest friend. It's a position of honor instead of one of servitude."

"I would very much like to hear more," Michael said.

"And we would very much like to tell about it," Davad

replied.

Davimon tapped Lishous's shoulder and urged him to fall back as Michael directed their course to the king's fortress. "You prefer Pisces Stragulum," he said.

Lishous, keeping his voice low, answered with a question. "You do not?"

"We are fools, my friend," Davimon said. "Though they are children, they are far wiser than we who call ourselves grown."

Lishous was not surprised when he glanced over to see that Davimon's left pupil had overtaken the white of his eye. "What do you see?"

"Superi has divided itself by not only race, but by station as well, and there are far more ranked low than high. If the low side with the Tristan and Anliac, the House of Angeli will become unstoppable by sheer number alone." He blinked several times as his sight returned to normal.

They had reached their destination without his awareness and now stood staring at Davimon, wondering at the words they'd heard him speak.

"That's good to know," Davad said.

"You weren't supposed to hear that." Davimon growled, glaring at Lishous, who'd failed to shut him up.

Lishous shrugged, but made no excuses. "Let's get this meeting over with," he said. "I want to go home."

Davad's molars showed for the size of his grin. "If I trusted you not to bite my head off, I'd hug you right now." His smile turned sickly when Lishous's black lips peeled away from rows of elongated, dagger-like teeth. "Okay," he said, "I...take it back."

Davimon threw his head back, laughing. "That's his grin."

Michael held the front door open and stopped Set before he could walk past. "Make him stop," he pleaded, smiling.

The group entered the king's foyer a moving mass of laughter, drawing the eyes of the servants and clerks darting about the marble-tiled floor. Others watched from over the balustrade at what had come through the doors with disdain.

Sobering, Davimon said, "You three should stay here. I'll escort Set and Davad to the king's office."

"No, sir." Nathin squared his shoulders. "Davad is under my protection. I will not be separated from him."

"Nor I from my charges," Michael said with determined timidity. "I swore my sole loyalty before having met them. Now that I know them, I mean it all the more," he ended with conviction.

"Looks like I'll wait alone then." Lishous smirked.

"Why?" Set asked as resentment punched out of the fera hard enough to knock his breath.

"I am to blame," Davimon said, taking them aback. "An errant decision during my youth placed me in a position of needing discipline. Lishous, ever loyal, came to my defense. He only growled, but…"

"But it was at the king," Lishous finished, "and now I am banished from his sight on promise of execution should I be seen."

Davimon's shoulders dropped as he released a deep sigh. "It was the best I could manage."

Set knew that the two friends were leaving something out, but he was not one to begrudge secrets. He held many himself.

"You don't have to wait here," Davimon told him. "I'll find you when we're done."

Stiff with pride, Lishous nodded and turned towards the exit, while Davimon said, "Let's go."

They crossed the open floor to a winding staircase. As they mounted the steps, Set aligned himself with Davimon. Eyes forward, he stated, "When you first came to Pisces Stragulum, I found you pompous… arrogant, and too formal. Before we left on this journey, I saw you as a man of pride and standards that others should aspire to."

"And now?" Davimon asked, as they walked half the length of the upper hallway and came to a stop before the king's ornately etched metal door.

Mindful of the servant waiting to announce them, Set said, "Lishous is more than your protector, more than your friend. He is your family, your brother, so to be honest, Davimon, your best was not nearly good enough. He follows you, and the life you've offered him is demoralizing. Right now I cannot see who you are through my disappointment."

Speechless, Davimon fell on ceremony to save himself. "Davad Jacobson and Set Matthewson to see the king."

The servant dipped his head and opened the door. "Your Majesty." He bowed at the waist. "Davad Jacobson, Magistrate of Pisces Stragulum, and Set Matthewson, head advisor to the angeli, members of the Five, and the House of Angeli."

As the servant stepped back, they entered. Michael took up position on the opposite side of the doorframe from where the servant moved to stand after closing the door.

Nathin flanked Davad's left side, while Davimon stood at Set's right, and together they came to a stop midway into the room.

Arched glass windows dominated two walls, while shelves of books lined the others from floor to ceiling. King Normis stood from behind his massive, square, stone desk to greet them. "I bid you welcome," he said. "Please, sit." He gestured to the two high-backed chairs facing him.

Davad locked stares with a mortalis man to the left of the king's desk, leaning casually against one of the shelves. His smile showed too many teeth.

The man nodded politely enough as he and Set took their seats. "We appreciate your interest in our cause," Davad said. "Superi must be united in its effort to face the gods of Earth." In his peripheral vision, he watched as Set surveyed the room, eyes squinted as if trying to see beyond the obvious.

Seated, Normis leaned forward and braced his muscled torso's weight on his forearms. He pressed his fingertips together as his iron-grey eyes considered them. The silver streaks at the temples of his shoulder-length black hair, tied back by a strap of leather, alluded to his age, but his sun-darkened flesh was free of lines or wrinkles. His goatee, neatly trimmed to a point, moved as his mouth did.

"Had you not come alone," Normis said, "your presence here would be cause for celebration. However, I will not hide my disappointment from you. Sir Davimon's orders were to bring the angeli to discuss terms."

"Before you offend by questioning our age," Davad replied, "let me assure you, we speak for the House of Angeli.

As members of the Five, I can guarantee our authority."

Normis slammed the side of his fist down atop his desk. "I am the king," he shouted. "They should have come."

"Tell me, King," Set gritted out from between clenched teeth, "what carpenter built your shelves? I would very much like ones of my own."

"What?" the king snapped.

"Their shape is an illusion. Is it not?" Set said. "We do not fear you, and you are not our king. Confess your purpose for the seven men you have hidden behind them, and you'll know why we have come in place of the angeli."

The guard beside the king's desk came to attention. A sharp look from Davimon prevented him from reaching for his sword.

"They are here for my protection," Normis replied, indignant, "and to suggest otherwise would be to question my integrity."

Stiff in his seat, Davad said, "Let there be no doubt that your integrity is very much in question. Is that not how new alliances are formed?"

"If I may, Your Majesty," the guard said, stepping forward, "I would speak to your guests."

Normis nodded after a curious pause, while staring at them with blatant amusement.

"Young masters," he began, "I am Claude Frankson. I am the king's chief diplomat and war advisor." He gave a curt bow, as if afraid to wrinkle his fancy, green silk robes. "The added men were placed by my order. You must understand. Word of the angeli has spread far and wide. Already gleemen have written stories of the destruction in Imbellis. The Five

Who Broke the Tower," he said, "is among my favorites."

"What is your point?" Set asked.

Claude, elbows bent, held his hands out wide and shrugged. "Considering the power of the transcended angeli, can you fault our caution?"

"I suppose not," Davad replied.

"Can you verify that you have the authority to speak on behalf of the angeli on matters of trade, peace alliances, and the matter of war?" Claude asked.

As one, Set and Davad tugged free the silver linked chains from beneath their black uniformed shirts and held aloft the V-shaped signet bejeweled with a single gem provide by Anliac.

Turning to the king, Claude nodded. "The signet is sufficient, your majesty."

"Then show them the document," Normis ordered.

Claude lifted a long, wide piece of parchment from before the king and handed it to Davad, who reached for it. He dipped a quill into an inkwell and held it out.

Davad's face skewed. "What is this?"

"The terms of peace between Regia Aquam and Pisces Stragulum," Claude answered.

Set snatched the paper from Davad's hands and stood to his feet. Glaring at Claude over the edge of the parchment, he said, "Your vacuous expression betrays you." His eyes dropped as he scanned the words. "So we are to: Surrender our arms…grant full access of Pisces Stragulum to Regia Aquam's forces…" As his anger grew, he began to pace. "We are to swear fealty to you…." His arms dropped to his side, the parchment dangling from one hand. "We are to obey you in all things." His pacing stopped as his head turned in slow motion to Davad and then to the king. "Is this some kind of joke?"

Normis shoved his chair away from his desk and stormed from behind it as he took a position before them that would force them to look up. "Would you prefer war?" he asked, lording over them. "The might of my armies would crush your ragtag Angeli Guards beneath their heels. I would give you a war that would stir the graves of your parents. They would turn in pity as I made you suffer for your insolence. I am king!" he bellowed, "And you," he sneered, "are children."

"And there it is," Davad said, coming out of his seat and retrieving the parchment from Set.

Nathin and Davimon exchanged an uneasy glance as men filed from behind the shelves to line up along the front of them instead. Davad's focus remained steady, prompting Nathin to lessen the distance between himself and his charge.

"My first matter of business," Davad said, then ripped the contract in half and let it fall. "The House of Angeli will never bow. Not to a magistrate, not to a ruler, and not to a king. The House of Angeli will never sign terms such as these, and your audacity in presenting them to us clearly speaks of your integrity. Such an insult could be seen as cause to collect our ragtag army of Angeli Guards and give them the arms you would have us surrender. The Five would lead them against your House, and of course, the angeli would take point."

Losing some of his bluster, Normis said, "Let us calm

ourselves, and—"

But, Davad wasn't finished. "And for what future yet remains to you," he interrupted, "you should bear in mind that if you ever speak of my father like that again, I will see you placed in a grave of your own."

"You would dare to threaten the life of the king?" Claude gasped as the seven men reached for hilts at their waist.

Davad slung back his father's cloak and freed the dracon sword from its sheath. Back to back with Set, they kept careful watch on Normis as they waited for the guards to make the first move.

Davimon became Nathin's sole focus in case the man's loyalty to Normis overloaded his good judgment.

Michael, still by the door, showed no outward sign of concern.

Set rolled his head along the back of his shoulders. He shook out his arms and asked Davad, "I wonder what is held in the mind of a king?" He could hear the smile in Davad's voice.

"I don't know."

Normis planted one foot backward before he caught himself and held his position. Something in the epoto's eyes had changed. The hunger for knowledge reflected in the boy's stare made his skin crawl.

"If one man draws their blade," Set vowed, "I'm going to find out, and according to the laws of Regia Aquam, I would then be king."

"Ha," the king laughed. "Ha, ha…" He drew curious stares from those in the room perched on the edge of a fight. "It would appear you were correct, Davimon," he said. "The

House of Angeli will not be strong armed."

"No, Your Majesty," Davimon replied, "they will not."

Claude snapped his fingers, and after sharp salutes, the seven guards filed from the room. "Your Majesty," he said, "should I have terms drawn?"

"Yes, yes," Normis replied. "You are dismissed."

"Your Majesty." Claude bowed, pivoted around, and left at a quick clip.

Returning the dracon sword to its sheath, Davad scowled. "Explain yourself."

"As a king," Normis said, "I do not explain myself. However, this once I will make an exception. The Five are young and inexperienced." He held up his hand when Davad's face reddened. "Those are the facts. You have entered the political arena and your opponents are far more experienced. Strong arming what appears to be a weaker player is part of the game."

"We're not interested in playing games," Davad told him, "and I hope the question of our strength has been put to rest."

"Indeed." Normis smiled. "Now that we have a better understanding of one another, I have no doubt that we will be able to reach a realistic accord of mutual benefit. New terms will be drafted tonight, and on the morrow we will meet again."

"Come, my lords," Davimon urged. "I will escort you back to the inn."

As Normis returned to his seat behind his desk and picked up a quill to continue his day's work, he said, "They are young men, Sir Davimon. You should take them to the

King's Ladies."

Davimon's eyes popped wide. "I fear they are not of age to enter a brothel, my King."

"Hmm. Perhaps you are correct, but we must do something to celebrate the impending peace accord between Regia Aquam and Pisces Stragulum." He paused to think. "We will host a party in the courtyard in their honor. See it done, Davimon."

"Yes, Your Majesty." Davimon bowed, ushering Set and Davad before him as the servant held open the door.

The last out, Michael locked eyes with Nathin.

"You didn't seem worried, Michael," Nathin said. "Are your nerves made of steel?"

"The king winked at me which is code to read his mind," Michael confessed, "he then told me of his plan. I was ordered not to react."

Set and Davad's animosity was a force of energy boring into Davimon's back. They did not speak, nor did he, until they were outside. Lishous, sitting on his haunches and leaning against a tree in the king's yard, stood when he saw them and tucked a book he'd been reading into his pack.

"Michael," Set said, "would you escort us back please?"

"Of course, my lord," Michael replied and started off at once.

"Set," Davimon said, falling into step beside him, "you must understand—"

"Oh I do," Set replied. "I understand that you led us into that room knowing it was a possible ambush. I understand that you stood silent as your king first tried to manipulate us and then threatened us with bodily harm." He stopped and turned to face the other man. "I understand that your emotional grid read the same as your king's when we refused his terms."

Davimon stood thoughtful before he countered, "Normis is a king with many enemies. Guards surround him at all times. He is right in his assessment of your inexperience. Set, he could have summoned you to the audience hall where dozens of guards are posted, or he could have just as easily had you detained under guard until it was convenient for him to meet with you. You came unannounced with insufficient means to protect yourselves." He cleared his throat when Set and Davad stared up at him with narrowed glares. "For truth," he said, "manipulation and strong arming are as great of weapons as blades in politics, sometimes greater, and King Normis did you a service by exposing you to that truth. If you need proof of his honor, look to his words. He revealed the intent of his action when doing so took away his advantage."

Disgusted, Set looked at Michael, who nodded and started off again.

"As to my anger," Davimon said, refusing to relent until he'd said his peace, "you are correct, but what you cannot know as an epoto is the source of an emotion. The others in that room may have been angry about your rejection of the king's terms. I was angry that the terms had been laid out in the first place."

Set refused to acknowledge him, so he dropped back to walk with Lishous, who in turn shook his head and fell back to join Nathin. Davimon found himself caught between his betters before him and the better men who walked behind.

Michael stepped onto the boardwalk of the inn and held open the door as Set, Davad, and Nathin entered the foyer without pause. Davimon came through next with Lishous following.

"What?" Davimon snapped when Lishous drew him aside as they paused in the foyer.

"I don't know what you did," Lishous snarled, "but you need to fix it."

Set was hit hard with Lishous's fear and it stole his ire. At the base of the stairway leading to their room, he stopped. "Don't be angry at him, Lishous," he said. "Davimon was only doing his job. The lesson today was ours to learn. We are friends, but our loyalties do not align."

Pained, Lishous replied, "What Davimon cannot say, I can. Yes, we are friends, but our loyalties align closer than you think. As with all things, there is a season, and now is not yet the time."

Set relaxed. "That, I can understand," he said.

Davimon exhaled heavily. "Then we are okay?"

"Yeah," Davad assured him. "All is well."

"Excellent." Davimon grinned. "Michael, see them well rested and well dressed. Tonight we will have a party."

"Yes, my lord." Michael grinned.

"You'll come too, won't you?" Davad asked.

Michael froze. "I, umm…well…" He scratched the side of his head.

"Servants must be invited as a guest," Lishous offered at Davad's confusion.

"I will make sure every eligible daughter in Regia Aquam will be there"—Davimon's brows wiggled—"and so will their mothers."

"Michael, Nathin," Set said, "consider yourselves invited. I'm going to need the company when Davad becomes distracted." His eyes twinkled. "I'm already spoken for."

"If you'll excuse us," Davimon said, "we'll take our leave to see to the arrangements."

"We'll be here," Davad said.

"Very well then." Davimon dipped his head and gestured for Lishous to follow.

"Could you tell me more about life in Pisces Stragulum?" Michael asked as they headed for the stairs.

Davimon and Lishous knew what Davad's reply would be, though they were back out the door before the answer was given. There were menus to plan, spirits to order, musicians to hire, and Houses with daughters to put on notice. It had been too long since they'd had an excuse to blow off steam, and with the war coming, it might be a while before another excuse came along.

XV

Revenge

Tristan stretched and turned sideways in the feather bed to admire the beauty that lay beside him on her stomach. He trailed the sharp point of a nail down her spine and delighted in the goosebumps that rose on her translucent, olive skin. A grin tugged at the corners of his mouth when her perpetual golden swirls became brighter at his touch.

Opening his senses, he absorbed the tranquility of early morning. Most in the town still slept, and those who stirred kept their voices hushed, or spoke only in their minds, beyond his ability to hear. Soon, the cacophony of shouted orders, raucous workers, and companionable conversations filled with laughter would drown together. In a way, he would become deaf, but for now he could hear for miles.

He could hear Micah's and Lynette's pacing steps beyond the front door. The gentle waves as they lapped at the shoreline. He could hear hearths being stoked as fires were set, and water, boiling for coffee no doubt as more people roused.

Beyond the city's perimeter, boars grunted too close to the herb garden Shashara had started there last week. The guards were patrolling; he could hear their brief conversations as their routes overlapped.

"I thought this place was supposed to be abandoned?"

The question was out of place. Tristan held his breath and commanded his heart rate to slow. Shutting out the other noises, he focused in the direction the question had come from, but a second voice responded.

"From the new construction, it would appear they've been busy."

"This could complicate our plans."

A dark foreboding tightened Tristan's chest as a vague remembrance tugged at the edge of his mind. He'd heard the familiar tenor of the second man's voice before. When again the man spoke, he was sure of it.

"Nonsense. So a few more people will have to die for me to have my vengeance. I could not care less, and neither will you if you want the information I have."

"What is it?" Anliac asked, stirred awake as Tristan bolted upright in the bed. She shielded her eyes when Tristan's illuminated marks burned brighter. "Ugh, babe," she groaned, "turn them off."

"Shh."

Gathering the quilt and tugging it up beneath her chin, she sat upright as well and laid a soothing hand on his back. Tense, she waited for him to explain.

The first man, the one with a voice that whined through a pinched nose, spoke. "It will be hard to find her before we are discovered."

Tristan closed his eyes and downed his head to concentrate. *Who were these men after?*

"Leveling the whole of it might be our better option."

The familiar voice's response ripped a growl from Tristan's chest.

"Awk!" Anliac shouted, as she became the anchor point for a quilt blown smooth off the bed to drape like a tent over her head. "Tristan!" she shouted, as she clawed her way free. Whatever else she would have said died on her tongue when she looked at him again.

Standing in the center of the room in only his brown cotton trousers, he clutched the sides of his head and glared her way as the pain summoned by her bellow lanced through his skull.

"Sorry," she whispered, wincing.

"No," the familiar voice said. "She could survive and slip through my grasp again during the chaos. I won't risk it. I want to witness her death."

"Tristan, talk to me," Anliac demanded when his markings began to pulse.

"I'll deliver you the angeli's head, but know this," the first man said. "If you fail to make good your promise… yours will be the next I place upon a pike."

"Save your threats, Bengim," the familiar voice replied. "Kill Anliac, and you'll have all the information you need to extract your own vengeance."

A wave of visible energy exploded outward from Tristan as his marks solidified with power. The threat made against Anliac unhinged him. Moving faster than sight could track, his image vanished. The exterior wall of their room exploded as he crashed through it without slowing, showering the guards below with chunks of stone and wood. He landed on the balls of his feet, and his image flickered before the guards. A mound of terra piled high behind his feet as he pushed off. Like a torch, light trailed in his wake as he raced to destroy Anliac's enemies.

Buildings shook, their windows rattling, as he passed. The rush of wind his speed created stirred a cloud of dust and overturned a number of wagons. He paid the havoc no mind as he focused on the two men who'd dared to threaten his love, and his city, just beyond their gates.

Blood gorged his muscles, swelled to giant proportions, as he came to a stop. He could hear their heartbeats, one pounding in anticipation, while the other held the steady rhythm of one used to battle. He saw everything—the blades of grass that quivered at their feet, and the loose stones that danced upon the ground, as the one called Bengim wiggled calloused fingertips that controlled the stones. His filthy brown trousers, bare feet, and tattered white shirt gave him the appearance of a vagabond, but his eyes were those of a killer.

Tristan's voice boomed with angelic force. "Say again who you're here to kill," he said. "I dare you."

"I admit I'm curious as to how you knew we were here," Bengim said. "However, your appearance is expedient. If you wouldn't mind summoning your female counterpart, I can take her head and all will be well with your city."

"That's not going to happen," Tristan said, eyes narrowing as his voice deepened even further.

"I'm the one that wants her dead." Zadyst grinned, standing tall in his fine, dark linen outfit. "Fetch her and I'll let you live." Flames erupted from his hands and caught the long sleeves of his linen shirt on fire as it raced towards the neckline. The material of both sleeves burned and fell away, but his flesh remained unharmed. "Refuse, and I'll gladly go through you and fetch her myself."

Tristan's speed carried him forward, his hands curved to wrap around the ignis wielder's throat. They punched their way through a two-foot-thick rock wall instead, as Bengim attempted to protect his cohort and failed. Once through the barrier, Tristan struck out with both fists.

Zadyst made a desperate grab for Tristan's wrists. Finding purchase, the force of the jar yanked his feet from beneath him. Both men hit their knees, though the cause for Tristan was pain. "I'm not what you're used to, boy," Zadyst taunted over Tristan's screams. "I'm a true wielder."

Tristan was beyond hearing. Lost in a world of agony, his pale white skin turned black, and then to ash that blew away from the heat waves pouring from the fire. The muscle beneath sizzled like frying meat and then shriveled away from the bone, as his tendons snapped and recoiled.

"Ugh," Zadyst grunted, toppled sideways by a fist-sized chunk of terra that smashed into the side of his head.

The ground rolled at Anliac's bidding. It carried Tristan clear of the ignis wielder so she could concentrate. "Touch him again, Zadyst," Anliac warned, "and I'll bury you."

Zadyst pulled back his arms, and with a forward thrust, two rolling balls of fire flew towards her head.

"You missed." She chuckled, standing barefoot in her

purple cotton pajamas. Fury then filled her golden eyes. "I won't."

Zadyst was spared her immediate retaliation when the ground opened beneath Tristan. Feeling the boulder he'd landed on, she raised it up to find him clinging to consciousness. His arms were a bloody, charred mess, but already the bones were being hidden beneath new muscle growth. She turned to the terra wielder, keeping close watch on Zadyst, determined to buy Tristan time to heal. She felt him shift the plates beneath her feet and used her control of gravity to keep from dropping into the pit he opened there.

"Impressive for an untrained terra wielder," Bengim said, "but as an angeli, I find you both pathetic. I'd expected so much more."

"Is that so?" she retorted, when in her peripheral vision she saw Zadyst go for Tristan. Turning the ground beneath him into a catapult, she sent Zadyst and a square section of terra into the air, where he flew over top of Tristan, who was just coming to his feet.

Mid-air, Zadyst curled into a ball as his body was thrown into the city's outer stone wall. Thanks to Bengim, the density of the wall softened to mud, and his life was spared. Standing up, he caught Tristan's stare and grinned.

Tristan followed the trajectory of Zadyst's malicious stare and bellowed, "No!" His plea fell on deaf ears as the ignis wielder launched a fireball into the city. "You cur," Tristan cursed as it smashed into the building beside the mess hall, and people began to scream. His blood ran cold when Zadyst turned for the opening in the wall. "Don't do it," he shouted.

"Try and stop me," Zadyst said.

Tristan, intent on giving chase, found his path blocked by a vortex of swirling dust and rock. He turned his focus on Bengim, who was levitated from the ground with a sour visage pinching his leathered face.

"I can't let you hurt him, boy," Bengim said, throwing up a terra shield to ward off the girl's next attack. As a volley of stones slammed into it, he added, "If you want him, you'll have to go through me."

"Done," Tristan said, blurring forward. Bending his knees, he jumped for all he was worth. His heightened sight revealed the rotating gravity shield encasing his enemy. Unsure of how strong it would be to break, he tucked his shoulder and prepared for impact.

The BOOM that followed was like thunder in a lightning storm, but neither the shield nor Bengim were affected. Tristan, on the other hand, suffered through a violent marriage of his plummeting dead weight and the stone wall that intercepted him.

"Boy," Bengim said as Tristan groaned and struggled to his feet, "I'm losing patience with you. Do you enjoy slamming into things?" Rolling the ground before Anliac like a wave crashing in on itself, he knocked the girl flat on her back. "And honestly, little wielder, you are like a gnat: annoying, but ultimately ineffectual."

Screams of panic echoed in their ears as homes were set ablaze and chaos was loosed on their people.

"Tristan," Anliac said, seething, "our people need you."

"Can you do you this?" Tristan asked, his head whipping back and forth between the two wielders' locations.

"No." Bengim smirked. "She cannot, nor will I allow you

to enter the city."

"Trust me," Anliac hissed. "I can handle him. Go!" she shouted, then used every ounce of speed she possessed, launching boulders and stones alike in quick succession, to ward off Bengim as Tristan made for the city.

"This is not personal," he said, squaring off with Anliac, "but should Zadyst die…it will be."

"That man is a treacherous snake!" Anliac screamed, slinging rock after rock, which he deflected with minimal effort. "He thrives on the suffering of others!" She hefted a large chunk of stone and launched it towards his head as her yellow, illuminated eyes narrowed. When he clenched his fist, and the stone became dust, she hissed, "It's personal for me."

"He has information I need, and the cost is your life. That much is assured, but do not fret. I will kill you quickly."

"Know now," Anliac retorted, "I do not offer you the same vow. The only one who will suffer more…is the monster you brought into my city."

Regret crossed over his weathered face, but by the time he'd squared his stance, he wore a mask of stone. "So be it," he said and opened the ground beneath her feet.

Prepared for the move, she hovered over the opening. "You'll have to do better than that," she said, cresting a wave of terra from behind him that crashed down, hard and fast, over the top of his head.

The wave of terra split its path and washed to either side of him. In return, he fired a steady round of small stones that should have punctured holes clear through her body, but she deflected his attack with a solid rock wall.

Levitating over her creation, she taunted, "You may understand this ability better than I, but I'm still stronger." The planet groaned as it heaved stone boulders to the surface. With them, she returned fire, throwing her shoulder behind her open-palmed shove as she directed her attack.

Bengim held is arms straight out before him. His features pinched. The veins in his temple and neck throbbed. Palms open, he found himself reaching the limit of his power as the boulders were caught between his ability and that of the angeli's.

The boulders hovered between them, until the stone gave way to the pressure and exploded. They both threw up shields to protect themselves from the violent spray.

Anliac recovered first, and her long legs ate up the distance as she raced for Bengim's position.

He opened a trench as wide as three wagons between them and then cursed despite his awed appraisal of her perfect form as she leapt with absolute grace over the obstacle. Such beauty was difficult to mar, but her vulnerability in mid-air was too great an opening to ignore.

Anliac cried out as her body was peppered by a myriad of rocks. She made it over, but landed on her side. Rolling, she came up on her feet and snarled. He was within reach. Knowing her physical strength to be greater, and now close enough to swing her fist, she let it fly…and then found herself sprawled, belly first, where Bengim should have been.

She rolled to the right as a giant spike punched upward from the surface. On her back, she tightened her stomach and pulled herself to her feet just as a second spike emerged where she'd been. She danced around spikes that shot up, that tried and failed to skewer her, as Bengim hid beneath the surface.

"Enough!" she bellowed. She launched herself in the air and descended with an arm reared back. When she landed, she sent her fist slamming into the ground, creating a shock-wave through the terra that forced Bengim to the surface.

He shook his head to clear the disorientation. "That," he said, "I was not expecting."

She didn't hesitate, but he thwarted her at every turn. Every punch she threw was met with a boulder, and every boulder thrown was turned back on her. Every kick threatened her footing as Bengim shifted the plates, forcing them apart to deny her the contact she craved, or worse, turned the ground to quicksand beneath her feet.

Her right arm shot out to the side and a geyser of aquis spewed from the crack in the terra she'd created.

The ground trembled behind him. He turned to see the eruption of a second geyser. The distraction served its purpose. He didn't see the thick rope of clear liquid that came at him from his rear flank until it had wrapped its way around his waist. He was tossed into the air as whips of aquis sliced open his flesh and beat him back to the ground.

***

Tristan passed through the entrance as patrolling guards rushed forward. He spotted Zadyst at the same time he was seen.

"Come and get me," the nox taunted, launching a series of fire balls.

Tristan dodged them and moved closer.

Zadyst responded to the advancement by encasing himself in a sphere of blue flames that burned white hot at the edges.

Tristan pulled up short and circled, searching for a way past the flames protecting the wielder. "Hold!" he shouted to the Angeli Guard when arrows flew only to be charred before reaching their target.

Huge, rolling spheres of ignis flew into the air, setting fire to other parts of the city as they landed. The crops went to flame. Buildings burned. The number of injured was mounting, and yet from the chaos came order.

From where Tristan stood, he saw the citizens of Pisces Stragulum come together. Thick streams of aquis flowed through the air to be dumped upon the flames burning their food source. Aer wielders were lifting those trapped within the buildings out of windows and from off of roofs. The healers were bombarded with burn victims, as those stout of back carried them over, but many hands offered their aid.

Zadyst, wishing to spread his brand of misery, rounded a corner that brought him to the old marketplace, but was cut off from going further by the Angeli Guard that poured in around him.

Tristan tracked him as his mind raced for a way to put out the man's flames. They were hot enough to melt steel. He didn't see a way, and his failure was hurting his people.

"Form a perimeter," Triton shouted. "He doesn't leave this square!"

Lan snarled, his white feathers darkening to grey as ash and soot fell like rain, and positioned himself a step ahead of Triton.

"Aquis wielders! Get some water over these buildings! Soak them down!" Lan bellowed. "Ignis wielders, divide! First unit, do not let the fire spread! Second unit, let's see if you can cool this boy down! Drain his heat!"

Zadyst felt their abilities pulling at his own. "Stand down," he warned, "or people are going to die!" When they did not listen, he made good on his threat. Men, women, young or old, he did not care. With tails like comets, the fire balls flew and the death count mounted.

"Stand down," Tristan snarled as his power returned. "This is between me and him."

Zadyst laughed. "Dance for me, angeli," he said, bombing fire balls at Tristan's feet. Thinking to trick him, he changed tactics mid-flow and fired two shots at Tristan's chest.

Tristan twisted his torso on his hips and dodged the attack, but his cry was none the less one of unequivocal pain.

"No!" he shouted when the flames meant for him crashed through the walls of Shashara's infirmary, and those trapped within began to scream. The aquis wielders were pulling and pouring water as fast as they could to save them, but the dry wood became an inferno.

The upstairs glass window shattered outward. A mother's head popped through. Peering down, she caught sight of the aer wielders. Without hesitation, the mother tossed her daughter out before jumping through herself.

"Thank you," Tristan said out loud to the aer wielder. His relief was so great that he thought he might vomit, but it was short lived.

"If I can't hit you," Zadyst snarled, "I'll hit them."

"They are my people!" Tristan bellowed in panic as he blurred forward; the wind stirred in his wake, knocking down a burning house, to spare the woman and child from the fate Zadyst would hand them. He was too late. Their screams ripped through his heart as he slid to stop in front of them and slammed his palms together with all his might. The concussion put out the flames licking over their flesh, but their lives had already been taken.

Their pain became his pain. Tears pooled in his eyes as he looked around at the burning carnage he couldn't stop.

Once before, when he'd attacked Jacob, Tristan had found himself trapped in an emotionless void. Then…it had terrified him, but not this time. Fear of the unknown would not hold him at bay, and he welcomed the power the void offered. "What kind of person…" His jaw clenched.… Words were lost as his blood ran cold, yet energy radiated from him like sheets of hot wind. Hate illuminated his eyes as the markings on his flesh glowed like a yellow sun. The last of his injuries healed, the hairless skin knitted, and the flesh returned to normal. His muscles bulged, engorged with the blood pounding in his veins, demanding retribution.

Zadyst was not the only one to stop and stare as the angeli grew in height before their eyes, gaining several inches. His jaw dropped when Tristan's sharp nails widened and elongated into claws.

When the golden marks on Tristan's skin stopped pulsating, Zadyst cursed and then held his breath as the angeli transcended before his very eyes.

Tristan's voice rumbled through his people, shaking Zadyst to his core, and vibrating their chests as he delivered his promise to their enemy. "I'm going to kill you…slowly…."

Fear replaced Zadyst's arrogance as he gulped but stood his ground, allowing anger to be his anchor, and redoubled the heat of his fire shield. "You can't touch me," he growled.

Tristan's image disappeared and reappeared next to the sphere of flames. His right arm shot through the shield of fire, and his claws wrapped around Zadyst's throat. He refused to let go as the entire front of his body was engulfed in flame. He didn't scream, and if pain was visible on his face, it couldn't be seen through the fire. His skin turned crisp, but when it fell, a fresh layer was already in place. The wielder's element proved to be no match for his transcended healing.

Zadyst's eyes bulged, and his breathing stopped, but his fiery shield held fast.

Tristan applied more pressure, sinking Zadyst to his knees and freeing his vision of the flames. Screams and gasps of horror filled Tristan's hearing as his nose and ears began to regrow. They regained their shape as his lips filled back in, but his eyebrows and hair did not return. His skin was left bare. A sharp rock cracked against his temple, and he turned to find Bengim being ushered before Anliac with a dagger of ice pressed beneath his chin.

"Do that again," Anliac swore, "and I'll slit your throat."

Kicking Bengim's feet out from under him, she barked, "On your knees." Against her will, her gaze strayed from Tristan's eyes to his flesh within the fire. She covered her mouth as her tears welled and spilled. "Sweet Superi…" It was both a curse and a plea for mercy.

She watched as his blackened skin peeled away, revealing fresh, blood red muscle, before bald, pale skin rushed over it. Distracted, she lost Bengim. He dropped into the ground and then resurfaced halfway between her and Tristan.

Having found a target, the Angeli Guard surged forward at Triton's command.

The marketplace became a sink hole, its edges rising to throw back the guards. "I can't let you kill him! He hasn't told me what I need to know."

"Then you will have to die first," Tristan said.

Zadyst gasped in great heaves as Tristan released him. The breath he'd gained was used to scream, when Tristan latched on to both his wrists and with a vicious turn, broke both his arms at the elbows and then again at the shoulders. He fell back on his haunches, his weight resting on his calves, with his arms hanging uselessly at his sides. His flames extinguished as Tristan walked away, and he found himself at the point of a dozen spears.

Bengim watched as his attacker vanished, and wrapped himself in a gravitational force field as fast as he could.

BOOM!

Tristan felt no pain as he slammed into it and sent the wielder three hundred feet, east, away from the city. "Anliac," he shouted, already moving.

Knowing what he wanted, she leveled the marketplace so he could give chase.

Bengim landed outside of the city, his shield down, and had only seconds before Tristan solidified in front of him and struck with a double uppercut that sent him airborne again.

Tristan bent his knee, his head back to track Bengim's trajectory, and then he jumped. The ground beneath him cracked and caved beneath the pressure.

Bengim rushed to throw up another shield as Tristan's body collided into him. The force of impact tossed him higher and further south.

As gravity reclaimed Tristan, Anliac, still hundreds of feet away, gouged a giant chunk of terra from the ground, and with it, swatted Bengim sideways in the air. A rope of aquis wrapped around his neck, and she drew him in like a dog on a leash.

With the space between them quickly diminishing, Bengim mixed his element with her own. The water turned to mud and cracked as it dried before becoming dust. He pivoted around, searching for the next attack, and then pushed against gravity to rise as high as his ability allowed.

Anliac joined him with much greater ease, and then clawed her away through the gravitational force field around him. She grabbed him by the throat and squeezed until his eyes bulged while pummeling his face with her free fist. The skin on her knuckles split wide, red with both his blood and her own.

Bengim's body went limp, a dead weight that dragged them both down to the surface.

Anliac softened the impact by changing the density of the ground into that of a bog and then groaned, "Yuck," as she sank to her waist, while Bengim landed face first in the mud beside her.

She hardened the terra so fast that to Tristan, it appeared as if the planet had spewed them out like a bad taste. He chuckled.

Her eyes narrowed at Tristan for his mockery and then

they flared as she flew at Bengim, thirsty for his blood.

"Stop," Tristan said. "Don't kill him." He rushed forward to capture her wrists in one hand. "Not yet," he urged when her upper lip furled. "We need to know what all this was about."

Her chest heaving from exertion and unspent fury, she relented. "Drag him to the city," she snarled. "Let's put him next to his comrade and see what truth we can discover, and then," she said, already storming towards the city, "I am going to kill him."

Bengim was still bleeding when Tristan dragged him into the square. Triton had Zadyst under guard. Lan's voice was raised in the background as he gave direction to those battling the fires. Jonas, Shashara's guard, had his arm around her waist to steady her. Her right arm, blistered and raw, was cradled in her left.

Zadyst wiggled on the ground, much to the people's pleasure, as Anliac and Tristan dumped Bengim beside him. He glared up at them through his pain, but time and again his eyes narrowed on Anliac.

"I hate you," he hissed, struggling to rise to his knees without the use of his arms. "You left me in that cage!"

"You were intolerable," she retorted. "Your eyes on my naked flesh while those in the tower tormented me… You deserved worse."

"I want you dead," he shouted. His stare moved to Bengim, who lay unconscious at Tristan's feet. "Worthless assassin." He spat in the wielder's direction. "He'll never know who killed his family now."

Anliac kicked Zadyst in the gut, doubling him over.

He vomited violently.

"Was it you?" she demanded. When he did not answer, she snatched a handful of his spiked black hair and yanked back his head, forcing his blue eyes to meet her own. "You sorry sack of dung. Did you kill them?"

Zadyst laughed through teeth gritted in pain. "The one who killed them is untouchable. He commands the Pero."

Anliac released him and moved to stand beside Tristan with Bengim's prostrate body between them. "Nutrine," she said, "of Certamen. He controls the Pero."

Chortling, Zadyst added, "I was using his desire for vengeance to kill you."

"Why then"—Anliac smiled—"would you give us the only information keeping you alive?"

Zadyst's grin slipped. "Wait.… What? No!"

A collective gasp ran across the crowd as the ground beneath the ignis wielder opened and swallowed him whole. His screams were cut short when the crack closed tight.

Anliac and Tristan stepped back, prepared to end the terra wielder, but the tears coursing down his aged face gave them pause.

Spitting blood and chunks of teeth, Bengim groaned as he sat upright. "That is all I needed to know." He looked up at Anliac with blackened eyes. "Thank you," he said through swollen lips.

"You did all of this to avenge your family?" Tristan asked, then waited for further explanation.

"In my youth I was a soldier," Bengim began. "I fought against many people in the last war. Being the only level three terra wielder, I was sought after by all sides of the struggles. I even worked with your fathers: Matthew Suxson, Jacob Davadson, Montilis Aquam." His eyes shifted to the massive nox standing off to the side. "I even worked a prison run with a pirate known as Triton."

They turned to Triton for confirmation. "Then he tried to kill us."

Bengim didn't deny the charge. "I cannot claim to have always fought honorably, and perhaps I am in part to blame for switching sides to flow with the current of most coin." His visage crumbled. "My enemies grew apace with my wealth." His shoulders slumped. "I tired of bloodshed and battle and retreated to Satio Mapalia to be with my family, but someone had killed them before I arrived. I was denied knowledge of who did the deed, but"—his tears came in a torrent—"they left their bodies for me to find. I could not even recognize their faces."

"And now that you know," Anliac asked, softened by his tale, "will you remain our enemy?"

"I was never your enemy," he replied, blowing away the blood running from his nose into his mouth. "He wanted you dead, and I needed to know the truth. Please, let me go. I'll leave your city." His head turned in the direction of Certamen. "The head of the one I want can't be found here."

Tristan knelt down to get face to face with Bengim. He stared into the man's eyes and then spoke as if he wasn't there. "Shackle him, and put him with the others who've been hurt tonight while we decide his fate."

Lan and an Angeli Guard stepped up and heaved Bengim to his feet.

"If he so much as wiggles a stone," Anliac commanded,

"kill him."

"Got it," Lan replied as they carried him away.

Shashara collapsed.

"Woah there." Tristan blurred across the thirty feet between them, catching her and lifting her into his arms. "Are you okay?"

Shorlynn entered the circling of people. "Has anyone seen Skylar? I can't find her anywhere."

"She was here a moment ago," Triton said. "She's been busy putting out fires."

"But she is okay?" Shorlynn was holding a fist to her chest, her worry palpable.

"Come." A nox with caramel-colored skin and steel grey eyes, dressed in the uniform of the Angeli Guard, stretched out her arm. "I'll help you find her."

"Hey, you?" Shashara whispered and then winced. She shifted in Tristan's hold, bringing a weak hand to her smoke-damaged throat. "Your marks," she croaked. "They're different."

"Yeah," Tristan said, "but, don't worry about that right now. You just stay calm and we will get you some help." He stood with her in his arms and headed for the dock.

Triton, head cocked to the side and hands on his lean hips, asked, "Are we going to address the fact that Tristan now looks like Anliac, or the fact that the fire didn't kill him?"

Anliac gave him a sharp look and raised her voice to be heard by all. "The Five could not be more proud of their people. Today, you protected each other regardless of race or station. You bound together and protected our home"—her voice cracked—"leaving the angeli free to face our enemies. Let us follow Tristan's example and see to our injured. There will be time enough later to celebrate the transcendence of Superi's first angeli reborn."

Triton watched Anliac move to follow Tristan. "So... that's a no on talking about it?" He shook his head and looked to Riker, who shook his as well.

"When they decide to discuss it," Riker said, "you be sure to let me know. That's a conversation I want to hear." He turned his back on the scowling pirate to help the guards put out the last of the fires.

XVI

Pieces of Meat

Davad couldn't stop smiling at his reflection in the mirror. His shaggy brown waves had been shortened, tamed, and made shiny with some type of goo by the barber Michael had called to the inn. He glanced at Set, who wore a bewildered visage of his own.

Set ran his hands over the close-cropped sides of his hair, over the white markings on the left side that stood in contrast to his ebony strands. He shook his head to see if the goo placed in the top, where longer hair remained, could hold it in place. He smiled when it did.

Davad had tucked away his father's cloak to don the silver cloak of the Five. Refusing Michael's offer to purchase clothing, they wore the solid black uniforms Anliac had designed, wearing their silver V signets on the outsides of their shirts. Their boots, freshly polished, finished off their outfits.

Michael, dressed in simple black cotton trousers and tunic with a braided silver rope tied at the waist, moved across the room to open the door when he heard a knock. Taking a step back, he bowed. "Master Davimon, Lishous. Welcome back, my lords."

"Thank you, Michael," Lishous responded. His soft blue linen shirt, the string loosened at the neck to show off four or five inches of his chest, was shoved into tight-fitted brown breeches. The pants were tucked into leather boots laced up to his calves. Sticking his hands into the pockets of his dark brown long coat, he entered and moved aside for Davimon to do the same.

"My young masters," Davimon said, "the king's court-yard has been prepared for the gathering in your honor."

"You look...not at all yourself," Davad teased.

Davimon glanced down at the loose-fitted, dark blue linen shirt and pants he wore that paled his skin, yet exaggerated his yellow and silver, four- and five-pointed stars connected by thin black and silver lines, that ran from his hairline to his chin along the left side of his face. The linen touched upon the contours of his muscled torso and thighs without clinging to his flesh.

"I think I look dashing and roguish." He grinned. "Do you not agree?" he asked, pulling a strap of leather from around his wrist to tie back his shoulder-length brown hair, as with one eye of the same brown and the other milky white one of an oracle, he stared and awaited their reply.

"You are sure to have all the single ladies vying for your favor." Davad chuckled.

Davimon wrapped his arm around Davad's shoulder and led him from the room. "And you will have your way with all their daughters. Ha!"

Set waited for Nathin and Michael to exit, assuring Michael he was capable of closing a door for himself, and asked Lishous in a whisper, "Is he all right? He does not seem himself." He flinched when the side of Lishous's mouth twisted.

"He insisted on sampling every wine that is to be served tonight," Lishous told him. "He found them all to his liking."

Davad laughed and hurried his steps from the inn, out onto the street, to fall in beside Set. "Are you excited?"

"More like I'm concerned," Set said, tugging at his collar. "You know Shashara's going to find out I went to party a without her."

Davad shrugged. "It's a matter of official business. She'll understand as long as you behave yourself."

"Excuse me?" Set stiffened.

"Oh, come on." Davad rolled his eyes. "You know how this works. Look, but don't touch...or taste...or even smell for that matter."

"Right." Set sighed.

"Hey." Davad grinned. "If you mess up, I'll be in more trouble than you will for letting it happen."

Set laughed and it felt good. "Oh, you think so, huh?"

"Yup." Davad nodded. "She likes you more than she likes me, so in her world, I'm the easier target."

"True." Set chuckled and looked up.

Twilight had fallen, and the multicolored moons over Superi added beautiful depth to the multitude of stars hanging in the clear grey sky. The cobblestone streets between the inn and the king's fortress were awash in color as well, as the citizens of Regia Aquam came forth in great number to partake in the party paid for by the king's coin.

Delicate ladies in yards of silk and lace, escorted by men in fine tailored clothing, kept their marriageable daughters front and center as they made their way with the flow of traffic. The colors they wore were as varied as gems and appeared equally expensive.

A red and white carpet fed the courtyard. Trumpets sounded at their approach and the music died as quickly as the conversations. A mortalis in the king's colors heralded their arrival.

"Announcing…King Normis's honored guests, Davad Jacobson, Magistrate of Pisces Stragulum, a member of the Five, and of the House of Angeli!"

Frozen and at a loss for how to respond, Davad held up his hand and twitched his wrist back and forth, as only half his mouth obeyed when he told it to smile.

Set fared little better when the herald bellowed, "Announcing… Set Matthewson, head advisor to the angeli, a member of the Five, and of the House of Angeli!"

Set's grin mimicked a snarl until Davad rammed an elbow into his ribs.

"Stop smiling," Davad said. "Eesh…Yours is as bad as Lishous's."

Applause erupted as they moved forward to join the fray. The grey stone courtyard was littered with carefully placed tables and chairs, adorned with white cloths, bouquets of fragrant red flowers, and flickering candles, set around a cleared area for dancing. A quartet of musicians sat upon a wooden stage and played a lively rhythm that brought laughter and a lighter step.

Red and white stone pillars, wider than a man and taller than a two-story inn, lined both sides of the courtyard. Each stone pillar was wrapped in green garland, and scented oil lamps hung suspended from silver ropes tied between them. Wine and spirits flowed like water, and servants flittered unobtrusively throughout the gathering to see to the needs of the guests. There was food in abundance, weighing down long, rectangular, wooden tables that were lined with men and women who waited to serve it.

"Shall we sit?" Davimon suggested.

"Preferably in a corner where I can hide," Set said.

They never made it that far.

"Davimon," a petite brunette, with a spattering of freckles on the bridge of her nose and cheeks, purred as she sidled up next to him, "rumor said you were back in the city." She laid her open palm on his chest and rose up on her tiptoes. "I've missed you."

Wrapping his hands around the tops of her forearms, Davimon eased her away. "It's good to see you, Isabella. I take it your husband is away again."

"Indeed." She smiled.

Set choked with laughter. "I'm going to find a table."

Michael followed, leaving a scarlet-faced Nathin behind to stand with his charge.

Davad, rooted in place by his fascination over the woman's boldness, made no move to follow.

Isabella tossed a coy glance over her shoulder and a younger version of herself pulled away from a group of eager young men. Drenched in red silk, with auburn waves cascading down the curve of her back, she worked her baby blue eyes as she crossed the edge of the area sectioned off for dancing to curtsy before Davad.

"Your description does not do you justice, my lord," she said. "I am Kareen." She held out a gloved hand. "Dance with me."

Struggling to keep his eyes away from the daring scoop of her neckline, he swallowed hard and allowed himself to be led away, as Nathin took up watch on the sidelines.

"Well," Lishous said, "with everyone else occupied, I think I'll see what trouble I can get into."

"Enjoy your night, my friend," Davimon replied. "You deserve it."

Lishous nodded and then was gone.

Set and Michael, unsettled by all the eyes that tracked them, decided they would rather starve than brave the food line. One of King Normis's men took note, and after seating them in a place of honor at an elevated table, he had the food line brought to them. After an embarrassing few moments of having platters carted before them—a nod for yes and a shake for no—they found themselves alone while their plates were prepared.

"I would very much like to visit Pisces Stragulum one day," Michael said. "The picture you've painted of it resonates with me. The idea of status being gained through works and not lineage, Master Set, that alone is invaluable."

"Where is such a place?" a voluptuous, pale-skinned girl, with volumes of thick, rich blonde curls and yellow-green eyes, asked.

Set thought her smile cruel. "We were discussing the

foundational reformation of Pisces Stragulum to abolish racial segregation and to unite the denizens of Superi under the banner of equality, while redirecting status away from lineage and towards those who are willing to serve."

Her eyes flicked toward Michael, but she was careful not to leave them there. "You would discuss such matters with your servant?"

"Michael is my friend," Set countered. "Would you care to join us?"

"I don't care how much my father desires to see you and I wed..."

"Excuse me?" Set gulped, but the girl was on a roll.

"I'll not marry a man who would steal our future children's birthright and give it to an undeserving commoner." She stiffened her spine and pulled her shoulders back until Set feared her bodice would burst. "I beg your leave, my lord." She gave a shallow curtsy and left without waiting for his reply.

"Please do not be offended, my lord," Michael said. "Those of higher rank will balk at the revolution sparked by the House of Angeli. To them it seems the beginning of the end, but to those like me, we see only a new beginning."

"Then why wait?" Set asked. "Come back with me to Pisces Stragulum when we depart tomorrow."

They were interrupted again by a bashful, doe-eyed beauty in a pink gown adorned with white pearls. Her sand-colored hair was piled atop her head with a few strands left to dangle down both cheeks.

"Forgive me for interrupting," she said so quietly that both men leaned forward to hear. "I am Violet." She held out her hand.

Set took it and kissed the back of her fingers before releasing it. "I am Set Matthewson," he said, "and this my friend, Michael. Would you care to join us?"

Michael stood to pull out her chair.

Smoothing her gown, she perched on the edge of her seat. "Thank you, my lord. You are as kind as the rumors suggest."

Davad veered from the dance floor, his arm held aloft and Kareen's hand trapped within his own, as he swerved his way through the onlookers to Set's table. Without slowing his shuffle, he leaned towards Set and grinned, saying, "Look, but don't touch."

Kareen's laughter melded with Davad's as he gave her a twirl, placed his hands on her rounded hips, and shimmied them all the way back to the dance floor.

"Are you spoken for, Master Set?" Violet asked, her gaze traveling along the line of envious girls wishing they were in her position.

"I am," he said, dashing her hopes along with all the others'. "Her name is Shashara Jacobs. She is Davad's sister and my closest friend."

Picking at an imaginary piece of lint on the table cloth, she forced a smile. "She is quite fortunate to have gained your favor."

"Ha," Set chuckled. "No, my lady," he said, "I am the lucky one."

As their plates arrived, Violet took her leave. Her exit opened a floodgate, and Set found himself overwhelmed by bright dresses, perfumed necks, and alluring smiles. Unfamiliar hands pawed at him as compliments flowed.

His markings were stunning. His hair was so soft. His eyes so blue. His muscles so hard. Even Michael fought laughter over that one.

"Enough," Set said, brushing them off as he stood. "Do you know what these marks mean?" he asked. "I am an epo-to. Despite your words, I know your truth. Half of you loathe being paraded out like slaves on a block, and the other half are reaching for deep pockets and power though a marriage alliance. Well guess what? That is no way to live, and no way to find love."

"Is there a problem?"

"Geez." Set jumped. "I didn't see you come up, and yes there is a problem. I feel like a piece of meat, left hanging over a lake full of flesh eating fish."

Davimon swept his gaze over the gaggle of females and said, "Leave."

They scattered.

"Oh, thank you." Set sighed. "Please," he said, "take no offense, but this party is not for me. The risk to my future, here, is far greater than ever it was in the king's office chamber."

"Davad seems to be having a good time." Lishous appeared at Davimon's side.

Set tracked Davad to the other side of the courtyard, where he had Kareen's back pressed against a pillar and his face tucked into the hollow of her shoulder. Her chin was lifted, her hands resting on the outside of his shoulders, as her eyelids drooped.

"I'd say so," Set concurred with a goofy grin and a shake

of his head. "There is no reason for you and Lishous to leave the party. That is, of course, if you don't mind walking back with me." He looked to Michael.

"It would be my pleasure, sir." Michael pressed his hand over his heart. It was the highest honor shared between equals. It was also his answer to Set's invitation to join them in Pisces Stragulum.

"If you're sure," Davimon said, "then sleep well, young lord, and I will see you in the morning."

"Keep an eye on Davad for me," Set said as he and Michael fought through the throng to the open road.

Back in the inn, with dinner brought up from the kitchen, Set and Michael spoke of things great and small. Time passed and the candles burned low and still Davad had not returned. As streaks of pinks and blues broke across a morning sky, he dragged through the door.

Plopping face first into the mattress, he moaned, "I can't hold my eyes open, and my feet will scar from the blisters, but"—he flopped over onto his back—"that was the greatest night of my life."

"I guess Kareen treated you well." Set smirked, blurry-eyed himself.

"Who?" He paused. "Oh, you mean freckles." He grinned. "She was only the first of many, my friend."

Michael's laugh was more a series of grunts that turned to snores when he made the mistake of oozing to the floor.

Nathin slid down the wall and leaned forward to rest his forehead on crossed arms over bent knees. "I'm so tired."

Set swayed. "You're pathetic," he told Davad.

"Mmhmm," Davad mumbled.

Giving up, Set eased himself backward. As soon as his head touched the mattress, he was asleep.

XVII

No Deal!

If Davimon knocked, they didn't hear, but his boisterous greeting jerked them awake. "What a glorious morning!" he shouted, entering the room. "Rise and shine, my young masters. The king awaits with a paper to sign and then we can go home."

Wincing, Davad peered through the window of their room. The suns had shifted, so time had passed, though it felt he'd closed his eyes only a moment before. "Right now," he said, "in this moment…I hate you."

Davimon laughed. "Lishous is in the common room, ordering coffee and sweet cakes to go. The nourishment will grant you the energy you need to get through the meeting."

Set's stomach growled at the mention of food.

As Davad headed towards the door, he paused to ask, "Do we wake them?"

Michael and Nathin were out cold.

"No," Set said. "Let them sleep."

Lishous met them downstairs. White glaze matted the fur at the corners of his black lips as they turned up in greeting. "Ready to meet the king?" he asked as he handed the boys their morning meal.

Dubious, they took what he offered and dodged the question by slipping out the front door.

The streets were quiet. Shopkeepers only now opened their doors, while city workers poked along, picking up random pieces of food and trash from the night before. The noise level rose as they approached the courtyard, and Set paused a moment to see it in the light of day.

The grey stone was littered with trash. Tables and chairs were overturned, and the carpets had been trodden to frays. Oil lanterns, their glass shields singed black from extended use, hung in sorry condition from sagging ropes.

"What happened to them?" Set asked, pointing to the musicians passed out on the stage in the midst of broken instruments.

Lishous crossed his arms over his chest and tapped his booted toe as he stared in irritation at Davimon and Davad.

"The more liquor they consumed," Davad explained, sticking his finger in his ear and shaking it, "the worse their playing became."

"In all fairness," Davimon added, "we gave them fair warning to quiet their racket."

"And when they did not," Lishous concluded, "these two yanked free the garland from the pillars and swaddled them it. They passed out from the booze before they managed to untangle themselves."

"And their instruments?" Set asked.

Lishous cocked his right brow. "Their instruments broke their fall."

"Davad," Set said, "seriously?"

"I blame all the sweets," Davad said.

"Sweet kisses, you mean." Davimon winked.

"And," Set said with a giant step forward, "we're moving on."

They entered the fortress, crossed the wide-open foyer without delay, and followed the winding staircase to the above floors. Lishous went as far as the end of the hallway, where he snarled at two guards with quarterstaffs before sitting on the top stone step.

The servant attending the king's door turned at their approach and stuck his head into the king's chambers. Only then did he turn to them and say, "The king will see you now."

"No secret guards today," Set noted aloud as they entered, "and your war counselor is absent. Have you decided against signing terms with us?"

"On the contrary," Normis said, rising from his desk to hand Davad a parchment covered in careful print. "The contract is more or less standard, but please, feel free to take your time in reading over it."

When Davad accepted the parchment, the king asked, "Master Set, did you enjoy the party?"

"It was an unforgettable experience," Set replied.

"Ha. I dare say it was far more memorable for young Davad, or so I hear."

Davad's ears turned red, but he kept his eyes glued to the parchment.

"And what of the other orders I issued, Davimon?"

"Handled, Your Majesty."

Davad looked up. "This document states that Pisces Stragulum, under the command of the angeli, will be obligated to assist you in any upcoming wars."

"Yes," Normis confirmed.

"It should not be stated as to who will be assisting whom," Davad said. "The war with the gods has to be a united effort without division of authority. We must be of one mind and of one accord."

"Agreed," Normis said. "However, this document includes wars other than that with Earth."

"What other wars?" Set asked, taking the parchment from Davad.

"The one we will wage against the fulgo," Normis said, "for their boundless greed. They have infested the waters with their high-priced ships carrying lightweight cargo and claim that the speed of the delivery is worth the coin. That's nonsense. The mortalis have bulbous, bellied ships with great holds. Yes, it takes us longer to cross the oceanus, but we do not pilfer the pockets of our citizens to deliver their goods. As the fulgo build more ships, the less cargo we have to haul. If allowed to continue, we will soon be unable to afford for our own ships to leave port."

"The fulgo's shipping business is a lucrative one," Davad said. "I've had a chance to study their marketing plan. It's ambitious, but if pulled off, it will change the way the two continents barter forever."

"Exactly," the king said, snapping his fingers. "We must stop them now."

"You mistake my words for agreement," Set said. "We will not punish a race for its ingenuity despite the curse."

The king's countenance darkened.

"Nor will we start a war with a singled-out race," Set said, "directly after fighting to unite the races to stand against the gods. Especially not for a single king's gain."

"Not mine alone," Normis countered. "It's in the document. I will give you Certamen. It has more angeli dwellings than any other city, and it is one with a long history of power. Consider it my gift—and one of sacrifice," he stressed, "considering I've waited a decade to crumble its stones beneath the might of my army.

"You will give it to us..." Davad's mouth was set in a pensive line. "With all due respect, King, it is not yours to give."

"It will be once we've taken it," Normis said. "When the war with gods commences, all we must do is place the fulgo at the front lines and smash them between the gods and the mortalis army we will have at their backs. When the dust settles, the fulgo will have too few men to stop us."

"What you are describing is horrific," Davad said, "and against everything the House of Angeli stands for."

Leaning against the edge of his desk, Normis cocked his head. "This is what it means to come to terms. You want the contract to state that we unite as equals? Fine, then take Certamen, and give me your word that you will stand with Regia Aquam against the fulgo."

"I'm not signing this," Set said, holding out the parchment for the king to take.

Davad beat him to it. "Nor am I," he said as he set the

parchment to flame. The ashes fluttered to the floor in a room gone silent.

King Normis erupted. "Davimon, you unappreciative cur! You swore they were not working with other Houses! You vowed that if I offered them fair terms, they would sign and all would be well!" He turned to Davad and Set. "Tell me," he said, "which House seeks my throne. And explain to me while you sit upon your high horses and accuse me of manipulation—and contemplation of ambush—that the House of Angeli felt it honorable to send a foul beast to destroy a section of a city within my region! To take advantage of my hospitality and then presume to judge my character when my sole interest is in the greater good of my people."

Davad and Set shared a look of confusion made clear by their drawn brows and flared nostrils.

"We made no effort to hide our visit to the House of Terra," Davad said, "but I assure you, we have no plans to align ourselves with Mitable beyond what is necessary in conjecture with the coming war." He glanced away, as if considering, and then added, "I was approached by a handful of people last night with interests in land rumored to soon become available along the Eastern Continent's coast, but none spoke of over throwing your rule."

"And as to an assault on any portion of Regia Aquam," Set said, "by beast, or man, was not ordered by any member of the House of Angeli, nor by any of citizen of Pisces Stragulum."

The king nodded to Davimon, who spoke.

"In Media Forum," he said, "a portal opened. What came through was something no Superian alive today has ever seen: a giant, hairless, one-eyed beast came through and wreaked havoc. Captain Nutruminson and his men brought it down, but we lost many men in the battle."

Set nodded to Davad and they both stood.

"Draw up a contract that simply states your vow to send your armies to aid the angeli in the war against the gods of Earth," Set said.

"And what of my war against the fulgo?" Normis demanded.

"Should you choose to proceed with that course," Davad said, "our signatures will be among those rallied against you."

"And if I refuse," the king snarled. "If I chose to stand aside and let the angeli face the gods without my aid?"

"Then when the gods turn their eyes to your city," Set told him, "you will face them without the aid of those who fight beside the angeli. We will not lose precious lives protecting those who will not act to protect themselves."

Silence stood as a sentinel in the room.

"I underestimated you," Normis said, "and it has left me without recourse, but when this war is over, a peace accord between our two cities will need to be drawn. You say you will not bow to a king"—his stance widened, his shoulders squared, and he became the image of the title he wore—"but neither do kings bow."

"Understood," Davad said. "Now, with your permission, we would like to see for ourselves the site of what happened and perhaps speak to your Captain?"

"If it will get you out of my sight until this cursed contract can be drawn…granted," Normis sneered.

Davimon escorted them from the chamber.

At the end of the hall, Davimon called out to Lishous. "Make ready horses. We're taking them to Media Forum."

"It's about time they were told," Lishous said as he darted down the staircase.

Outside of the fortress, Nathin and Michael wore matching scowls, though while Michael kept his head down to hide it, Nathin worried less about sparking ire.

"You are one of the Five," he said to Davad. "The angeli—and the entirety of Pisces Stragulum—depend on me bringing you home in one piece. How could you leave the inn without me?"

The spark of angry emotions Michael directed at Set said he felt the same betrayal.

Without defense, Davad said, "You have our apologies and our word that it won't happen again."

Their smiles were instantaneous.

"Where are we going, my lords?" Michael asked as Davimon cut from the street to cross back onto the king's grounds, where a path led to the stables.

"We were told about an incident in Media Forum," Davad told him as Lishous exited the stalls, leading three horses. A stable boy followed him out, leading three more.

"I was informed by the network," Michael said, eyeing the beast he was supposed to mount. "The houses were mostly spared, but damage to the businesses was extensive. Young masters, would it not be better for me to walk? There will be talk otherwise."

"Mount up, Michael." Set grinned. "By tonight it won't matter what others think."

"Yes, my lord," Michael replied, doing as he was told.

Settled into the saddle, Set inhaled as a rush of someone else's adrenaline poured through him. He tracked the energy back to the man in black he'd met in the alleyway. With his head down, buried deep in his hood, he approached.

Davimon, Lishous, Nathin, and Michael closed rank around Set and Davad.

"Do you know him?" Davad asked.

"Remember I told you I had something to tell you later?" Set said. "Well, apparently later came too late. Let him pass."

"As promised, my lord." The man lifted a black, leather-bound journal. After Set took it, the man bowed deeply at the waist and backed several feet away before turning and standing upright as he rejoined the meandering citizens coming and going from shops and houses.

"One missing from Calstar's collection?" Davad asked. "Why did he give it to you?"

"Later," Set said, squaring his shoulders when Davimon's considering stare collided with his own.

After a brief pause, Davimon said with a half-smile, "You're learning," as he reined his horse towards the street and nudged its flanks.

By midday, they'd reached Media Forum. The town could not have been more different from Regia Aquam. It was clean, of course, but filled with quaint little homes that reminded Set and Davad of their home in Exterius Antro. One was as likely to see a pig in the front yard as a chicken, and though the people wore exhaustion like a second skin, they smiled readily as the small group made their way through their territory.

"Captain, Nutruminson," Davimon greeted the wolfish fera in a dark blue uniform riding point before his in men in red.

"Sir Davimon." The captain dipped his chin. "Lishous we see often enough, but it is rare to see you here."

"Allow me to introduce Set Matthewson and Davad Jacobson from Pisces Stragulum."

The captain's eyes dropped to the silver, V-shaped signets hanging from their necks. "Welcome, my lords." He bowed deeper than before. "How may I serve?"

"We're here to see the damage wrought by the creature that came through the portal," Set said, "and if you are willing, we'd like to hear your account of what happened."

"Follow me," Nutruminson said.

Two right turns from where they'd entered the town, the charred remains of wooden building spread their ashes across an open square, whose ground had been crunched and ripped.

"One man did this?" Davad asked, sliding from his saddle as the others did the same.

As a unit, they made their way around the wreckage and came to a stop in front of… Was it a tavern…a shop? They couldn't tell by what little remained.

"My lords," the captain said, "I fear I do not have the words to recreate the horror that was this beast, but unless I'm mistaken, my lord, you are an epoto."

Set's chin lifted. "Most run from what I am."

"I am a captain in the king's army," he replied. "I do not run. And if what came through that portal is the beginning of war with the gods, then all should be warned of what we face. Take my hand, my lord. See for yourself the strength of the beast."

The part of him that was Set feared reaching into the Captain's mind. The part of him that was Calstar was salivating. "Brace yourself, Captain," he said. "This is not always pleasant." He took the man's paw in one hand and placed two fingers to his temple with the other. "Bring the images to the forefront of your mind, and it will help if you don't try and fight me."

Set stiffened, and so did the captain. Set's eyes, though closed, squinted as his lips pressed thin. The captain's jaw was busy clenching and unclenching, but he remained silent. When Set gasped, the captain fell to his knees, breaking the connection.

"Set," Davad said in concern at the horror-filled rounded eyes, staring without seeing. "Are you okay?"

"Lishous, watch out," Davimon said, lunging through the air to crash into Lishous's side, knocking them both to the ground.

A portal opened where Lishous had been standing, behind Set, who caught hold of Davad's wrist in a death grip and yelled, "Nathin! Michael! Move!"

"My lord!" Michael rushed forward, jumping without hesitation through the portal.

Nathin had grabbed hold of Davad's other arm the moment the portal had crackled to life, and so was in no danger of being left behind when Set dragged them all through. Davimon and Lishous, however, found themselves alone.

"What do you think you're doing?" Davad shouted.

"Have you lost your mind? Where are we?" he asked, turning in a circle to scan the area and noticing only huge trees blocking his line of sight. The ancient forest triggered memory. "Turris Cavae! Well, that's just great!" Davad paced in pounding, boot-slamming steps. "No wonder my skin feels flayed." He got up in Set's face. "That jump was too far for you and you know it!"

"Shut up," Set said, swaying on his feet. "Just shut up and let me think."

Michael, having narrowly escaped face planting one of the great trees upon exiting the portal, dropped to his knees and vomited at its base upon the lush, green grass that grew there.

"About what?" Davad snarled. "About how you left the king hanging without a signature? Or are you considering the physical pain that you just put Michael through that has caused his guts to twist? Tell me, Set, what presently weighs most upon your mind?" Disgusted, Davad moved to kneel beside Michael. "Are you okay?" After receiving a weak nod, Davad asked the same of Nathin. "How are you doing, Nathin?"

"I'm fine, sir," Nathin replied, but gave away the lie as he lost balance and fell to his backside.

"Davad," Set snapped and latched hold of his hand.

"Oh, no, no, no, no..." Davad gasped as his plea went unacknowledged. Against his will, the information Set had gleaned from Nutruminson's mind copied itself into his brain. Fear, unlike anything he'd felt before, numbed his flesh. "Superi help us," he said. "What do we do?"

"We do not control the gateways anchored to Superi

by the gods of Earth, but we do know where at least one of them is."

"You don't think Regia Aquam was the only city assaulted," Davad said.

"No. I do not."

XVIII

Friends

Set fainted cold, his flesh as pale as his brother's.

"Curse you, Set," Davad said as he dropped to kneel at Set's side. With trembling fingers, he checked for a pulse at Set's neck. He released the breath he'd been holding and gave the answer to the fearful question in Nathin's and Michael's stares. "He's still alive, but just like his brother, one day his arrogance is going to get him killed."

"I think it was not arrogance," Michael replied, "but abject fear that forced his action."

Nathin cleared his throat. "He shared with you what he saw through the mind of the captain. Was the Earthling really so terrifying?"

Swallowing hard, Davad looked up from his position beside Set. "Yes."

With a stiff nod of acceptance, Nathin said, "Then may Superi grant the angeli the strength, and will, to save us."

"We must first reach them." Davad smacked the side of

Set's face with an open palm. "And to do so, we need this one awake."

"Ow," Set groaned as his ice-blue eyes cracked open, and he raised a soothing hand to cover his reddening cheek. "Was that really necessary?"

Davad stood. "It made me feel better," he said, "and it served its purpose."

Nathin and Michael stood quiet, scanning the spaces between the great trees for signs of concern and allowing those in charge to converse.

"How much energy did you use to bring us here?" Davad's head tilted as his eyes narrowed. "And do not underplay, or the next jump we make might be our last."

"More than I would have had I been in my right mind," Set admitted.

"With a straight head you would have known better than to make such attempt," Davad said. "We are too close to the gates of Exterius Antro for comfort and too far from the shores of Catena Piscari to seek sanctuary." He shook his head. "It will take a while for you to recover your strength. We are sitting ducks."

Set's shoulders tensed, as did the skin around his eyes, but then a smile turned the corners of lips pressed thin as he propped himself up on his elbows. "Another option presents itself," he said. "We have company."

Nathin drew his short swords.

"Put them away," Set told them. "They are friends."

Trepidation saw their swords to scabbards with slow speed.

"Do you hear that?" Michael asked.

"It's like the clicking of a beetle," Nathin answered, "only with greater volume."

"It's Rupert," Davad laughed, as Set grinned. He stood and leaned against the trunk of a tree with one hand to brace against the vertigo that hit.

Nathin's eyes widen as a pack of fera topped a low-lying area in the landscape and fully revealed themselves. "Thank Superi they wear smiles," he said.

Rupert was at the head, his long arms swinging at his sides, with Dunhold and Luce flanking him a step behind. Dunhold's wide nostrils flared. He gave orders to the feras at their flank, but Davad and Set could not hear them. Luce's feline tail flicked like a whip, and then she bounded forward on all fours.

"What trouble do you bring to our territory this time?" she quipped, sitting back on her haunches.

"We are not at fault this time, Luce," Set replied without humor, "but trouble still comes."

Michael stiffened. His eyes jerked from one fera's face to another, unaware that he'd been backing away until he tripped over a root protruding from the ground.

The lot of them turned towards him, but it was Set who found his way over. "Michael? You good?"

"Forgive me," Michael said and then grabbed hold of Set's hand.

As stolen images flowed into Set's mind, he looked to Rupert. "You've been set upon by a beast."

Dunhold and Luce exchanged stares before turning them to Rupert, who answered on behalf of their pack. The other feras remained on the peripheral, neither engaging in conversation nor lowering their guard against an unseen threat.

"We have," Rupert said, checking for Michael's mark. "Your friend is a telepath?"

"I did not mean to take information not given," Michael rushed to assure the grey-eyed fera. "The aether has a way of acting of its own accord," he added as he and Set helped each other back to their feet.

Set made quick introductions among those he knew.

With that done, Davad said, "Rupert, we need to know exactly what happened. Turris is not the only region to be attacked."

"Char will want to exchange information," Dunhold said. "Much is changing, and quickly."

"I agree," Set said. "We need to hurry."

Luce smirked. "You are grey as ash and can barely stand."

Davad concurred. "He's drained."

Set winced but couldn't deny the claim.

Rupert stepped backwards with a grin. "Don't look at me," he said. "You're not touching me, epoto."

Davad looked around the pack. "Anyone feel like sharing a little energy?"

"Make Bentinup do it," Luce said. "At least he will finally have a use."

A green-eyed fera with quills stepped forward. "I am smaller, and slower, than the rest." Bentinup squared his shoulders and then said, "Luce is right. Maybe this will help me earn some credit." He held out his hand to Set. "I offer a portion of my strength to speed our journey—and in so doing, I hope to please my tribal alpha."

"You remind me of my friend Totalis," Set said with a weak smile.

The watching feras growled their approval as Set took what was offered.

Luce stretched her long back into a graceful arch as she shook out her hind legs one at a time. "If you men are done chatting"—her black lips pulled away from sharp teeth in a crooked grin—"let us run."

Davad and Set ran at Rupert's side while Michael and Nathin fell in with Dunhold and Luce, leaving the others to guard their rear flank. It didn't take them long to leave the great trees of Turris behind and to reach the gently rolling plains of wheat-colored grass.

Char's camouflaged home was surrounded by a pack swollen in number. Two dozen eyes followed them in.

"What's with all the new faces?" Set asked at their approach.

"Donnin's men," Luce answered. "These are unsettling times, and our alpha's new mate wants to keep his bride swaddled against threat."

As Dunhold and Rupert went to inform Char of their arrival, Davad chuckled. "You don't approve," he said.

"You cannot marry a soldier and then take their blade," she said, "nor mate an alpha and then clip their claws. It leads only to discourse and division, and that"—she lifted her whiskered muzzle—"is dangerous."

The front door swung on its loose hinges as Char stepped out into the suns' light, a visage of concern on her white-furred face. Red eyes caught and held their own as she made her way to where they stood. "As always, you are welcome to share the shade of my home," she said, "but first I would hear what news you bring."

Set scanned the perked ears that were pointed in their direction. "We should speak privately."

Char's fur rippled with unease. "Is what Rupert tells me true?" she asked, ignoring his suggestion. "Has another monster attacked Superi?"

"At least one that we know of," Davad answered. "King Normis of Regia Aquam requested an audience with representatives of the House of Angeli. We were sent."

"During our discussions," Set interjected, "he said that Media Forum was similarly attacked."

Char turned towards Rupert with one brow arched.

Rupert shook his head.

Set, sensing Char's unease, questioned it. "Would you not have told us?"

"I would rather have informed Donnin first," she admitted. "The Alphas have emerged topside."

Set's and Davad's eyes widened.

Michael opened his mouth to speak of the images being held secret in the tribal alpha's mind, but gave Char the opportunity to answer honestly when Set asked the question.

"Even Tristan's rebirth and peril from the tower was not enough to flush them out," Set said. "What was strong enough to do so?"

"Dura Mortis received a visitor from Earth as well," Char told them. "Your news of Media Forum brings the count to three. Have there been others?"

"We're not sure," Davad told her. "We're on our way to Pisces Stragulum."

"Are you taking a ship?" Luce asked. "Last we heard Triton wasn't there."

"We don't need a ship." Davad grinned. "That's what we have Set for, but the jump from Regia Aquam would have been too great."

Char met Set's stare. "I would come with you if you can handle a portal large enough for me and my pack."

Set's eyes scanned all those standing in the clearing. Pensively, he said, "I need a moment," before he turned to the side and placed distance between himself and the others. Only Michael followed, having appointed himself Set's guard.

XIX

A Lesson in Aether

"I am no gate maker," Michael told him, "but I do have an idea of how aether reacts to being manipulated. Share with me your thoughts, and perhaps I can shed light on the shadows of doubt troubling your mind."

Set squatted, his fingertips pressed against the hard ground for balance. "When I returned from Exterius Antro, the others told me that I had taken out two guards whose only crime was standing too close to the portal."

Michael nodded. "That makes sense."

Set's head pulled back on his shoulders. "How?"

"Aether is not like the ground," Michael told him. "It's not fixed in place. Nor can it be compared to the air we breathe, for even when air is absent, aether is present. Our entire world consists of manipulated aether. The wind moves it, water carries it, the ground holds it, and fire ignites it. You are an epoto. You control it. You can bend it to your will, drawing it in or expending it as you see fit."

Set rolled his neck to relief building tension. "It would be more accurate to say it controls me."

"Forgive me," Michael said, "for speaking plainly, but young sir, therein lies your problem. As an epoto, you *are* the ground. You are the air we breathe. You are the conduit that moves the aether that controls our world. Once you stop trying to fight it, you will be able to control it—at least that is how the telepath training worked."

"So if I stop trying so hard…" The grass around Set's fingertips withered. Seeing it, he lifted his hands and dropped back to the ground, knees bent and head hanging. "I wouldn't know where to begin to even try."

Michael situated himself on the ground, facing Set. "When first my power manifested, the noise inside my head threatened my sanity. To hear thoughts as clear as voices, to see images of the mind as sharp as those my eyes perceived…it was consuming. There was no room in my psyche for myself, and I feared I was lost in the chaos."

"A sentiment I know well," Set said. "How did you gain control of it?"

"I stopped trying to control it. I let the thoughts and images of others flow through me. I store the information I need and discard the rest as empty noise. You fear your power, and thank Superi for your caution, but if ever you are to become a true rift maker, you must embrace what you are."

"That is easier said than done."

"Truly it is not. One must only choose to begin." With one hand, he reached out and touched upon the withered grass. With the other, he clutched a handful of that yet living. "These represent what you fear and what you hope for.

This is where you start."

Michael stood, forcing Set to look up at him. "I don't understand. I don't see what you're trying to show me."

"Stop looking with your eyes, epoto. See with your power instead." With that, he turned away and rejoined the others.

Set touched upon the dead grass as Michael had done, scraping a handful of the dry terra into his closed fist, and let it slip like water from his hold. His touch brought death to vitality. In anger, he grabbed hold of the living vegetation and uprooted the wheat-colored strands. Clutching it like a talisman to his chest, he closed his eyes and laid an open palm to the dead patch.

The terra was dead, but just beneath its surface, life remained. He could feel the torn roots that had supported the grass he'd pulled free. It was a start. Sweat beaded on his forehead as he focused, not on the roots, but on the aether surrounding them. From nothing came small clusters of dim energy, like miniature stars. Pushing with his animus, he willed them to brighten, to do his bidding, and to breathe life back into the death he'd created.

"How did you do that?"

Davad's voice broke his concentration. He opened his eyes and gasped, his hand now empty. A circle, ten feet in diameter, was cloaked in a lush carpet of new growth. A seed hidden beneath the ground had emerged as a sapling, bearing flowers and soon to bear fruit.

A smile split Set's face wide. "I understand," he said, rising to his feet. "Come." Rejoining the others, he said to Char, "I think I can open a portal large enough to carry us all to Pisces Stragulum, but it will probably come at a cost."

"As do all things in war time," Dunhold said.

"Agreed." Char nodded. "Luce, gather the pack. Tell Donnin's men that they are free to travel with us, or to remain behind as their conscience dictates." To Set, she said, "Do what you must to see us to where we must go. The angeli must be warned."

Unsure of what would happen, Set said, "We need to move away from here. Where is the closest water source?"

"There is a small pond," Rupert said, pointing to the west, "there. Where you see that cropping of trees."

The pond was no more than a few hundred feet away, hidden by the grass. He turned to those gathered. "Move away from me until the portal stabilizes, and Char," he said, "forgive me."

Seeing Set's plan percolating within his mind, Michael offered encouragement as he urged the others back. "You do what you must." He nodded. "Bring your thoughts to fruition and we will join the angeli."

"What is this cost of which he speaks?" Char asked with mounting concern.

She was not alone in her disquiet. Her pack shifted with restless nerves as they stood alongside Davad and his two companions, watching out across the plain at Set's shoulders and head that rose above the tall grass.

Set could feel their rampant emotions, despite the distance separating them—their doubt, their fear, their desperation to reach the angeli and the aid offered there. He did his best to block it out.

Instead, he closed his eyes and focused on the accumulation of elements surrounding him. The suns heated his flesh from overhead, while a breeze cooled their touch with a gentle caress that ruffled his cloak and hair alike. The scent of still waters filled his nostrils, as did the fruit trees gathered at its bank. The ground, formerly a dead thing, was alive beneath his feet with ants, insects, snakes, and other creatures who'd dug holes in it. Pangs of regret threatened his concentration, for he knew that all such life would soon be forfeit as the aether did his bidding.

There was no help for it. He did not look upon the devastation as he unleashed it, but held his eyes closed and clasped his hands together.

Those who bore witness had no words to describe the monstrous wave of death that flooded forth from the epoto. In an ever-expanding circle, the spreading decay encroached upon their location. The grass turned black and fell as ash, leaving them no choice but retreat, or be overtaken.

"Uh…" Davad said, "We should back up. Now…."

As a unit, they did so, fighting the urge to break and run.

Char's mouth hung open as the trees lost their leaves, bark, and branches, turning grey as if decades dead. With the landscape cleared of obstacles, the pond, or at least the dry crater left behind, became visible. The life held within now lay still upon cracked, dried ground.

Set forced two points in the aether to bend towards each other, and when they connected, the portal to Pisces Stragulum stood open. The standard purple lightning barely crackled before the image of the portal stabilized and stood perfect. It was massive, ten men wide and at least ten feet tall. Its purple edges were clearly defined, and the image on the other side was flawless. He opened his eyes to the majesty of what he'd created, but his pride was dashed when he was hit with Char's sorrow and grief.

Tied to the land, her spirit was torn by the cost of their passage, and he felt it as if she had smashed him with a war hammer. The fear and awe that flowed from the pack added salt to the open wound in his heart.

Davad would have given much to share the burden that drooped Set's shoulders, but it was the cursed part of being an epoto. He went to him. "How are you holding the portal open?" he asked to distract him.

Slow to answer, Set first sought Michael, who stood with the feras and nodded his thanks. To Davad, he said, "I cannot image a world where epotos are plentiful. The more I learn of the destruction we are capable of, I begin to understand why we were hunted down and killed." He took a deep breath. "Everything I have done up to this point has been according to the strength of my own animus," Set told him, "but I am a conduit for much greater power. I understand that now. The aether does not struggle to complete such a simple task as opening a hole for us to pass through."

A cold chill crept down Davad's neck. Having no idea how to reply to Set's words, he asked instead, "Did you know this would happen?"

"Come," Set said as he started across the meadow towards the others. "Char's question will surely be the same."

When he reached her, Set knelt with her and said, "The distance across the oceanus is great, and the number of people you would have cross…" He lifted her tear-streaked face by the chin. "It required a sizable portal and it needed stability against collapse. Small things require little to no sacrifice, but endeavors such as this…" He shook his head.

"They require more," Char finished for him as she gained her feet. "You did as I asked," she said, her voice as stiff as her spine. "I have no right to be angry, but I am. The cost to my pack was the life of our land. What was the cost to you, epoto?"

Set understood the way she felt. One of the first lessons he'd learned as an empath was that emotions lied. People hid their grief behind anger, but as the sorrow passed so too would the ire. This knowledge was his shield against her burning eyes. "The cost to myself is the way you are looking at me now. The cost is in the fear radiating from those around me. The cost"—his voice broke—"is knowing my touch brings death."

For a moment, who they were ceased to matter, and Char snatched him forward in an embrace meant to shelter him from the pain reflected in his pale blue eyes. She was a woman, and he was but a boy forced to face trials meant for men.

Set clung to her and cried, though in his mind it was the loving arms of his mother that held him close. "Forgive me," he said as he pulled away, wiping the tears with the back of his sleeve.

"There is nothing to forgive," she said. "We do as we must."

"Tristan!"

At Davad's shout, they turned towards the portal and watched as Tristan came through.

"What are you doing?" Davad's sprint towards the opening slowed to a trot and then stalled altogether. "Why…are you bald?"

"We've had unpleasant surprises of late," Tristan replied as the gathering of people converged on the portal. "When a portal this size opens just beyond the walls of our city, it warrants investigation."

"Brother," Set said, clasping forearms with Tristan as he walked up, "you've fully transcended…and…you're bald…"

Tristan rolled his eyes. "And you find my hair loss the more interesting of the two, huh?" He draped his heavy arm over his brother's shoulders. "A lot has happened, and yes"—he lifted his free arm and brought it up to where they could examine the markings—"a few things have changed."

"You have no idea how much has changed," Set said, "but I intend to tell you."

Nathin and Davad did what they could to ease Char's fears when she and her pack found themselves surround by Angeli Guards with Anliac at the forefront of their defensive positions.

"Stand down," Set heard Anliac order the guards as he and Tristan came through.

Trees were broken. A section of the wall was crumbled, and the level ground he remembered was a battlefield of gouges and upheaved mounds of terra.

Set asked the obvious question. "How did Pisces Stragulum fair against the beast?"

"How do you know about the attack?" Tristan queried as Anliac came up.

"It is good to have you both home," she said, "and better still that you brought Char with you, but this portal needs to be closed."

"I would suggest we carry ourselves within the city first," Char said, "and hope the distance enough to spare us the cost of the closing."

Her pack readily agreed, as did Nathin, but his words left those of Pisces Stragulum confused.

"No." Set stepped in front of them. "I took something precious from each of you." Staring into Char's eyes, he said, "I would now give back."

He could feel the energy of aether circulating between himself, Superi, and the portal. He redirected its course. The grass beneath them, from where they stood to the stone wall, turned vibrant green and covered over the surface wounds of the terra with new life. The trees, broken but standing, flowered. Their boughs grew heavy with fruit that budded and ripened before their eyes.

More surprising was the influx of energy into those who stood close. The golden marks glowing upon Anliac's and Tristan's skin and their yellow eyes flaring were all clear manifestations of the transfer of power. The portal closed as smoothly and soundlessly as a greased door, and the people were left renewed.

The people's fear of the epoto's touch far outweighed their gratitude. Their silence spoke volumes, but of it all, the look of concern shared between Davad and Tristan cut the deepest into Set's psyche.

"Come." Anliac gestured Char forward. "Let us see you and yours settled within the walls."

"You did good, Set," Davad said. "I'll see you two inside."

Tristan draped his arm over his brother's shoulders as they began to walk. "So tell me what you meant about the beast, and then you can tell me how you learned to make the grass grow." A wayward thought made him laugh.

Set cocked his head and with an arched brow and asked, "What?"

"I was just thinking." Tristan grinned. "Shashara is going to have you in the garden forever now. You know that, right?"

Set sighed, but his grin said he didn't really mind at all.

XX

Out of Hiding

As they made their way past the exterior wall of Pisces Stragulum and headed towards the marketplace within sight of the docks, Set asked, "Did the Earthling wield fire?"

The question was expected, considering the damage. The building beside the mess hall had been gutted with fire. The whitewashed walls of the infirmary were blackened with soot, and the upstairs window had been shattered. Homes were destroyed. The ground where they walked sank beneath their feet as if newly turned, and the farmland on the outskirts of the city had been charred.

"There was no attack from Earth," Tristan explained. When Set opened his mouth to speak, Tristan cut him off. "We have enemies on Superi as well, Set. It was a hard lesson to learn, but we won't be caught off guard again."

Pisces Stragulum was not the only thing to carry the marks of battle. The Angeli Guard was hypervigilant. The people were on edge, and Set couldn't stop stealing glances at the changes in his brother. The silver and black uniform Tristan wore made his pale, bald head stand out all the more.

"What?" Tristan asked, rubbing the top of his head. "Does it look that bad?"

"My entire life you've had long hair, and I come home to find you transcended and bald… It doesn't look bad." He chuckled. "It's just going to take a bit to get used to. The, uh, lack of eyebrows is kind of creepy, though."

"Shut up." Tristan laughed.

"So"—Set's smile slipped as reality stole in—"are you going to start talking about the battle, or what?"

"When we went to the tower with Jacob," Tristan said, "do you remember the man Anliac told us to leave in the cage?"

"I think so."

"He got out and found leverage that turned a level-three terra wielder against us."

"Seriously?"

"Yeah. Anliac's head in exchange for information about who slaughtered his family."

"Is Shashara okay?" Set grew nervous.

"We lost a few, but yeah, Shashara is fine." Tristan's eyes dropped to the ground.

"Where is she?" Set demanded, seeing the worry in his brother's eyes, but before he could panic her voice cried out in answer.

"Set!" Shashara, in a blue sundress, came at a run and threw her arms around his neck, kissing him soundly on the lips before cupping his cheeks between her hands and pulling back to smile at him. "I'm so glad you're home."

He captured her right wrist and lowered her arm to inspect the reddish, purple, scarred skin.

"It's nothing," she said, pulling free.

Set looked to Tristan. "Why didn't a healer see to this?"

"There were more severe injuries that needed tending," Tristan told him. "When she finally agreed to let the healers take a look, the scarring was permanent."

Davad's eyes lit up as he joined them and saw his sister's hurt for himself. "Someone better have died for that," he said.

"He's buried beneath your feet," Tristan told him.

Anliac, having come up in time to hear, added, "I assure you both, he suffered a great deal before he met his end."

"Is that Char?" Shashara asked. Rupert, Dunhold and Luce, she remembered, but the other fera faces were unfamiliar to her. She looked to Set for explanation. "What's happened?"

"The war has begun," Davad answered.

"What?" Anliac and Tristan asked as one.

Bells tolled on opposite sides of the city before more could be said. Lan came up at a trot. "What would you have us do, angeli?"

"Split ranks," Tristan said, "and see our visitors guided here."

"On it," Lan said and then began barking orders to the men.

Davad turned to Nathin, who was never far from his side. "You and Michael clear the streets of civilians who are unable to take up arms. Quickly."

"Yes, sir." He nodded, and the two men hurried off,

shouting, "Clear the streets!"

Char joined the Five with Rupert at her side. Luce and Dunhold were a step behind.

"Shorlynn is coming," Tristan said, his eyes locked on the city wall. "Where is Triton?"

"Who is here?" Shorlynn asked, approaching hand in hand with Skylar. Looking towards the Eastern Road, her yellow eyes grew round.

The rest of them tracked her line of sight. Five fulgo men led a group of thirty more through their streets, guarded by angeli forces. Dressed in light, black chainmail, overlaid with red silk uniforms, they wore matching stoic visages. They carried themselves with the grace of predators. Though they were fulgo, they moved as a pack.

"Anyone know who they are?" Tristan asked.

"No idea," Davad said, "but from the looks of them, this should be fun."

Anliac provided the answer. "They are they Pero—assassins loyal only to Nutrine of Certamen."

"Nutrine? As in the one Bengim and Zadyst were talking about?" Tristan asked, but no one answered.

"I count two bearing aether marks," Set said.

"Three," Shorlynn corrected. "The man on the right. Check his hand. He's a telepath."

"You know them," Anliac said. "Why are they here, Shorlynn?"

"I'm betrothed to the one with the golden rope marking his rank on his left sleeve," she confessed. "His name is Maltris, and I'm assuming he's here to take me back."

"Yeah, well," Skylar said, "that's just not going to happen."

"We might have bigger problems," Davad told them. "Look." He pointed towards the opposite side of the market-place. "The Alphas have arrived, and they are well guarded."

Lan's white-feathered neck was stiff. His beady black eyes were unblinking. Following behind him were the Alphas, with three solid lines of feras crowded at their backs. Sole, the grey wolf with white wings, was of impressive size, but the two feras flanking him and the diminutive, orange-furred Lunam made even Sole appear child-like.

"That is a creature of rare beauty," Razoran said, walking up.

There was no doubt of whom he was speaking. On all fours, the sleek black-furred fera, from nose to tip of tail, was at least eighteen feet long. Purple, wide-set eyes scanned for threats amongst the people of Pisces Stragulum. White whiskers twitched as triangular, pointed ears turned to catch all sound. With each stride, the muscles in her powerful form bunched and released.

"It would appear she is taken," Davad teased, though trepidation deepened the creases around his eyes and mouth.

The female's grey-furred male counterpart was massive. His head was that of a hyena. His neck was as thick as that of a boar, and it sat upon shoulders twice the length of an axe handle. He was as tall as the female, but stood erect on two feet, his arms swung wide, unable to rest against his sides because of the bulging muscles that rippled his torso. Black leather pants hugged slender hips that punched into legs resembling tree trunks.

"I think they are related," Shashara said. "They share the

same eyes."

Char had eyes only for the man walking a pace behind his father. Donnin, in a dark green linen shirt left to hang open, had a hand on the hilt of his short sword strapped to his waist. The suns' light caught the gold flecks in his eyes as he returned her stare.

Tristan chortled and Anliac smacked his shoulder in response.

Davad and Set shot him a look that questioned his sanity.

"I fail to see the humor here, brother," Set said.

"Socmoon said Pisces Stragulum would soon be a powder keg of power ready to ignite." Tristan chuckled. "He took off early this morning without word or reason. I guess he saw this coming."

Caught between two forces, the Five were relieved when Triton's entire crew came up from the docks. As Lan moved to stand with them, and the Angeli Guard took up position on the peripheral, awaiting instruction, Triton gave a slow nod as he and his men evened the odds.

Sole was the first to speak, but it was not to the Five. To the feras of Pisces Stragulum, he said, "It is time for you all to retake your place among our number. Fall in."

Not a single man or woman moved to comply. Instead, Donnin broke rank and joined Char beside her pack, asking, "What are you doing here?"

Lunam smiled. "Donnin, your new mate is quite lovely."

Char blushed, but answered Donnin's question loud enough for everyone could hear. "The Turris region came under attack. Rupert ran into Set and Davad the following day to discover that Media Forum had suffered worse."

Sole growled. "The attack in Dura Mortis makes three, then."

"Certamen brings the count to four," Maltris said. "War is upon us, and I've come to claim my betrothed. I would know she is safe before true battle begins."

Tristan broadened his stance and crossed his arms over his chest. "And you thought it would require a contingent of men to see it done?"

Taking note of Tristan's golden line markings along his pale skin, Maltris replied, "Stories of the angeli's prowess are becoming legend, but I have orders to follow, and if it requires testing the truth of such claims to see it done, then I am prepared to do so."

Anliac's matching golden marks were not missed on the fulgo. She spread her glare evenly between the Alphas and the Pero leader. "The people of Pisces Stragulum are free to make their own choices. We couldn't care less what race they come from or what promise was made before they arrived. They are here now and fall under our protection."

Maltris found Shorlynn in the crowd, standing beside a fiery redhead with a fierce scowl. His gaze slid downward to their laced fingers. "Get your filthy hands off my betrothed."

"She doesn't belong to you," Skylar retorted.

Snapping his fingers, he ordered Shorlynn, "Get over here. Now."

The ground trembled as Anliac's temper flared. "You should choose your words with more care," she said. "Shorlynn is not a dog, nor is she leashed as one, but if you talk to her like that again you will find her protectors have very sharp teeth."

"Shorlynn," Skylar shouted as the woman pulled away and began to walk towards the Pero.

"It's okay," Shorlynn said, barely above a whisper. "There are greater battles on the horizon. I would not see blood shed over me."

A curving wind conjured by Skylar spun Shorlynn around. "Don't leave me," Skylar said, as she hurried forward to recapture Shorlynn's hand. "I love you. If you can't say the same, then go, but do not walk away because this brute snaps his fingers."

"She's right," Anliac said. "We are in the thick of it here. News of Earth's strategic attacks across Superi is of concern, but right now, you are our focus. The feras who've joined us, they are our focus. This is the bigger picture. The right to live as we choose as long as we leave others to do the same. The right to live without fear of slavery or persecution because of race, gender, or station. For this cause, above all others, the House of Angeli stands, because we know that winning the war against Earth will be for nothing if Superi is found to be no better."

"Angeli, or not," Maltris sneered, "you are just a woman. Shut your mouth and stay out of fulgo affairs before I shut it for you."

Maltris felt a ripping wind before Tristan appeared inches from his face, snarling. "Try it, you stupid…Agh!" Tristan hit his knees, screaming, his hands clasped to both sides of his head as pain lanced through it.

"Tristan!" Anliac shouted, rushing forward.

Inside Tristan's head, he heard, '*No one touches Maltris*!'

"Back off," the telepath said aloud before Anliac could

escalate the situation into bloody territory, "before I scramble his brain permanently."

"I'll kill you for this," Anliac vowed.

Lunam didn't waste time with words. She brushed up against Sole's side. He delivered the energy she required, and she released it into the telepath's mind. His screams took the place of Tristan's as blood vessels burst in his eyes, nose, and ears, and blood flowed from them.

The men of the Pero stepped forward. The Angeli Guard did the same in counter. Triton's crew had circled behind the men from Certamen and made a racket to let them know they'd been flanked.

Released from the pain, Tristan stood with Anliac's aid. He looked first to Set, who shook his head, and then to Lunam, who said, "No one touches the angeli reborn." Having made her point, she loosed her hold on the telepath.

Maltris glared. "You should have remained hidden, Alpha," he sneered. "Now you've made an enemy."

"No," Sole growled, as the two giant feras did the same, "but you have." The other pack- loyal feras moved, forming a half-circle that flared out on both sides of their Alphas.

The fulgo of Certamen were forced to divide; half to face the pirates behind them, half to face the fera before them, with the Angeli Guard cutting off any chance of retreat.

"I did not come here to incite a war Superi cannot afford," Maltris said. "I've come to collect my property."

"I am not your property," Shorlynn hissed.

"Calstar and Nutrine would disagree," Maltris countered. "Come with me now, and you'll not be punished for your insolence. Make me ask again," he said, "and you'll suffer for it."

Hot tears sprang from Shorlynn's eyes and coursed down her ashen cheeks. "I am a person," she said. "I have feelings. I have desires of my own and a life I envision for myself that does not include the submissive servitude forced upon fulgo women. Do what you must, Maltris, but I'm not coming with you." Capturing Skylar in a fierce embrace, Shorlynn looked over the other woman's shoulder at the man that would be her husband. "And there's nothing you can do about it."

"You have your answer," Tristan said. "Leave, while we still allow you to do so."

Maltris let out a heavy sigh. "Trust that I would, if it was my choice, but Nutrine would have us discuss terms."

"If they are on par with King Normis's demands," Set spoke up, "know now that you're wasting your time." Goose bumps rose on his flesh as tensions mounted and anger flared from those who ruled.

"You've had dealings with the mortalis king?" Lunam asked. "That is unacceptable. What terms did you agree to?"

"Nutrine will not be pleased by this turn of events," Maltris said, "but if sides have already been chosen, the fulgo will respond accordingly."

Riker, in full military dress, came up from the docks. He cleared his throat as he walked through to the heart of the gathering. "It would appear my brief absence this morning has placed me outside of current events," he said, "and I would not choose to interrupt, but the news I've been brought bears weight on the conversation."

"Let us hear it then," Anliac said.

"Palus Regia was attacked," Riker told them. "General Aquam has taken over the city and has sent word. The nox stand ready, without condition, to fight beside the House of Angeli against the gods of Earth."

Anliac raised her voice and spoke with clear confidence. "Those are the only terms the angeli will accept. We do not see male or female. We do not see rank or race. We see only Superians. We act only on behalf of Superi. If you choose to stand with us," she said to the Pero and Alphas both, "then it will be without condition, or you will stand alone."

Maltris stood slack-jawed. "You would let a woman speak for your House?"

The women of Pisces Stragulum took offense. Shorlynn and Skylar moved to Shashara's side. The female Angeli Guards advanced ahead of the men. Women, who'd been listening from doorways, took up what weapons they could find and sacrificed the safety of their dwellings to stand with the rest. Lunam, along with the giant female fera, moved deliberately to the forefront of the brewing conflict.

The men of Pisces Stragulum began to chuckle. The sound grew to hearty laughter, as Tristan replied, "I do not see women, Maltris, but fighters who stand ready to take your head. Go back to Certamen, and deliver our words to your master. Do not…come here again unless it is to offer full support towards the cause without condition."

"That's never going to happen," Maltris retorted.

"Then we are done here," Anliac said. "Guards, see them removed."

"You're just a bunch of ignorant children." Maltris growled when it was the women in black and silver uniforms that escorted them back past the walls, laughter reverberating off their backs.

Davad cupped his mouth and yelled back, "Children with an army bigger than yours!"

In the Pero's absence, tensions lessened, and proper introductions were made. As Sole was officially introduced to his son's wife, Lunam made her way over to Lan.

"Why did you not respond to the order of your Alpha?" she asked him.

"In coming here," Lan told her, "in meeting the Five, I have discovered who I am. Here, I am more than a sword to wield, more than a pawn to be placed in the maneuverings of others. I am a free man, one worthy of respect, one fighting for a cause I believe in. I no longer answer to the Alphas, and I speak not only for myself, but for all the feras who ignored that order." Braced for rage, he was surprised when Lunam smiled.

"Excuse me," Lunam said to Lan before calling out, "Young Tristan," and then waited for him and Anliac to make their way over.

Shashara—hand in hand with Set—Triton, Razoran, and Davad gathered together to greet the Alphas. Riker approached alone, but would be privy to the conversation.

"It would appear you've transcended," Lunam said, "at last coming in to the full power you will need to face what comes next."

"As well as taking command of the nations of Superi," Sole added, "a necessity if you are to achieve victory over your enemies."

"Thousands traveled to Earth," Set said, capturing their

attention, "and they were beaten back and cursed. The an-geli are but two. If we are to protect Superi, it will take more than those of us gathered here. We are prepared to lead, but your wisdom far exceeds our own. Your counsel would be greatly appreciated, as would that of Riker, Triton, and Shorlynn. We must unite as one…or history will repeat itself."

"Only this time," Tristan said, "there will be nowhere to run."

XXI

The Summit

The location had been agreed upon by the gods. It was neither on Earth, nor in any of the heavens, but in an in-between that they came together to discuss the threat of the angels of Superi.

The room was formed of a void and possessed an ethereal life of its own. It breathed. Its edges pulsated like a steady heartbeat. A square table made of wood and stone had been conjured with aether energy built into it. The rainbow of aether colors marbled through the table provided them with light, for there were no suns in the room.

Pillars of stone were placed around it, whereupon the gods took their places upon arrival and allowed their temperaments to be exposed as the stone changed colors according to it.

The Greek gods were the first to appear. Zeus took his place upon a pillar at the center of one side of the table.

Apollo sat at his right side, dressed in the same white toga as Zeus.

Apollo's presumptuousness angered Ares, who was adorned in full Spartan armor and glared at the god who'd taken his rightful place. He paced behind the seat of Zeus.

Hermes, his winged, serpentine staff propped against the edge of the table, kept his own counsel as the other gods began to arrive.

Zeus turned to Apollo. "Where is my brother?"

"Hades refused to come, uncle." When Zeus glared at him, Apollo added, "Oh, Poseidon…. You meant…" He cleared his throat. "I believe he will be here any second."

"He'd better be," Zeus snarled.

Four Egyptian deities arrived for the meeting.

Bes, the dwarf with the skin of a lion and the head of a mortal, tapped the stone pillar with the hilt of his jeweled dagger to get its attention. It lowered itself so the god could take his place before it rose again.

Ma'at, a pendant of weighed scales lying between her breasts, checked the single, blue-plumed feather that protruded from her head to assure it stood erect. She sat daintily at the opposite side of the table from Zeus and caddy corner from Shu, who smirked as he shook out his full headdress of brilliant colored feathers before perching upon a pillar of his own. Horus entered with them. The legs of a man carried him forward, but as he took his place at the table, he viewed them through the eyes of hawk. The pillar went red.

Zeus took note of it. "You come to us angry, Horus?"

"My place is in Edfu," Horus told him. "I do not like being absent from it. The current Egyptian Pharaoh is an idiot, and yet it is my duty to see him safe."

"No other god will cause discourse in your country to-day," Ares grumbled, "as we have all been summoned."

"My country is ripe for war." Horus glared at the war god of the Greeks. "Rumor has it your hand has played a part."

"You flatter." Ares grinned.

"No. I warn of what will come to pass if rumor is proven truth."

Ares threw back his head and laughed. "And now you tease."

Balder, a Nordic god, shimmered into the room.

Apollo's golden bow appeared in his hand as he stood from his place and loosed an arrow at Balder's chest.

The arrow swerved. Thanks to his mother, Frigg, and the absence of the weed mistletoe, the projectile had no chance of hitting its mark. Still, it was an aggravation. "Seriously," Balder said, "even here I am to be target practice?"

"Forgive me," Apollo said without real remorse. "The wait grows long. I thought perhaps you were the entertain-ment."

Tyr materialized, missing his right hand, and tossed a tiwaz to his fellow Norseman with his left one. As Balder caught it, Tyr said, "I offer you strength and the hope of a good outcome should you choose to challenge the arrogant archer."

The gathered gods held their positions as Thor, son of Odin, shimmered into the room. It took but a single glance for him to sum up the situation. He loosed his hammer. The spelled weapon arched around Apollo's head and then re-turned to its owner. "I offer my services, Balder, if you'd prefer I take up the challenge in your name."

Munsin, the only Korean god at the table, sat stoic and unimpressed with the temperamental display. He instead watched the doors for more egresses to appear, as he waited for those yet to arrive.

Apollo, unaffected by the weapon that had weaved its way about his head, snarled. "We are just having a little fun, Thor. Try to lighten up."

"Boys," Allatum said as she made her entrance, "let us play nice." Adorned in black silk that left little to the imagination and dark flesh drenched in gold, the raven-haired beauty stole their thoughts of aggression and ignited an altogether different kind of heat in their stares.

A demon goddess, little more than black shadow, appeared at Allatum's side. "Where is the fun in that?" she asked and then became corporal. Allatum's beauty paled in comparison to the wanton lust permeating from Qandisa. Male and female alike were affected by her luscious curves, whether in her ethereal or corporal form. She grinned. "I say let them fight."

"A goddess after my own heart." Ares grinned. "Come," he said, taking the pillar to Zeus's left and gesturing to the one next to him, "sit by me."

The light exuding from the aether in the table dimmed. The room itself held its breath when, on a wave of rage, Poseidon arrived. As he took on solid form, and his eyes narrowed on those gathered, he demanded to know, "Where are the archangels?"

"We are here," Michael said as he and Raphael appeared. "Let us begin."

"The Hindu gods have yet to arrive," Zeus told them, "and the lesser gods of the Native Indians have requested time to send a representative as well."

"We exist outside of time," Raphael said, bringing in his white, feathered wings as he took his pillar next to Michael, whose wings were folded down his broad back, "but of patience we have little."

Ares snorted. "The gods of the Hindus have far more influence over the Earth than does the evangelical deity you serve."

"And yet those who worship at the feet of our god far outnumber those who worship at yours." Michael growled, his wings unfurling. The span of them reached to both ends of his side of the table. "The Greek Pantheon is naught but history. Sit quiet and let those who still hold sway discuss our course."

"That is all you do," Zeus sneered. "Talk. When last we faced the denizens of Superi, your presence was absent. They usurped your title, claiming heaven as their home and hanging the banner of Angels around their necks, and still you did nothing."

"Peace, brother," Raphael said, laying a calming hand on Michael's shoulder when the archangel looked ready to call forth a host of his warriors to see Zeus dead for his insolence. To break the tension, Raphael asked, "What do we know of the Superian race beyond what history teaches?"

Poseidon answered as his image solidified behind Ares. "We know they do not stand whole, but the curses cast by the Egyptians, and my brother, have been circumvented. Though born incomplete, what remains has been strengthened. Their elemental abilities have been perfected. They've become warlike. The division we created in their blood served only to forge them together. Though individually weaker, they pose a greater threat now than before."

"The problem," Apollo said, "is their planet. They hold the advantage there."

"How do you know this?" Thor asked.

"Because I've been there. The gravity of their world is like carrying a mountain on your back, and the powers we wield are adversely affected, though the cause remains unknown."

Balder's brow furrowed. "I was under the impression that the true Angels had been reborn."

"We are the true Angels of Heaven," Michael said.

"Of the celestial heaven, perhaps," Bes answered, "but we are speaking of those of Superi."

"Our preliminary reports have only revealed two," Zeus told them, "that carry the markings of the true Angels."

"Two?" Allatum questioned with a high feminine chuckle to follow. "If that is all, then you boys rest easy, and Qandisa and I will handle the matter."

"I would caution against such arrogance." Poseidon glared at her. "I've lost five of my children. Only one returned. He was bloodied and cursed. His skin blackened and rotted before my eyes. He spoke of a monstrous people and then died in front of me."

Hermes chimed in, "Magic is beyond their reach. Trickery is not. Perhaps alchemy has been a skill they've acquired."

Ma'at countered, "Or, when their genetic code was fractured, they could have become more instead of less."

"They do not wield magic," Ares reiterated Hermes's comment, "but the elements they have mastered a control over."

"I grow bored," Shu said. "From what I hear, you Greeks have been rattled by pale shades of the past, and in fear of their return, have succumbed to panic."

"I agree," Tyr said, "but then have not the Greeks always been thus? They would start confrontation and woe simply to assure they lead, and by striking first, they expect the rest of us to follow."

Michael did not try to hide his amusement, and his laughter drew glares.

"You have something to say?" Zeus growled.

"No," Raphael said, adding his own glare towards Michael. "He does not."

"Good," Zeus sneered, "for neither of you hold the title of god. You are but errand boys for a deity that refuses to show his face."

The stone pillars that had varied in color from calm blue, to bored yellow, to frustrated purple, now raged red as they were abandoned and the gods of Earth gained their feet. The shouting started and weapons appeared in more than a few hands.

Munsin alone retained a steady mind. "Enough," he said. The room fell silent instantly. "Bes, you and Horus are guardians. To protect, you must fight. Ma'at, Balder, you are gods of justice and balance, of reconciliation. You should be uniting us in a common cause not causing further discourse. Raphael, though not a god, you possess the power to heal, an advantage we will need if we find that our immortality does not hold on the world of Superi. The rest of you are gods of war." His head whipped towards Zeus. "Before you say again that Michael does not hold the title, remember that he commands legions of angels."

"What do you then suggest?" Zeus asked.

Munsin spread his hands, palms up, and shrugged his shoulders. "I am but a god of egresses. I show the way. I offer a path. I open the door so that others may walk through."

"Thor," Zeus asked, "what is your counsel?"

"I am a warrior," he said, "not a general."

Zeus turned to Ares. "You are my general. What council do you give?"

"I say kill them all," Ares replied.

Qandisa laid her palm upon her chest. "Oh, you and I will have great fun."

Thor laughed, as Michael, self-righteous as always, added, "I think the children should leave the room, so we adults can speak of actual strategies."

"Children?" Qandisa locked stares with Michael as she laid her hands upon the table, dimming the light it offered, as she absorbed a touch of its power. You already know I can kill you, boy. Your legions weren't enough to save you the last time we played, remember?"

As Michael stood and reached for his weapon, the Hindu goddess Kali shimmered into the room. All eight of her hands were filled with the tools of her trade—those meant to wage war and deliver death. "Is someone playing my song?" she asked.

Parvati, the divine mother of the Hindu, solidified next

to Kali. "Peace, my precious," she said as she laid a calming hand on Kali's grey shoulder. Turing her attention to those seated around the table, she smiled. "I see that no blood has yet been spilled. This pleases me." With her pleasure came a calming wave of tranquility that washed over them, cooling their ire.

Munsin's smile was genuine, as he dipped his head in respect for Parvati. "I thank you for coming. Perhaps your wisdom and guidance will further our cause. We must begin to make progress if ever a decision is to be reached here."

Kali snapped her fingers and two additional pillars materialized next to the Norse gods. As she and Parvati took their places, Ma'at spoke.

"Apollo should give us the account of what happened on Superi."

Ares chortled. "Yes," he said, "the story of Apollo getting dumped back on Earth beneath a mound of Superian soil is one I will relish in the retelling for eternity."

Apollo glared at Ares as he started from the beginning and told the whole story again.

When he was finished, Munsin shook his head. "After hearing your account," he asked, "why would we ever go there?" Including the others in his assessment, he added, "What would we hope to gain from further attacks?"

Nodding, Raphael concurred. "I believe your story, Apollo, but by your own account, they merely sparked a gateway. They never actually opened it. You did."

Murmurs began around the table as the gods spoke their thoughts to those seated close to them.

Balder cleared his throat...loudly. "We attacked them,"

he said. "Without provocation, it would seem. I see no reason to get involved here. They aren't attacking us. My counsel would be to leave well enough alone. Apollo is whole."

Michael and Qandisa laughed.

Apollo glared.

"Whole enough, I mean," Balder continued with a grin before turning serious. "First, the Greeks attacked them on their own planet, and then the Greeks sent Cyclopes through the gateways without the permission of a council. We should forget the matter before the Greeks' actions create further discord with the Angels."

Poseidon stood. His trident appeared in his hand. "Are you saying that the deaths of my children are of no consequence?"

"No." Balder shook his head. "But they were senseless deaths."

Horus asked, "Did Apollo not just confess to killing dozens of their people? Is it any wonder they attacked your children? Can the Greeks truly find fault with their actions?"

"I can't believe what I'm hearing," Ares raised his voice. "You don't want to attack because they haven't attacked us? Retaliation is the only cause for action?" He turned to Zeus. "Father," he implored, "tell me your reasoning is above such ignorance. The Superians will attack Earth, and when they do, they will kill millions."

"Millions?" Horus scoffed. "Really, Ares? You would satisfy your lust for war at any cost. However, there are those of us here who cannot risk war with another world."

Parvati looked to Munsin and sighed. "I see what you mean," she said. With a voice meant to calm, she suggested, "Those not interested in finding common ground should leave. It does not matter who struck the first blow. War is coming, and it is the duty of this council to determine our best course of action." She held up her hand. "Do not speak of turning the other cheek, Michael, or of leaving well enough alone, Balder. There are but two sides to any war: the victor and the fallen."

XXII

Indestructible?

Set and Shashara, feet dragging from the long days of late, followed behind Anliac and Tristan on their way to the mess hall where everyone had agreed to meet. Sole and Lunam intercepted them halfway there with their humongous guardians towering behind them.

"We are impressed with the progress you have made here, angeli," Lunam said. "The city of Pisces Stragulum has returned to its former glory."

Anliac smiled. "Your compliment is well received, but not deserved. This place is not what it once was—a city of peace and prosperity. It is a base for war."

"Yes it is." Davimon walked up. "But a fine base it is."

"When did you get back here?" Tristan asked.

"We just arrived," Lishous answered over Davimon's shoulder, as his hand went to his stomach.

"You okay?" Set asked.

"Oh, he's just being dramatic," Davimon teased. "I'm

277

going to start calling him Terra if he doesn't man up."

Set smiled but it never reached his eyes. Instead, he asked, "How mad is your king?"

"Ah, well, we kind of didn't tell him you left." The side of Davimon's mouth turned up in a crooked grin. "We didn't exactly tell him that we left either."

"Is that going to be a problem?" Anliac asked. The silence that followed was her answer.

Reaching the entrance to the mess hall, Belua asked Sole, "If you feel safe enough, we would stay outside," he said, peeking over their heads, but ducking to see through the door. "The open, beamed ceiling would allow for our height, but the crowd inside would shrink the space."

"I agree with my brother." Torren dipped her head in respect. "We would follow you anywhere, but we've been a long time away from people not of our race. We fear our presence would replace the people's hunger with trepidation."

"You have my word, they are in no danger here," Anliac assured them, "but feel free to leave the door open so you can see for yourself."

"Thank you," Torren replied as she and her brother took up post, while the rest of them entered.

Sole growled as he surveyed the room.

Shashara jumped.

"Ignore him." Lunam scowled at Sole and then smiled at Shashara. "He is not much for gatherings."

Shashara nodded in acknowledgment when Set squeezed her hand and led her to a table where they took a seat. A moment later, they were brought plates piled high with roasted meats caught by their hunters, fresh vegetables harvested from their own gardens, and sweet drinks made of fruit from their orchards.

There wasn't enough space for all those within. People lined the walls, balancing their meals on one hand and eating with the other, while setting their drinks between their feet to protect them from the traffic.

The long, wooden, rectangular tables were lined with people. The cacophony of boisterous laughter, and the rough conversations of fighting men and women, turned the inside of the building into a deafening roar.

Those in Angeli uniforms stood out from among the civilians, but even they did not congregate together. There were no lines of division; not by race, gender, or rank. A nox child was bounced on the knee of a grey-haired fulgo man giving her mother a chance to eat. A beast of a fera, with curved husks pulling up his top lip, made him himself smaller to make room for a mortalis with girth enough for two men. Shoulder to shoulder, they laughed as they bumped into each other with each lift of their arms.

"I do not agree with what you are about to do," Sole said. "Chaos is born from too much information given to those untrained to cope with the knowledge."

Anliac laid a hand on the Alpha's grey-furred shoulder. "I understand your misgivings," she told him. "Not long ago, I would have argued the same logic, but we lead a free people, and that obligates us to give them full knowledge of what we face."

"I cannot think past the noise," Sole snarled. He startled even Tristan when he bellowed, "Silence!"

The civilians quieted a degree. The others ignored the command after a quick check to see who'd barked it. A few scoffed before turning back to their meal and conversation.

Sole, eyes bright with aggravation, caught Tristan's humored stare. "There is no respect here," he said. "I am an Alpha."

"Not here," Tristan told him. Holding up his hands, his golden markings flared for a brief moment, allowing him access to a voice they would heed. "Silence," he said without the need to raise his voice. It boomed, reverberating off the walls and echoing from the ceiling.

Luce, ever the dramatic feline and easily startled, screeched and launched herself into the air. She caught a beam, flipped herself up on it, and glared down at Tristan. His smile stole her ire, and she rolled her eyes instead of biting his head off.

"We know it's crowded in here," Tristan said, causing all other conversations to cease, "but we would have everyone present before we begin. Luce gives good example. If those who are able would join her aloft, we can seat those who remain outside."

The majority of those who went topside were feras. Their animalistic qualities gave them an edge, but before Sole's superiority could manifest it's self as fera pride, the feras began to reach down from above to aid others.

Children, anxious to experience the height, were lifted overhead and perched on beams, protected from falling by those already there. The men, stout of arm and back, lifted the lighter females, who in turn braced the men and enabled them to pull those without claws to the rafters. As space was made available, those who'd tarried behind Belua and Torren beyond the door, and those hovering outside of windows to hear, made their way inside.

The creak of shifting leather, the rattle of settling chain-mail, the giggles of the young, and the cooks banging around in the back kitchen were the only noises as all eyes turned to Tristan.

"There has been much excitement and upset over the last few days," he began, "and with it fear and uncertainty have found their way into your animus. We would have it removed."

Set, sitting beside Shashara with the heels of his palms pressed against his temples and his eyes clenched tightly closed, said, "Talk about an understatement. Everyone is afraid." He braced himself against the onslaught of emotions captured within the mess hall.

Shashara blushed as a laugh escaped her throat. "I'm sorry," she said loud enough for everyone to hear. "I know we are about serious business, but I can't get the look on that sexist Pero's face, as the women of Pisces Stragulum escort-ed him beyond our walls, out of my head. He…was afraid. Our people"—she shrugged—"we are simply concerned."

Hoots and hollers, and gales of laughter, followed her assessment.

Anliac held up a hand to quiet them. "It is true," she said. "The fearlessness that you've each shown in the face of conflict inspires pride. We, the House of Angeli, are proud to call you our people. We've gathered you together to share what knowledge we have of other conflicts that have struck other cities. We've gathered you together to speak truth.…

The war with Earth has begun."

Tristan gestured to Riker, who sat with Donnin and Char at a table off to the right. "Riker," he said, "give your report."

"Have you been touched by the Cruxen Clave?" Sole questioned. "It is insanity to tell the whole of what we face to the masses."

"Ha!" Davimon's outburst had heads turning. "Pay up," he said, wiggling his fingers, palm up, towards Lishous, who laid an orange jewel in it. "Sorry for the interruption, Riker, but a bet was laid that the mortalis were not the only race to balk at the Five's tactics."

A wave of laughter followed his words.

Lunam cast a private thought Davimon's way. '*Your friend may carry fera blood, but he knows nothing of our ways. He is not one of us.*'

The pointed look Davimon shot her from across the mess hall was clear. It said, '*And your point is…*'

Riker chortled. "The nox outside of these walls have issues understanding it as well," he said, growing serious, "but the Five have shown us a better way. They've shown us that secrets lead to division and that truth keeps us whole. Let us all give thanks for their wisdom and guidance."

"Unbelievable," Sole uttered as the people lowered their heads for a moment of reverence to the Five.

"I've received word from Palus Regia. A beast emerged from a gateway…" Riker began to give his account.

As his story unfolded, the citizens of Pisces Stragulum did their best to hold themselves together. Palms covered gaping mouths. Brows furrowed with concern. Hands found hilts of weapons, though no immediate threat loomed. Women whimpered. Children cried. Old men gave comfort as young men found their resolve. Those in uniform, men and women alike, were stoic.

Though colors representing almost every region of Superi were displayed upon the people, though every race…every age group…was present, they turned their fear to fire and forged themselves as one weapon to be wielded by the hand of the angeli, ready and willing to serve.

"…and that is when your father took control of the city, ma'am," Riker concluded.

"Relay my message to General Aquam," Anliac said. "Those who lived to tell the tale, and those who sacrificed their lives in defense of Superi, are heroes. They, along with all those who will follow, will be remembered and honored by the House of Angeli for their bravery."

"Ma'am." Riker nodded. "I would add," he said, "that General Aquam does not believe the beast was of this world."

"Thank you for your report," Anliac told him. "Please, take your seat." She turned to Tristan. "Now we should tell them."

Tristan nodded and raised his voice to carry. "General Aquam is correct. Though we have not seen one for ourselves, through Set we have seen enough. The beast is a creature of Earth, and it did not come alone." He turned to Sole. "Give your report."

Sole growled at being given orders.

Torren stayed where she was when Lunam summoned Belua telepathically to her side. Already cramped, the people of Pisces Stragulum scrunched together to make room for the gargantuan fera who entered. And though his progress was slowed by the attempt to not step on anyone, he obeyed his Alpha and moved as close to her as space allowed and stood with his head down and his shoulders hunched to avoid the rafters.

"We were not present in Dura Mortis when the village came under attack, but with my ability, the transgression of the Earthling was made clear. If it is the will of the Five that you be fully informed," she said, "I will acquiesce to their desire, but know that we believe the truth to be a greater burden than you can bare. Brace yourselves, for from the images I give you will nightmares born."

"Not the children, please, Lunam," Shashara pleaded.

Nodding in agreement, Lunam began: '*A family of three tops a snow covered rise. A mother clutches her infant son to her chest, as her mate falls into a defensive stance. They are the first to see the one-eyed beast.*'

Another mother, one safely inside the mess hall but blinded by the telepath's ability, reached for her young daughter, who'd begun to cry. Pulling the child into her lap, enfolding the child in her arms, she gave thanks that she was spared the other woman's fear.

The man goads the beast into chasing him, buying his mate time to escape as he runs full out for the village, shouting an alarm.

Heartbeats accelerated as the people of Pisces Stragulum got caught up in the scenes unfolding in their minds' eyes. Their muscles grew tense as instinct drove them to run or to turn and fight, and yet there was nothing they could do.

Memories could not be altered, but growls of approval issued forth when...

At the edge of the village, two feras attack the beast. The first, a woman, latches on with teeth and claws. A hammered blow to the top of her head snaps her neck. She falls, her blood splattering the snow-covered ground.

Gasps sounded throughout the building as tears began to flow.

The second defender, jaws clamped around the forearm of the beast, is shaken about as if the weight of child. With a vicious sling of the beast's arm, the fera is sent flying. His body crashes through a domed, mud home.

Three young children stare through rounded, terrified eyes as a body crashes into the hearth and scatters coals and flames that burn their mother.

"NO!" The word was shouted from multiple locations as people surged to their feet, weapons bared, but the images could not be destroyed by might.

They watch their father bolt through the hole in the wall, intent on retribution. Peeking from the destruction, they see the protectors of the village helping some to flee, while others of their rank converge on the beast. One gains its attention. The beast gives chase and is led to Belua.

A slow, steady pounding of closed fists into open palms began like a solemn chant throughout the mess hall, as the beast of Earth met the beast of Dura Mortis. They howled in righteous approval as fear entered the invader's eye.

A single blow, a direct hit to the Earthling's face, plants the beast on his back. From over his shoulder, Belua pulls free his spiked axe. The axe falls, pinning their enemy to the ground and severing it from its life.

The sound of fists to flesh grew as voices were raised with accolades. "Belua! Belua! Belua!" the people chanted.

Tristan raised his arm and silence descended. "Thank you." He nodded to Lunam. "I think that the images help everyone to better understand. Set," he said, "you're up."

Shashara tugged at Set's hand when he rose from his seat.

Set squeezed her shoulder and made his way to where Anliac and Tristan stood with the Alphas. "I would not show them the images, brother," he said. "The carnage was far too great."

"Understood," Tristan said. "But, they need to know what happened."

Set faced the crowd. "Media Forum was attacked as well. The city guards were able to take the beast down without any civilian casualties."

"So much for the truth," Sole said.

"What does that mean?" Set said.

"Who is keeping secrets now?"

"There are no lies being spoken here," Set snarled between clench teeth before addressing the people again. "The battle was devastating. Buildings were destroyed. Nearly a dozen guards lost their lives in defense of the city, but," he stressed the word, "the beast was killed."

Questions sprung up from the people. "Have there been other attacks? How many more are to come? From where?"

"One other was seen," Char said from beside Rupert and Donnin, "but the coward ran into Rus Elisium before we could kill it. The poison of that place surely accomplished the task for us."

The questions continued to pour from all sides of the room.

Davad stood from his place between Hammy and Razoran, with Triton's black eyes staring up at him from across the table, and said, "Calm yourselves! We've known we were at war with Earth. It should come as no great surprise that they sent warriors to ascertain what threat we Superians hold. Rejoice, for our message was delivered loud and clear. Not a single beast returned with its life."

Anliac's marks flared. "These beasts were taken down by a handful of nox, a group of city guards, and a single fera." Glancing sideways, and looking way up, she added with a grin, "Large though he may be…" She waited for the laughter to die to down. "He is still but a single man. They could send a hundred of such warriors, and Tristan and I could face them alone and win, but with you at our backs…they could send a thousand, and victory would still be ours."

At their people's dubious stares, Tristan's blood heated. His marks flared to match Anliac's, and then he said, "Do you need proof of the strength of the angeli and of Anliac's claims?" When many of them nodded, or cast their gazes to the floor, Tristan said, "So be it." He turned to Belua. "You took one down with a single blow. Your strength and prowess in facing our enemy has been witnessed by all. Would you be willing to aid me in a demonstration?"

Belua checked with his Alphas. When neither spoke to stop him, he agreed. "You are a little man," he teased. "I will do my best not break you."

Tristan laughed. "I've been called many things, but little…well…" He slapped the guardian on his back. "That's a first," he said as they made their way outside.

The building emptied out behind them. A circle of on-lookers formed around them, as Triton came up to ask, "Are you sure you wouldn't rather choose the smaller of the two guardians to make your point? It would be bad for morale if you were knocked on your arse, and fear would be born instead of the hope you aim to give."

"A voice of reason," Sole added.

Ignoring the Alpha, Tristan clasped forearms with Triton and smiled with genuine affection. "You are among a small number of those we call friend," he said, "and yet you need to witness this as well as they do. In your eyes, I remain the boy carried upon your ship by Jacob, but it is time you see me as the man I've become."

To make clear his intention, Tristan asked, "Belua, who is stronger, you or Torren?"

If a fera could blush to the point of their fur turning red, Belua would have. His chest puffed out. "I am tougher, but…" He paused. "She is stronger."

A smattering of laughter followed Belua's admission, but curiosity and fear were around the edges of it. If Tristan lost this battle of brute strength, Triton was right—the people's morale would be shattered.

"Torren," Tristan said, "I need your help." His neck was forced to bend as the big girl obliged and came forward. "I need you to hit me as hard as you can. Our people need to see that a single blow that would kill one of our enemy has no effect on an angeli."

"My brother's right," she said from her towering angle above him. "You are a little man, and despite your confidence, I fear killing you."

As the crowd settled to bear witness, he grinned. "I'm a hard man to kill," he assured her. "I'm much more durable than I look." When still she was reluctant, he added, "I tell you what," he said, "strike a few lesser blows and test my words, and then, you will put your weight behind your swing."

She laughed out loud. "Belua asked to play this game once upon a time." Torren's grin was lopsided and goofy. "He changed his mind after the first strike."

Shashara came up on Tristan's right side. "I'm not sure this is a great... Whoa!"

It happened too fast to track. A blur of movement brought back Torren's arm. She released it like a catapult, backhanding Tristan across the chest, considering his face was too small of a target, leaving his neck at risk.

The air pushed ahead of the strike had knocked Shashara to the ground. She landed with a harrumph and shook her head to clear it from the jolt to her spine that had rattled her brain.

Tristan leaned into the blow, and his feet skidded backward a few inches, but he remained standing and unharmed. He lifted his shirt. Not even a red mark bore witness to the hit. He looked up at Torren and grinned. "Maybe you can make the next one hurt a little? I'm trying to make a point here."

Torren laughed. Digging in with her hind claws, she balanced her forward weight on one front paw and struck out with the other.

Tristan absorbed the hit. The gush of wind created by the

force of Torren's blow pressed against those standing behind him, yet he was unaffected. "You've got to do better than that." He smiled.

Not used to feeling inferior in strength, Torren raised up on her back legs and formed a giant fist with both paws clasped together, intent on hammering Tristan into the ground.

With a collective gasp, the crowd caught and held their breath.

The decision was fast. The move was faster, but there was no one alive who possessed Tristan's speed. He caught her wrists in his left hand on her downward swing, creating a funnel of loose sand that spiraled outward and slung into the faces of the onlookers. The breath they held was released. Some laughed, while others stared, slack-jawed, at the blow that would have buried normal men.

"Thank you, Torren," Tristan said, releasing her and stepping back. "You've been a great help."

Belua pointed at Anliac. "Is she as strong as you?" he asked Tristan.

Tristan's head cocked to the side as he winked at Anliac and replied, "Just about."

With a gulp that had his Adam's apple bobbing, Belua said, "Then I no longer volunteer to help make any points."

The crowd laughed along with Anliac and Tristan.

Set drew close to Tristan's side, and for his ears alone, said, "That was a foolish stunt. You even had Anliac worried. If you had lost…" He shook his head.

"I know, brother," Tristan told him, "but it needed to be done."

"I suppose. They aren't as afraid as before." He turned to the people of Pisces Stragulum and raised his hand to gain their attention. "Like cowards, the Earthlings snuck in the back door, and yet Superians proved they were ready. The one-eyed beasts were slain to the last."

"Ahoo!" the voices of the city rose as one.

"Anliac and Tristan are ready."

"Ahoo!" Clenched fists punched into the air to punctuate their agreement.

"Their strength and skill is greater than anything Earth can bring, but," Set waited for the crowd to calm and then said, "should they come at us in number…remember… We are now thousands strong, and we…are ready!"

"Ahoo!"

"I stand ready." Set grinned. "We will meet them on the field of battle. I will delight in draining a god and bringing him to his knees before the might of Superi!"

"Ahoo! Ahoo! Ahoo!"

Davad shouted over the crowd, "The Alphas have come. The nox stand with us. The mortalis king has joined rank, and the fulgo of Imbellis have our backs. We are indeed ready, so let us celebrate our unity today…and our victory tomorrow!"

Amongst the cheering crowd came hasty orders. "Where are the musicians? Someone start a fire. Who's doing the cooking?"

Davimon was chuckling when he approached Davad. "One party this week wasn't enough to satisfy you?" He laughed a full-bellied, shoulder-shaking laugh, and Davad went beet red.

Shashara laced her arm through Set's and asked with a quirked brow, "What is he talking about?"

"Huh…"

Davad and Davimon laughed harder.

XXIII

Matthew's Journal

"We've begun expansions on the dock," Triton said as he and Davad made their way to Tristan and Anliac's home, "but it's not going to be enough."

"What do you suggest?" Davad asked.

"I think it's time we consider having two ports. The fishing vessels are a hindrance to the merchant ships."

"And the coin to pay for the new build, from where shall it come?"

Triton shoved his hands into the front pocket of his trousers. "The House of Angeli are going to have to start collecting taxes."

"No."

"The town of Pisces Stragulum will, before long, be a full sized city. And as Magistrate, the citizens will look to you to see it cared for, and you can't do that without coin."

Davad rolled his eyes. "Anliac is a terra wielder. There is wealth enough in the ground, but Anliac doesn't have the

---

time to go mining right now, so unless you can find another way to raise the needed coin, your endeavor will have to wait."

Having reached the house, Davad nodded to the guards as he opened the door and soothed Triton's ruffled feathers with a pat on the back as he passed. He entered the house and closed the door and found four sets of eyes pinned on him from the living room.

The squeak of Anliac's rocking chair ceased, as Tristan stood from where he'd been leaning against the wall beside the fireplace. Shashara sat next to Set on the sofa with their fingers intertwined. In Set's other hand was a black journal that he gripped hard enough to turn his knuckles white. It appeared to be one of Nathon Bealson's from Calstar's description.

"What's going on?" Set asked and looked askance at Triton when he stiffened at Tristan's side. "You okay?"

Triton ignored him. "You have your father's journal."

"Wait," Tristan said. "What? Is that why we are all here?"

That got Triton's attention. "You didn't know?"

"No, I didn't know. Set, where did you get it?"

"He got in Regia Aquam," Davad answered, "from the man that stopped us on our way to Media Forum."

"He's right," Set said. "I don't know his name, but he told me if I refused to give King Normis wanted he wanted, in exchange he would deliver a journal that had personal meaning to me. I'd assumed it was one of Calstar's. I shoved it in my pocket and forgot about it. It wasn't until later that opened it to discover the name on the inside cover." His throat grew thick. "Matthew Suxson."

"Well…" Shashara nudged his shoulder. "At least now I know what you've been doing since your return. I was beginning to think you'd tired of me." She smiled.

"That will never happen," he replied as his eyes swept the room, catching others as they passed. He had to clear his throat before he could speak. "Part of it reads like a training guide for epotos. I think"—he dropped his gaze—"that he knew he might not live long enough to teach me." He looked up at Tristan with tear-filled eyes. "He talks about you as well."

Tristan blinked rapidly, but try as he might to hold it back, a tear escaped to slide down his pale cheek.

Anliac saw that Set and Tristan were lost in a connection only they shared. To fill the silence, she asked, "Triton, how did you know it was their father's?"

Triton smirked. "Matthew was never without it. The scratches and blemishes all over it have a history of their own. He carried it with him even into battle, and that's how I know that Set is holding out on us."

Set never broke eye contact with his brother, but he'd heard Triton clearly enough, and his reddening face gave evidence of his guilt.

"The journal predates even Beth." Triton pointed at it as he continued, "Rulers have sent mercenaries hunting for it, and it holds more personal secrets than it has the right to."

Shashara giggled. "Triton you're as red as he is. Let me see," she said reaching for it.

Set held it over his head. Tristan blurred.

"Hey!" Shashara laughed. "No fair." Tristan was already carrying it towards the kitchen with Anliac in pursuit.

"I need to read that journal," Triton growled.

Loud enough to ensure that Tristan heard, and complied, Set said, "No one other than me and Tristan is going to read it. I'm sorry." He held up his hand to ward off Triton's objection. "But that's the end of it."

"There is a name likely to be in it," Triton told him, "and if I hear it uttered from either of your mouths…I will gut you from navel to gullet." Spinning on his heels, he stormed to the door and yanked it open. "I'll feed your innards to a dracon," he vowed before slamming the door on his way out.

Shashara was in a full-bellied laugh, curled over on the sofa in a ball. "Did you see his face? Oh," she groaned, wrapping an arm around her middle as she laughed some more. "You have to tell me what the journal says."

A victim of his sister's mirth, Davad sported a goofy grin, but said, "I'm glad you guys found a piece of your dad. Really, I am. And if you find something in it that will help us, please, let me know, but right now I've got so much work to do…"

"Go," Set told him as he started a tickling match with his giggling girlfriend. "I just wanted you to know we had it."

Seriously uninterested in watching the play between Shashara and Set, he nodded and headed for the door. Before he could escape, he heard, "Ha! What? Tristan, what does it say? Looks like the pirate has some moves… Let me see… Ask nicely… Ow!"

Davad saw Triton and Shorlynn up ahead. Triton was storming off. Shorlynn was headed for the house. The sway of her hips was distracting. She was nearly upon him before his eyes traveled upward again.

"Hi." She smiled.

He caught her hand. He should have dropped it. She should have pulled away, but the touch lingered. "Now's not a good time to visit," he said, gesturing with a tilt of his head towards the house.

"Well…" She stepped closer. "It wasn't a wasted walk. I got to see you."

Davad leaned in. "Shorlynn," he whispered her name.

Her lips parted as her eyes dropped to his mouth.

"If you don't stop me," he said, "I'm going to kiss you… again." He dipped his head to level their stares. "And if Skylar finds out…"

She flinched. "You're right." She blushed. "Some habits are hard to change. I'm sorry," she said. "I'm taken." Lowering her eyes, she maneuvered around him. "I should learn to act like it."

"Where are you going?" he asked.

"To fetch Shashara," she said. "Razoran thinks he's been poisoned and won't let anyone touch him but her." At his panicked expression, she added as she walked away, "He drank too much, Davad. I assure you he'll be fine."

As the sound of her steps upon the dry leaves carpeting the ground faded, Davad found himself standing between the ancient, angeli dwellings and the town. He was between the couples at his back and the clustered groups that lay ahead. How had he become the one to stand alone? He chuckled to himself at the thought and started towards the marketplace, where preparations for tonight's party were underway.

Lishous was standing off to the side, watching as others sat up tables and situated chairs around them. They had set up bonfires, and already the aroma of roasted meats wafted across the open space.

Lishous glanced over as Davad came up at his side. "Glad you could make it," he said with a grin that showed a disturbing amount of teeth.

Davad laughed. "Stop smiling, Lishous. You're scaring people."

Lishous tugged his upper lip down over his teeth.

"I need this party," Davad confessed. "I need a distraction, and there are enough beautiful women here to see it done."

"You are starting to sound just like Davimon and me," Lishous chuckled. "You should be warned. The life of a bachelor has its downfalls."

Davad sighed. "Yeah, well, it seems everyone close to me is pairing off. It's ridiculous. We're too young for relationships meant to last a lifetime." He turned to face Lishous directly. "What's wrong with having a little fun first?"

Lishous nodded. "Nothing at all."

Davad raised an eyebrow. "Your tone would suggest otherwise."

Lishous's brow furrowed in thought as his eyes tracked Torren. "We've discussed this before," he said as he lifted two mugs off a passing tray and handed one to Davad. "There is a season for all things...including falling in love."

Davad held his mug aloft and said, "And until then...we party."

Lishous lifted his mug, his frightening grin returning as he said, "Indeed. In fact"—he gestured with a nod of his head to two women smiling in their direction—"I say we begin with those two party favors over there."

Punching the side of Lishous's arm, Davad grinned. "I'm willing to share if you are."

"What are we sharing?" Davimon asked as he escaped his conversation with Lan to join them.

"Party favors," Davad and Lishous said together and then laughed uproariously.

"I've no idea what you're talking about," Davimon admitted, "but count me in."

XXIV

With or Without YOU!

"You suggest that those of us who are about war should leave, Parvati," Thor said, "yet is this not a war council?"

"Superi is a world as old as our own," Parvati told him, "and history shows that a threat from the Angels should not be taken lightly." She turned her head towards Apollo, who'd risen from the pillar to pace. "Your actions have reignited a feud between our two worlds that has been fueled by hate for thousands of years." She sighed. "Now, though Earth has been the aggressor, we must decide if we are to invade their world." To Thor, she said, "They've done nothing wrong. There is no justice to exact."

"We broke the Angels when last they came to Earth," Apollo growled. "Was the lesson of humility learned? No, for they've spent the years recreating what we took from them as punishment for their audacity. When I stepped through, onto the world of Superi, what did I find?" He rushed forward to slam his fist down on the table. "They

---

were trying to open the gateway, Parvati. Perhaps they've not trespassed yet, but I swear to you, that is their intent. There was a small invasion force waiting. What more proof do you need?"

"We know where you stand," Munsin interjected as Balder nodded in agreement. "Which is why Parvati has asked that those of like mind remove themselves so other options may be examined."

"I am with Poseidon," Apollo said. "I'll leave when he does."

Standing from the pillar upon which he sat, Ares sneered. "A few thousand years ago this would not have required a debate. We would have slaughtered them all." Spinning on his heels, he headed for the new egress: two golden doors that appeared in the wall, courtesy of Munsin. "Thor…" Ares gestured with a tilt of his head.

The grin on Thor's face stretched wide as he hefted Mjölnir upon his shoulder. "The promise of war makes for unlikely alliances," he said as they exited together.

"Ma'at?" Parvati was not the only one surprised when she moved to leave the room as well.

"You are right, Parvati," Ma'at said. "The Superians did not start this. Yet Apollo speaks truth… They would have, had he not stumbled upon them. The only course of action is the one of which Ares speaks. We eliminate the threat on Superi before it becomes a threat on Earth." With nothing more to say, she left the room as well.

"You would leave this council to join the war mongers?" Parvati asked when Qandisa's black shadow floated over the table towards the exit.

"Each of you are tied to Earth in some way," Qandisa told her, "but I am not. My power comes from chaos, and it is universal. I would very much like to see this…Superi and the Angels given birth there." Even in her shadow form, her shrug was notable. "Call me curious, or war hungry. It is all the same to me." She smiled as the doors closed behind her without her aid.

Beyond the doors was a long, white hallway that stretched forth across the terrestrial heaven like a never-ending road. White stone pillars stood every twenty feet, a delicate glow emanating from them, yet there was nothing for them to hold aloft save for the pressing darkness.

Thor leaned upon one of them, his arms crossed, his foot tapping with impatience against the white-tiled floor. Ma'at, knees bent, sat upon a pillar, lost deep in thought. Ares's thoughts, however, were clear as he paced before the door. Qandisa chuckled at them in their various states of frustration before she floated outside of the pillars, off of the white-tiled hallway, to fall to slumber in the vast space surrounding it.

Time passed, and then the golden doors burst open. Poseidon emerged like a raging bull with Apollo yapping at his heels.

"Uncle, wait," he said. "We need the council behind us if we are to achieve victory."

"I will not wait," Poseidon bellowed. "My children will be avenged."

Apollo maneuvered himself in front of the elder god. "You weren't there, Poseidon. You didn't see."

"Move."

With a flick of his wrist, Ares sent Apollo flying through the air to crash into a pillar that shattered like dust in a windstorm. Such was the nature of the place that the pillar reformed, whole and complete, before Apollo hit the hallway floor.

"You heard your uncle." Ares grinned. "Back off, boy."

As fast as thought, Apollo regained his feet, and though he glared daggers at Ares, he spoke to Poseidon. "Give the council a moment," he implored. "They will reach the right decision."

"And if they do not?" Poseidon said. "What then?"

"You will start a war we can't win without them."

Qandisa woke from her sleep, stretched, and then translocated from beyond the hallway to where Thor stood. "War," she purred, tracing a lacquered nail down his cheek. "Such a lovely word." As Thor moved away from her touch, her gaze fell on Poseidon. "Are we done talking?" she asked. "I prefer action."

"Then follow me," Poseidon said before vanishing.

Ma'at remained seated. "I agree with your course of action," she told the others, "but I will not act against the will of the council."

"Then you are as weak as they are," Ares said as he, Apollo, and Qandisa followed the trail in the aether left behind by Poseidon.

They found themselves on the shore of an ocean, the place Poseidon had taken Apollo before sacrificing his children.

As Poseidon stared out over the open water, he said to Ares, "I should have listened to you, nephew. Perhaps if

I had, my loss would not have been as great." He turned
to Ares, whose clothes had become a heavy, black armor.
"Chaos, war, and death—these are things you are known for.
I beseech your aid in unleashing all of it upon the world of
Superi."

Ares crossed his arms over his powerful chest and grunted with a self-righteous lift of his chin.

"Spare me the mockery you would unleash," Poseidon
said, "and speak words that serve a higher purpose. I admit
it was foolish to turn from your counsel, but I am listening
now. How do you suggest we proceed?"

"Ignorance, brother—willful or otherwise—has been the
undoing of gods and humans alike. Information is the key to
victory, and might is the hand that delivers it. The Cyclops
that returned to Earth, what did he tell you?"

"That they are monsters," Poseidon replied.

"The Norse fear no enemy," Thor said. "If it is information you seek, send me. I will take their knowledge, and then
Mjölnir will take their lives."

"If they were that easy to kill," Apollo told him, "they
would be dead already, and we would not be standing here.
Your arrogance is your weakness, as was mine when I
crossed over."

"Then I will accompany him," Qandisa said. "I am not
arrogant. I am confident. I've tasted the souls of humans,
from bitter to sweet, and would know the taste of a Superian animus as well. I would know if their life source too will
scream for mercy as it travels down my throat." Her breathing grew heavy. "The possibility excites me."

"You are truly a frightening creature," Ares said. He

turned to Thor. "Can you obtain a squad of men without alerting Odin?"

Thor laughed. "If you think for one moment that Odin isn't listening to this very conversation then you are mistaken, Greek. His eye sees all."

Ares rolled his shoulders to shake off the instinct to attack the Norse god for his laughter. "Fine," he said. "Will Odin stop you from taking a squad?"

"There are those that follow me despite the will of even Odin," Thor said. "They go where I go. However, I will go into this battle alone." With a smirk for Apollo, he added, "If he killed dozens, then I will kill thousands."

Ares looked to Poseidon, who was quick to say, "I'll not send any more of my children unless I travel with them."

"I would not endeavor to convince you otherwise, Poseidon," Ares told him. "Thor, I will summon an army of the dead to aid you, as I fear Qandisa will be…distracted." When Qandisa did not dispute the claim, the corner of his mouth twitched as he fought back a grin. "Kill them if you can, but you must prevent your capture at all cost. Your mission is to gather information. Hey." Ares growled. "Are you listening to me?"

"Forgive me, god of war," Thor quipped. "I stopped listening when you uttered the words *can you*… If it can bleed, then I can kill it."

"So be it," Ares said, pulling free his lakonia. Pointing it skyward, he bellowed, "Come forth!"

The coastline trembled as sinkholes appeared along the beach. Smoke belched from the craters as molten rock shot into the air. What landed in the water hissed. What landed upon the sand turned it to glass.

The ghostly warriors who'd been summoned clawed their way out of Hades only to solidify and fall at Ares's feet. Some wore the ancient Greek armor of an age long past, others wore the camouflage of the modern soldier, yet all had proven in life that war was in their blood. The lack of it in their death had changed nothing.

To the thirty dead gathered, Ares said, "Your orders are simple. Protect Thor."

The Norse god grinned, threw back his head, and thundered, "Heimdallr, open a gateway to Superi!"

As Ares's minions gathered around him, Thor asked, "Is Qandisa to come?"

The sound of her laughter was evil incarnate. Poseidon's trident appeared in his hand. Apollo conjured his golden bow as Thor's grip tightened on Mjölnir. Even Ares shivered as the sound of it made his skin crawl.

"You look to Ares as if to gain permission for me," Qandisa hissed as her shadowed, demon form shifted into that of a human woman with spiraling, pointed horns protruding from her skull. "You forget who I am. To the Christians, I am Astarte, the goddess of nature. To the Greeks, I am Astarte, the daughter of Uranus." Her form shimmered and she became a goddess painted in gold, her eyes lined with coal, holding a Khopesh sword in each hand. "To the Egyptians, I am Astarte, the warrior goddess. To the Canaanites"—she began to grow until she stood seven feet tall, her bulging muscles mimicking those of a man—"I am the consort of the god El. They were a people who understood the true strength of women, and they worshiped us as all should." As she smiled, her form shifted with ease into an elegant, golden-winged woman adorned in golden plate apparel. "But it is my Moroccan worshipers who I most adore," she said. "To them, I am Qandisa, a simple goddess of Lust." Her smile was so wicked even Thor took a step back. "You see, Thor, my power comes from many sources. I cannot be killed in battle. Therefore, the god of war knows better than to dictate orders to me. Isn't that right, Ares?"

"Just remember whose side you're on, Qandisa," Ares replied. His feet lifted from the sand and, against his will, he was carried close, inches from the blinding beauty of the goddess.

Her full lips turned up into a beguiling smile that stole sanity. But then, those same lips pulled back into a feral snarl that revealed black, jagged teeth. "You want me on your side, Ares," she hissed. "Then kneel, as all men should, and I will be your goddess. You would make a fine addition to my harem."

At last, Heimdallr answered Thor's call. A gateway burned itself into the sand, and a moment later a vertical, glowing gateway appeared. As it stabilized, Ares used the distraction to put distance between himself and Qandisa. Poseidon's chuckle from twenty feet away was not missed.

"Well," Thor asked, spinning Mjölnir in his hand, "shall we, goddess?"

"I thought you'd never ask," she said, keeping the image of a golden-winged angel. With a last wicked grin cast over her shoulder towards Ares, she added, "This should be fun."

With the dead following and Qandisa leading, Thor carried his laughter with him through the gateway to Superi.

As it closed behind them, Poseidon said, "Your hatred runs deep for the goddess."

"Indeed," Ares replied, "but it is equally matched with desire, depending on her form of course." He grinned. "She is a source god, Poseidon. I almost pity the Superians now." His form shimmered. "Almost," he said and disappeared, leaving Poseidon to stand with Apollo.

XXV

Family Bonds

"Halt," a stout fera he hadn't seen shouted as he approached the main opening in the walls of Pisces Stragulum. "State your name and your business."

A bell tolled, though whether it was to warn the city of his arrival, or for some other purpose, he wasn't sure. "I am Calstar Luxson of the Asylum in Imbellis. I have come to see that my niece, Shorlynn, is well."

Coming up from behind him, a mortalis guard ordered, "Dismount, and you will be escorted in."

Calstar surveyed the land, having neither seen, nor heard, the first two guards before they'd been upon him. If stealth were an ability, he would have thought they were level threes. Tossing a leg over the saddle, he slid to the ground to comply with their order.

"How goes preparation for the war?" Calstar asked his escorts as they cleared the entry and made their way deeper into the city.

"The denizens of Superi are uniting," the fera said.

The mortalis added, "We are ready should Earth strike again."

"Good news indeed." Calstar grinned. "The Five of the House of Angeli have done well."

"Michael," the mortalis called out, addressing another of his race, one with the aether markings of a telepath on his hands, "would you mind tracking down Shorlynn and letting her know that she has a visitor?"

"No problem," Michael replied. "You're her uncle, right?" he asked Calstar. The man's apparel—a red tunic and dark brown trousers—was creating a bump in the informational flow coursing through Michael's ability.

"I am," Calstar said.

"Is there a problem?" the fera guard asked, picking up on Michael's hesitation.

"I've never seen him in anything other than the red robes favored by the lawyers in the Asylum," Michael told them, "but he is who he says he is. I'll go find Shorlynn."

"We're taking him to see Set," the mortalis guard informed him.

With a nod, Michael turned and jogged towards the docks.

Calstar sighed. "Telepathy is an amazing ability. I've never met the man, and yet he clearly knows who I am. I could have accomplished much more had I been born so gifted."

"Such abilities come at great cost," his mortalis escort said as they reached their destination.

The door to Set's office building was flanked by two

Angeli Guards, a fulgo man and a nox woman, who came to attention at their approach. As the woman ducked inside, the fulgo stiffened, placing himself squarely in front of the door, and then asked, "What brings you here, Calstar?"

"I am not here to cause discourse," Calstar assured him. "My reason for coming is personal."

The woman returned with Set beside her.

"Thank you," Set said to the two perimeter guards. "You can return to your post." To Calstar, he said, "Follow me." When his two guards moved to enter the building as well, Set stopped them. "I would speak to him privately."

"Set…" the fulgo guard objected.

"He poses no threat to me," Set replied, already turning from the door.

The nox woman caught Calstar's arm as he passed. "If one hair on that boy's head is disturbed, I will gut you on your way out. You have my word."

"It never ceases to amaze me." Calstar grinned. "The loyalty the Five inspire. I mean your master no harm."

The nox let him go with a sneer. "He is not my master," she said. "We are free people here. He is my leader. I protect him by choice."

Stepping into the building, Calstar replied without looking back, "And that makes you twice as dangerous."

Set sat behind his modest wooden desk. Maps and scrolls were stacked and scattered across it. He looked up with a lopsided grin. "Sometimes I think the paperwork will do me in before the gods of Earth have the chance."

Calstar chuckled. "May I?" he asked, gesturing to an empty chair.

"Please. Looking up at you puts a crick in my neck."

Settling into the straight-backed chair, Calstar crossed his ankles and smiled. "How are you doing, Set?"

"I can feel the sincerity behind the question," Set said, "but the reason for it alludes me."

Calstar winced. "I do not possess your ability, but neither am I completely ignorant of how it works." He paused. "You took something from me that you wanted, but in the taking of it, you took on the burden of my mind as well. You and I are the same. No." He held up his hand when Set would have objected. "Don't try and deny it. My life is inside your head. My secrets, my desires, my ambitions, there is nothing you do not know about me. In a way, you are the son I never had."

Tired of hiding the truth, Set took the opportunity to speak of it instead. "It is a paradox I cannot escape. Where I would choose caution you would throw it to the wind. Where I would act you would bide your time. I love Shashara, but you look at her as a little girl. You love Shorlynn—a different love, perhaps, but equally as strong—and I know that, because the emotion has become mine. You and I are not the same, Calstar. We are extreme opposites, and when I took the knowledge from your mind and it melded with my own, a war ignited." A single tear from an ice blue eye slid like a liquid crystal down his cheek. "I fear you will be my death though your hand never strikes me."

"Has the knowledge you obtained not aided you?"

"It has helped as much as it has hurt. Your years outnumber my own. Your life inside my head is bigger than the life I would choose for myself. You crave power." He sighed.

"And I crave only peace."

"First obtain the power, Set, and you'll find the peace you long for."

"Why are you here?"

"To see Shorlynn." Seeing that the explanation wasn't enough, he added, "Five days ago the Pero were sent by Nutrine to retrieve her. They returned to Certamen empty handed. I needed to know that she was okay."

"To punish her for rejecting the Pero leader, or to force her to return to Imbellis?"

"You say you feel my love for her, and yet you would question my intent?"

Set's smile never reached his eyes. "When we first met Shorlynn, you'd tasked her with the job of seducing my brother despite the fact that you'd tied her to a betrothal she did not want. So yeah, I'm questioning your intent."

"Seduction is an art form that fulgo women are taught from the cradle. You know this as well as any fulgo, Set. Yet she was not forced to take action beyond words. As for her betrothal, she requested that I speak to Nutrine on her behalf, and I did so because I can deny her nothing. It was about her elevation and protection. Now, I will not deny how keenly I have felt her absence, but again, returning to Imbellis would be her choice. I desire only to see her happy."

Set's eyes fell closed as he inhaled sharply. When they opened, he said, "She has brought someone for you to meet." Standing and coming out from behind his desk, he made for the door. "Let us see how much you desire her happiness."

Rising to follow, Calstar said, "Have you become a telepath in my absence?"

Running his fingers through his hair, Set said, "Thank Superi, no, but I've become attuned to those closest to me and the way their emotions flow."

Calstar grinned at the nox guard as he exited the building. "The damage to his hair was not my own. His fingers were the weapons used against it." He laughed at the woman's glare.

"Uncle Calstar!" Shorlynn was all smiles as she ran to him and threw her arms around his neck.

He leaned back, lifting her feet from the ground, and spun her in a circle. "You have been missed," he said, setting her down.

She placed her hands on his shoulders and asked, "Are you angry for the trouble I've stirred by rejecting Maltris? I can't imagine Nutrine was pleased."

"I've never found cause to be angry with you," he said, gazing at her through the eyes of a father, as he leaned in and kissed her forehead, bringing a smile to her face. "Erase Nutrine from your concern. I have."

"I'm pleased to see you, uncle, but why have you come?"

"I feared for you, for your safety, and could not rest until my eyes told me you were well and happy."

She tucked her long, black hair behind her pointed ears and smiled as a blush crept across her cheeks. "I have found more happiness here than I thought existed, and I would introduce you to her. Skylar…" She gestured over the red-headed fulgo beauty who'd stolen her heart.

Skylar offered her hand. "It's a pleasure to meet you."

"Handshakes are for those with whom we do business." Calstar bypassed her hand and caught her up in tight embrace.

"Oh." Skylar gasped, taken off guard by the affection.

"We embrace those we call family," Calstar said, squeezing gently before releasing her. "Your beauty rivals that of my niece. Wars have been fought over less." His smile stretched to his pointed ears. "The chaos in Certamen is but a small price to pay for your bond with Shorlynn. The happiness you've brought into her life…that is worth everything." He leaned forward and kissed her cheek. "I am in your debt."

Set chuckled.

Shorlynn turned to him and questioned, "What?"

"Nothing. Your joy is just contagious," Set told her. "Go. Visit with your uncle, but I would like to speak to him before he leaves. I'll check in with you three later."

"Okay." Shorlynn smiled, capturing Skylar's hand in one of her own before grabbing one of Calstar's in the other and leading them both to a gazebo where they were protected from the suns' heat.

"Hey you," Shashara said, getting Set's attention. "What's Calstar doing here?"

"He came to see Shorlynn."

They watched as Calstar hugged Shorlynn to his side as they took seats and began talking.

Shashara giggled. "I don't think I've ever seen him be… nice."

"Our enemies would say the same of us," Set said, looking to his right as Anliac and Tristan joined them.

Tristan planted his fists on his hips, a crooked grin turning one corner of his mouth. "You win, Anliac." He grunted when she punched him in the ribs.

"I told you it was him," Anliac boasted. "This proves my hearing is superior to yours."

"No." Tristan chuckled. "It just means I underestimated Calstar's capacity for good."

She nailed him in the ribs again.

"Ow." Tristan laughed, though her ineffectual hit caused no pain.

"I've told you in the past that he wasn't as vile as you all accused him of being."

Shocked, Shashara asked, "You…of all people…thought better of Calstar than we did?"

Anliac shrugged. "I had a feeling."

"A tender moment with his niece—and a momentary smile—does not detract from the wrongful things he did to us," Tristan said.

Calstar's barked laugh jerked their heads around to see Skylar, hands waving and face animated, telling a story that sparked humor. He had his arm wrapped around Shorlynn's shoulders, and from the looks of it, he wasn't going to release her anytime soon.

"We're sure they're related, right?" Tristan asked, looking to Set for confirmation.

"She's his niece by blood," Set said, "but she's the daughter of his heart. When he lost his wife to an infection that destroyed her lungs, he thought the grief would claim him as well, but then a year later Shorlynn was born. One look was all it took and Calstar was captive. When her parents died in the last war, I took her in as my own." The visage that overtook Set's face was one of pure fatherly love.

"I can't imagine what I would have done without her. She's my world."

Anliac didn't need to be a telepath to read Tristan's troubled thoughts, as his brother lost hold of his mind and spoke through Calstar's mind instead. She didn't need to be an epoto to feel his worried concern. She laced her fingers through his own and squeezed as she met Shashara's tear-filled eyes.

"What did I say?" Set asked as their sadness penetrated his psyche.

Triton's obnoxiously loud whistle saved them from having to answer. He and Davad, with Donnin and Char in tow, made their way over.

"And here I thought I'd seen everything." Triton chuckled, his stare locked on Calstar and the two women. "If he convinces Skylar to leave my ship for the tower, there will be war."

"Strong words," Char said. "Are we missing something?" She leaned her head against the outside of Donnin's arm. Triton's black, twinkling eyes suggested mischief over malice and alleviated her concern. "Is that Shorlynn's father?"

"What makes you think so?" Set asked.

"Are you kidding?" Char grinned. "Many emotions can be faked if the situation warrants it, but that…well, that is pure love over there. That can't be faked."

"Your perception is superb, my dear," Donnin said, tipping up her chin to kiss her, "but I still don't like him."

Char grinned. "Come then," she said. "Let us leave before you ruin their sweet moment with your negativity."

"We should return to the docks," Donnin suggested. "It

nears nap time and Triton has empty bunks."

With a wink for those who stood around, Char's grin grew as she took his hand and led him away, saying, "We both know it is not sleep you crave."

Davad and Triton made parting remarks to the couple that made Anliac and Tristan laugh. Set's ears turned red, however, and Shashara found sudden reason to study the tops of her boots.

"Well," Shashara's voice quivered, "that was awkward."

Anliac and Tristan burst out laughing again.

"Only for the innocent," Anliac teased.

"All jokes aside," Davad said, "Triton and I have been talking. We've given the Alphas, and the feras under their command, a few days to wrap their minds around what we're doing, but we think it would be best to have a course of action planned for when they agree to our terms."

"The boy is right," Triton said. "The Five will need to lead from the start or others will vie for the position—most likely the Alphas."

"I've been doing some reading," Set told them, "and putting the pieces together as I gain understanding of how my ability works. I think I've figured out how to open the gateway in Bealson's Grove."

Shashara's heart slammed against her ribs. "Set," she whispered, "are you suggesting we invade Earth?"

"It would put us in an offensive position," Set explained. "Up until now, we've only defended ourselves. It's not enough."

Anliac shook her head. "Nathon invaded Earth with an army of angeli. Tristan and I, we're good, Set, but we're still only two."

"I keep thinking about that scroll Socmoon shared with us. Remember? We were not ruined, merely broken. Repair the damage by placing the pieces together again, and we will be assured victory."

"Not even Socmoon knew what it meant," Tristan said. He sighed. "For now, can we not simply enjoy the peace and quiet?"

BOOM! Superi herself seemed to give answer as the ground shook and people began to scream. Though the world quaked, the sound came from the east, from the direction of Imbellis, and they turned towards it. Distance prevented them from seeing the tower, but not the massive mushroomed cloud that boiled above where it stood.

XXVI

Easy Target

People screamed and sought to hide as fear overcame them. Shashara clung to Set's hand and watched as a cloud of smoke billowed over Imbellis.

"What was that?" Davad asked over the noise of panic as the representatives to Pisces Stragulum fought through the people to reach him.

"The better question would be who that was," Triton replied, coming up behind Davad from the direction of the docks.

"As if we don't know," Tristan snarled as his marks pulsed with the anger burning in his gut. "If that golden god has returned, I'm going to shove that bow of his so far up—"

"Enough," Anliac growled back, her eyes flaring. "Now is not the time to become emotional, Tristan. Our people need us to think."

"Not just to think," Davad countered. "They need us to act." He turned in a slow circle, searching the faces that

---

323

rushed by in panic for one in particular. "Jaccoo," he shouted above the chaos, having caught a glimpse of the five-foot tall, dark-skinned, bald mortalis man with a level three speed ability.

"I'm here," Jaccoo replied, jumping with his hand in the air to reveal his location, but the people blocked his path. Speed would have only caused a collision, but his diminutive size was proving an equal obstacle. "I'm here," he shouted again.

"Move, people!" Davad yelled. "Let him pass."

"What are our orders here, Davad?" Davimon asked as he and Lishous made their way to stand beside him.

"Get a message to Normis," Davad told him, "and see that General Aquam is notified as well. Tell them there has been an explosion in Imbellis, and that we believe the war has begun. Let them know we'll send another message as the information comes to us."

"Consider it done." The two men turned towards the docks.

"Riker," Davad said, "you and Lan gather the Angeli Guard. Meet us at the wall."

"Done," Riker said as Lan gave a stiff nod and they took off.

"Shorlynn," Set said, "you and Calstar gather the civilians. They'll be safer in numbers should the fight come here before we can return."

Davad shook his head. "We can't leave them without defense. Triton, it's going to fall on your crew to keep them safe. Find Davimon and Lishous while you're at it," he said. "They'll help as soon as our missive has been delivered."

"You've given me no easy task considering the state your people are in." Triton smirked. "But I'll do what I can."

"Perhaps I can be of aid there," Lunam offered. Brushing up against Sole, she cast her thoughts to the people. '*Calm yourselves. Trust in your leaders. Trust in the alliances they've made. Follow the pirate to safety.*'

Triton chuckled. "The two words do not flow easily together, do they, little fox?"

Torren growled at the perceived slight to her Alpha.

The fera's noise made him chuckle. "Alright!" He raised his voice to be heard over the chaos. "If you're not going to fight, then follow me!"

"What can I do?" Jaccoo, who'd finally made his way to them, asked.

"I need you to…"

Jaccoo cupped a hand around an ear as he leaned forward to study Davad's moving lips. "I'm sorry, sir. What?"

The exodus of civilians as Triton took them to the new marketplace was drowning out Davad's words. Anliac, her patience thin, shouted, "Quiet!" as her golden marks flared as brightly as Tristan's own.

Everyone stopped talking, but the panic didn't ease.

Tristan grinned and tipped back her head to kiss the corner of her mouth. "Now is not the time to become emotional, Anliac. Our people need us to…ugh," he grunted as she soundly punched him in the gut.

Davad ignored them both. "Jaccoo, we need you to get to Imbellis as quickly as your speed can carry you. We need to know what we're up against. Do not engage the enemy," he said, "but head back with the information we need. We'll intercept you."

"I'll go with him," Tristan said.

"No!" several of those standing around, including Jaccoo, shouted.

"Sir," he said, "you are far too important to be used as a forward scout. You've told us that we each have a part to play in the war with the gods. This is mine." He took off at a trot, but blurred as he picked up speed and disappeared.

"I could have opened a portal and gotten him there much faster, Davad," Set said. "Your way wastes time."

"Think, Set," Davad said. "Opening a portal might alert our enemies to our location, or you could open it to find an army of gods waiting to pour through and most obvious…" He stepped close and laid both hands atop Set's shoulders. "In this fight, you are not a gate maker. In this fight…you are an epoto. Your ability makes you as valuable as the angeli."

"Sole," Tristan said, "you're an epoto as well, and combined with Lunam's telepathy, the two of you become a powerful weapon." Seeing Donnin standing with Char and Rupert, who were flanked by the feras of Turris, he said, "Not to mention between you and Char there are two packs to add to our number. Belua and Torren will frighten even the gods, but as a whole, the feras' presence will make an impact on our enemy."

"Let's get one thing straight, angeli," Sole growled as he came forward with a strip of grey fur rising along the ridge of his back. "I will defend this planet with my life." His wings unfurled and spread wide as he stood as an image of power and strength. "But I've lived longer than you. I know more than you, and I will never serve under your command."

"Then stay here," Tristan sneered, "or better yet, go crawl back into the hole from which you came. If you will not aid us, then you are useless to us."

Anliac shook her head at the fera leaders. "Come, Tristan, we have soldiers to lead."

XXVII

Front Line

When the oracle had told Sizon to be prepared to protect the city, he'd assumed the man had been referring to Exterius Antro, but his dream had shown otherwise. He'd summoned the city guards and told them of his fear, but only ten had believed him, and together they'd raced for Imbellis.

They'd bought passage through a portal that had taken them as far as Caterva Concentio. It was from the slave city that they'd witnessed the explosion over Imbellis and had gained the proof that his dream had really been a foreshadowing of what was to come, and so they ran. Their lungs burned. Their legs ached, and yet they pushed through in the hopes of not being too late.

He led his men through the open gate, sticking to side streets to avoid the main square, where chaos had overturned the city. He chose a high vantage point and stood with his men upon a section of wall. They gaped at what lay below.

Sizon's heart pounded in chest. His lungs tightened until

---

he could not breathe. His eyes saw what they did, but his mind refused to accept the images as real. Dozens of the city guard were clustered together in the center of the market square, their number slightly increased by the citizens who'd taken up arms, but they were not alone.

The enemies he could see were less than forty, but they seemed immortal, for they did not fall, not even when Superian blades ran them clean through. Without fighting skills, the civilians fell dead, one after another. The white stone streets were covered in the blood of the dead and dying. Felled soldiers, those who'd faced the invaders alone to defend the people, were among them.

Turning to his men, Sizon said, "The white-stoned city has become a tomb, so what say you? Are you ready to battle Death?"

"Hoorah!" his men shouted, raising swords and lances and shaking them in angry fists.

With a snarling grin, he unsheathed his own weapon and bellowed, "Then let us fight!"

The men of Exterius Antro dropped from the wall and entered the fray.

***

Jaccoo raced for the city, towards screams that would haunt him forever, but he did not slow. He had orders that carried him through the western gate of Imbellis. The streets were packed with shoving people, carrying what they could on their backs as they scrambled out of the city. Looters scavenged through the remains and carted off stolen goods by the wagonload. And the fires…they alone possessed the power to destroy the city, and they were everywhere.

The clash of iron carried Jaccoo to the marketplace, where he found guards fighting the invaders, but there was something about the Earthlings that wasn't right. Their appearance was of something already dead, yet despite it, these gods were lethal. That was not to say his people where not giving their best. He watched as a boorish guard cut off one of the enemies' heads, and then watched as it turned to ash. The enemy was not invulnerable to death, and that meant the angeli could save Imbellis yet.

He turned his head for a moment, and when he looked back, the boorish guard was nowhere to be found. He searched the marketplace for the guard, intent on offering hope. He'd tell the guard that help was on the way, and then he'd return to tell the angeli what they would face upon their arrival.

"Whoa!" he shouted as he was spun around like a top. "Hey!" His voice shook along with his body as he was jerked back and forth by the guard he'd been searching for.

"What are you doing?" the guard demanded. "We're dying out here to give you people time to escape!"

Jaccoo started to answer him, but Sizon grabbed him under his arms and hauled him behind a building that had not yet caught fire.

As soon as Jaccoo could find his voice, he said, "I'm a forward scout for the angeli. Help is coming. Who are you, so that I may tell them your name?"

"I am Sizon," he said, his head swinging towards the tower that rose from the heart of the city and then towards Pisces Stragulum. Nostrils flaring, eyes wide, he grabbed

Jaccoo by both shoulders and said, "You must go back. You must tell them to use their wielders to put out the fires. Tell them…to send their warriors into the marketplace."

"I will," Jaccoo said. "That is why they come. To face the gods."

Sizon stepped back and peered over Jaccoo's head to the last of his men and to the monsters they faced. "They are not the gods, merely minions. The gods are much worse."

"If they are not the gods, then where are the gods?"

Desperate cries called out from up above. They both turned to look as two beings hovered in the smoke grey sky above the turret atop the tower, each of them with a red-robed lawyer in their grasp. The lawyers seemed to shake, and then they were tossed to their deaths. One lifted a weapon over his head and called forth lightning to strike them midflight. The other, a woman with wings and golden skin, threw back her head in laughter. They watched as her image shifted into that of black shadow.

"Run…" Sizon said, drawing his second short sword. "Without reinforcements, the angeli will face not only the gods, but also their army of the dead. Run," he shouted as he moved to rejoin his men. "We'll hold them as long as we can."

XXVIII

Not Apollo

Blurring in and out of focus, Jaccoo ran for all he was worth back towards Pisces Stragulum.

He ran through the tree line and across the large prairie land before coming upon Anliac and Tristan, who led ninety of the Angeli Guard towards Imbellis.

"Where are the others?" he asked as Anliac lifted her hand to stop the Guards' advance. "You should have brought a larger force."

"Breathe, Jaccoo," Tristan said, "and tell us what you saw."

"The outer city is mostly burning," he told them, "and what is not on fire is being overturned with looters."

"I don't care about buildings and goods," Anliac snapped.

"I spoke with a guard," Jaccoo said, panting. "He calls himself Sizon and asks that you use your wielders to battle the flames and that you send your warriors to the market-place to fight the dead army."

"The what?" Tristan asked.

"Hack off an arm, a leg, it fights still," Jaccoo tried to explain. "Put a blade in its belly, in its neck…it does not fall. You have to take its head. They've gotten out all the civilians they could—at least all those that chose not to fight."

"And the gods," Anliac said. "What do you know?"

"I know we are wasting time," Jaccoo said. "The last of the guards have joined together in the square, but they will not hold for long. If they fall, we will have to fight our way through men who are troublesome to kill to reach the gods."

"It will serve no one for us to go in blind," Tristan told him.

"If we don't go now…there will not be a city left to save."

As if to give credence to his words, the main west gate blew apart. They heard the explosion and watched in a stunned stupor as pieces of stone flew above the trees in the distance.

The Angeli Guard, stirred to violence, surged forward.

"Hold," Tristan ordered. "Jaccoo, did you see the gods or not?"

"I did," he replied. "One is a blond male."

"Apollo," Tristan said. "He's mine." As his golden marks burned hotter, he added, "This time I'll finish what he started."

"The other is female," Jaccoo continued, "but…her shape shifts."

"What does that mean?" a guard on the front line asked.

"I'm sorry," Jaccoo replied. "She was too far away from to see clearly. I know only that she was golden and then she was shadow."

"Tristan, what do you see?" Anliac asked when his stare stayed locked on the smoke coming from the gate.

"We need to get closer," he replied.

When Tristan moved, Anliac moved, and the Angeli Guard followed. They moved across the open prairie and made it to the only tree line, nine hundred feet from the gate, Tristan came to a stop. The two angeli exchanged a pensive look. From this range, they could both see the obvious.

"If Jaccoo is right," Anliac said, looking towards the city, "then Imbellis's last defenders have fallen." She pointed towards the gate at something. "Whatever that is… It's not alive. From here, we must move quickly…"

"Wait here," Tristian said.

"Tristan!" Anliac shouted to no avail.

It was too late to do more than track the blur Tristan became as he ran full out for one of the dead chasing a woman and child just beyond the rubble of the gate. Anliac held her breath along with the Angeli Guard and waited.

The dead man was startled as a gush of wind stretched back his sagging skin against the bones of his face. He caught a glimpse of his destroyer's form and of the strike of his killer as it sliced through the air to catch him at the side of his neck.

Tristan gagged as his hand met a squishy resistance before the dead man's head popped free of its shoulders. Tristan cursed and leapt backwards as the man turned to ash and was no more. Two others stumbled through the broken rubble of the city wall. He didn't waste time announcing his presence. Using all the speed he possessed, he disappeared, removing their heads without showing himself, and then returned to Anliac and the Angeli Guards that waited for him.

Anliac attacked him with fists and feet when he returned. "You idiot! What were you thinking? You could have been killed!" She struck out at him again.

This time he caught her wrists and spun her around until her back was trapped against his chest. Into her ear, he whispered, "Our people do not need to see you lose it." When she struggled again, he said, "I would not send our men to fight without first knowing they could win."

Anliac stilled and then stepped away.

Tristan's eyes flashed gold. When he spoke, his voice carried the authority of an angeli. "Today," he said, "we will face opposition on three fronts. This is how we emerge from battle victorious: Wielders, find your quads. There is nothing Earth can throw at you that the collective elements cannot deflect. Your first objective is to put out the fires. Warriors, remember what you have been taught. Stay with your units. The Oracle has spoken. The key to our victory is our unity. To slay the dead, avoid their blades and remove their heads."

The Angeli's Pugnae Coetu, a five-man ignis team, broke rank and approached. Liam, the one who spoke for them, asked, "And what are our orders?"

It was Anliac who gave them. "Aid the warriors where you can, and search for survivors, but your objective is stop the looters and gain control of the city."

"That will leave us free to face the gods," Tristan told them. "Are we ready?"

The Angeli Guard slammed closed fists against their chest.

"Then let's go," Tristan said.

They moved as a unit. They reached their destination and entered through the crumbled wall. They had to force themselves to not stop and gape at buildings that had been leveled and at the bodies that littered the ground. They listened to the haunting screams of those who yet lived and vowed to save those they could.

A man screamed as one of the dead severed his arms with two quick strikes of a sword. When the dead man turned his blade against a woman, who'd hidden inside her home with her child instead of escaping, it met the steel of an Angeli Guard instead.

"Run," the guard told her as Tristan and Anliac pushed on.

Anliac rounded a corner with Tristan just in time to see more of the undead Earthlings attacking citizens.

"No!" Anliac shouted as one of the dead yanked back a woman's head. She moved to run to the woman but stopped as the dead warrior sank his teeth into the side of the woman's neck. Knowing she was dead from the blood that pumped from the wound, Anliac opened a crater that swallowed the woman and undead together, then repaired the damage to the terra.

Tristan yanked Anliac against him, curling his shoulders around her, as something caught fire and exploded in the building beside them. Glass shards pin-cushioned his back. He endured the short-lived pain as his transcended healing pushed the glass free and sealed his wounds.

As the angeli separated, two undead Earthlings stepped out into the street. Their rotted skin reeked of the grave. Hollow-eyed and sunken-cheeked, they ambled forward with skeletal grins on their putrid faces.

Anliac saw them first. Drawing moisture from the air, she formed a flat, circular disc of smooth ice and spun it towards them. Like a hot blade through warm butter, their heads were severed from their shoulders, disintegrating, but their bodies continued to advance.

"Tristan…" Anliac asked, "what now?"

"I don't know," Tristan replied. "The others dropped when their heads did."

Two squads of wielders rushed by on either side of them. The headless bodies burst into flames. The leader of the first squad spoke in a rush. "Leave the dead to the Guard and the fires to us," she said. "Do what we cannot. Find the gods."

"She's right," Tristan said to Anliac. "Let's move."

They left the guards to their duty and started down the street leading to the tower. "Where are they?" Tristan asked as they came to a stop in front of the steps leading up to the tower.

His answer was a heavy hammer that smashed into his chest, snapping bones as his feet left the ground. His arms and legs flew forward as the hammer stayed with him, propelling him backwards. The weapon smashed through the chainmail he'd been coerced into wearing, leaving the left side of his chest exposed. He grunted as he smashed through the stone wall of the building they'd rounded and groaned when his body punched through the opposite wall.

The brick wall of the next home stopped his flight. He hit hard, slid down it, and then watched as the hammer flew back towards where it had come from.

XXIX

Gods of Earth

"Tristan!" Anliac shouted, rushing to him as he regained his feet. "Are you okay?"

"Yeah," he said brushing himself off.

They turned as one to face the god in shining armor, the suns' light reflecting off his helm, as his hammer returned to his hand.

Anliac lifted her chin. "That is not the same god we faced before."

"No," the god smirked as he planted his feet upon the white stoned street that lead to the back of the tower. "I am not."

"We have no interest in taking prisoners today," Tristan told him, stepping away from the wall, "and I see no gateway to cast you through. So go home, god," he taunted, "or die."

Anliac caught the god's wayward glance and tracked it to a balcony where a golden-winged goddess hovered.

"Tristan…"

"I see her," was his reply.

"Retreat," the god's voice boomed, drawing their focus, "is not in my vocabulary. I am an immortal, the Norse god of thunder! Of lightning!" He grinned, returning his voice to normal as he shrugged and said, "But you may call me Thor."

Movement in Anliac's peripheral vision caught her attention. Three Angeli Guards were trying to sneak a group of Superians passed the god by staying between the buildings, but the damage done to them by Tristan's body had foiled their plan.

"Crap," she cursed beneath her breath. There were children among them. "You've got to move this fight, Tristan. Get him outside of the city."

Tristan's nod was imperceptible.

"You will die today, Superian," Thor said as Tristan and Anliac spoke, "but do not be troubled. You will feast in the halls of… Ugh!"

Tristan's right fist became the hammer, and it was Thor's turn to smash through a series of walls that carried him closer to the destroyed gate of Imbellis. The god did not stay down, but rebounded to his feet in a rush of power. Laughing, he said, "You throw a good right cross. This battle should be interesting."

"Go, go, go…" Anliac ushered the guards forward. Once they were in the clear, she shouted, "Now, Tristan!"

Tristan's image disappeared.

BAM!

Faster than even the god could track, Tristan appeared

beside Thor and slammed into his side with a right hook. Thor's body flew upwards at an arched angle and was rocketed to the north. Tristan followed.

Anliac did not. Instead, she turned to the golden-winged goddess and left Tristan to see to Thor.

Using her terra ability, Anliac pushed against Superi's gravity and levitated upward until she was staring into the coal lined eyes of the goddess. "Tell me," Anliac said, "is flying your only ability, or do you count hiding in the shadows as a talent?"

"You can call me Qunadisa," the goddess said, gliding through the air towards Anliac. "The golden markings running through your dark skin fascinate me." Tilting her head at an angle, she added, "I would know your name."

Behind the goddess, Anliac consolidated moisture into a solid block of ice, and then replied, "You may call me pain." She waited for confusion to cloud the goddess's stare, and then she slammed the ice into the back of her head.

Confusion did not last long. Qunadisa's face contorted in rage as she flung out her right wing to steady herself. Without pause, she released three golden feathers from her left wing.

Anliac watched as they became daggers. She dodged the first blade. The second she caught, but before she could send it hurling back, the third sliced through the outside of her left arm. Losing her focus, she plummeted downward into the strong arms of a female fera guard.

"Thanks," Anliac said, shoving back the hair that had fallen in her face as the guard lowered her to her feet.

"Don't mention it," the fera said as she and her unit

moved on.

Qunadisa tracked her to the ground, but did not settle upon it, as Anliac threw the captured blade. The dagger slowed, hovering two inches from her face, before she turned it to dust. "That was quite lovely, my little warrior." she smiled, dropping to the stone street to face Anliac. "I do enjoy the company of feisty females."

Anliac wasted no time with words. She attacked. Closing the distance between herself and the goddess, she threw a right hook…and missed. She braced her weight on her left leg and kicked out with her right, but the goddess moved effortlessly around it. She kicked again. Punch. Kick. Punch. Punch. But for all her effort, Qunadisa avoided the blows.

Fear tugged at the edge of her mind. What if the goddess couldn't be killed? What if this fight had been lost before it began? But then she saw it; a single bead of sweat rolled down the goddess's forehead, down the ridge of her nose.

Smiling, Anliac moved faster, determined to win. Cross. Kick. Sweep. Hook. Nothing landed, but she saw the sweat beading on the goddess's skin and redoubled efforts.

BAM! She landed an overhanded right punch.

Qunadisa was driven down, but she never touched the terra. It caved in as if Superi, herself, rejected her. Her golden skin took on a bronze cast, and her wings disappeared, as she conjured a golden mace to each hand. A trickle of blood oozed down her chin from a split in her lip. As her tongue snaked out to taste the red drops, she grinned and said, "You've just made this personal."

***

Tristan tracked Thor through Imbellis, beyond the city wall, and into the familiar orchard trees where it had all begun. Entering Bealson's Grove, he found Thor standing upon the back wall. His stare, and broad grin, spoke of an easy victory, but his bluster faltered when Tristan spoke. "Now," he said, "the fight can begin."

Thunder crackled from overhead, conjured by the god. "Mjölnir will teach you, mortal!" A bolt of lightning flew at Tristan with a second one following close behind.

Tristan's senses, always heightened, tracked the streak of sickly, yellow energy as it raced towards him. Though the world continued to spin at its pace, through his eyes, reality slowed. He sidestepped the first bolt and then ducked beneath the second.

"If that's all you've got," Tristan goaded, "you should have stayed home." When Thor launched another bolt, Tristan laughed. "Come down here, god, and I'll teach you the same lesson Apollo was given."

"You want me down there?" Thor growled. "So be it." He started forward one long stride at a time. "You are fast, Angel, and you may be strong, but I AM A GOD!" He hurled Mjölnir.

Tristan grinned and braced himself for the blow. As the hammer struck at his chest again, he embraced the strike, leaning into it. His feet slid across the terra until his back brushed against the outer wall of the grove. He reached for the hammer, cursing when it pulled free of his grasp to return to its owner.

Thor shoved Mjölnir into the air and the sky darkened. Angry clouds blocked out the suns as thunder shook the ground. The water surrounding the gateway site trembled, and the ignis pillars crumbled into heaps, as a barrage of lightning strikes lit up the grove.

Blinded, Tristan ducked when he should have dodged, and he took a solid hit. He flipped head over feet and smashed into the wall, landing splayed out on the ground, face first.

Thor raised his hammer as lightning struck it, and then he brought it down on the rising Angel's shoulder. The force of the blow flipped him over, stealing the breath from his lungs as he landed on his back. He grinned at the Angel's widening eyes, as his hammer pounded into his chest and his armor gave way.

When next he brought his hammer down he was rewarded with the crack of bones, but the warrior in him craved more. On an upswing, he charged his weapon with lightning and struck again…and again.

***

The goddess was tireless, and the weapons at her disposal seemed endless. Her wounds healed even as her ire grew.

"Cover me," Anliac shouted as she raced towards the ruined gate of Imbellis. "I've got to get her out of the city!"

Despite the odds, the wielders responded. They used their elements to slow her down. Tornadoes stirred sandstorms to blind her. They placed walls of frozen aquis as obstacles in her path, while coordinated strikes of ignis forced her to throw up defensive shields.

The goddess treated their attempts as an irritant and continued on.

Anliac worked her way towards the city's edge. When she reached the wall, she dropped into a forward roll to avoid the first of Qunadisa's maces. Coming up in a squat, she flinched as stone exploded like shrapnel from the shattered wall overhead.

Taking advantage, Qunadisa closed the distance between them.

Anliac came up swinging with an uppercut, but missed.

"I feel as if you're holding back, angeli," Qunadisa said. "I would suggest you do otherwise." She swung the second mace.

Anliac ducked, barely keeping her head. Gathering her strength, she released it, and shoved with all she had against the terra. Arching her back, she flipped over the city's thirty-foot wall and landed in the open plains on the other side.

Qunadisa floated over the top of it to stare down at Anliac. "If you'd have only asked to take this fight beyond reach of your city, I would have acquiesced. There is no victory in slaughtering those without defense. Taking the life of one possessing power," she said, descending until her feet touched the ground, "that is why I have come."

With Qunadisa where she wanted her, Anliac grinned, and then released her hold on her power. Waves of energy poured forth, her calico hair blowing away from her face, as she revealed her true self to the goddess. Unclasping her cloak, it flapped in her hand and then was lost to the wind.

With her shoulders bared, the blue aquis marks stood in stark contrast to the flare of golden ones that covered the rest of her body. The hue of illumination they created was nothing, however, compared to the twin spears of light that shot from her eyes.

Qunadisa fought the urge to shield her face, but the high pitched keen to the Angel's voice sent chills sweeping down her spine.

"Tell me," Anliac said, "are all the gods on your planet this talkative? Because we couldn't get the blonde to shut up either."

Qunadisa's hands curled into fists at the insult. "I am no planetary god, girl! My power is much greater!"

With a flick of her wrist, Anliac sent a jagged rock flying towards the goddess's face. "You're still talking," she said as, taken off guard, Qunadisa stepped back. When she did, Anliac softened the terra to absorb Qunadisa's weight, then hardened it, trapping her foot.

Blurring forward, she squared up on the other woman and delivered a solid body shot. She ducked left, under a wild swing of a re-conjured mace, and came up on Qunadisa's right side.

BAM! An overhanded left punch connected with the side of the goddess's face, but the blow had unintended consequences. Her foot was ripped from the terra before she rolled across the grass.

Anliac didn't hesitate. Her image shimmered as she advanced at a run, conjuring an aquis hammer that she hefted over her head. Just as Qunadisa attempted to rise, Anliac brought the hammer down. The goddess's shoulders pulled backwards as the hammer smashed into her back, but it was the spikes of terra Anliac had conjured that impaled the goddess and held her in place.

Hefting her hammer overhead again, Anliac put her

weight behind its fall, but it was the ground, not the goddess, that took the impact. "What on Superi?" She pivoted towards the sound of the goddess's laughter but saw too late the mace that had been thrown. Pain exploded in her temple, and she fell.

"So you wield the elements of your planet," Qunadisa said.

Clenching her jaws, Anliac groaned and forced herself to stand.

"Very impressive, little angel," Qunadisa praised. "Not even Ares would have recovered so quickly from such a blow."

A wide chasm opened up beneath the goddess.

Levitating over the opening, Qunadisa tisked. "Not twice, little one." She grinned. "Not twi—AHH!" The goddess glared at the spike that had risen from the chasm to stab through her foot. "AHH!" A second spike gored her through her right arm. "Enough!" she bellowed and shifted into her demon form, healing herself in the process.

"Oh no, goddess," Anliac countered. "I have only just begun."

Spreading her feet shoulder width apart, Anliac threw out her arms and called upon the ability of her first birth. Aquis fell from the sky. It gurgled its way from beneath Superian soil to the surface, flowing into the crater in an attempt to fill it, but Anliac had another use in mind.

Qunadisa did not think to put up resistance as Anliac lifted the water to encase her in a spinning orb of clear liquid. "I…" Her black, demonic eyes rounded. Her hands went to her throat.

Anliac chuckled. "Shadows don't hold aquis," she said, "and they don't breathe, but in any form, you gods talk too much. It was only a matter of time before you opened your mouth."

The orb burst. Qunadisa plummeted to all fours, but Anliac was not finished. She levitated the goddess over flat ground and slammed her into it. She ripped two boulders from the terra and lifted Qunadisa up, then smashed her between them. When the boulders fell away, Anliac cursed. The goddess had disappeared.

She turned in a circle, but instead of finding Qunadisa, she came to face to face with Luce. "What you doing here?" she asked. "You need to go."

"No," Luce retorted. "Char sent me to help you."

"This is not a fair fight," Anliac told her.

"I know." Luce growled. "I've been watching from the tree line. Your abilities are holding her, but you're not inflict- ing damage fast enough."

"What do you suggest?" Anliac asked from between clenched teeth.

"She'll be back," Luce replied, "and when she shows herself, we'll see how she fares against these." Flashing her dagger-like fangs, she unsheathed her claws.

A whizzing sound was the only warning they had. Anliac shoved Luce to the side as she tossed herself in the opposite direction. The goddess, having returned to her winged form, plunged like a meteoroid to land between them.

"I like you, Angel," Qunadisa said, ignoring the animal crouched at her back to face the one she'd come to battle. "I really do, but you're going to have to pay for that." She inhaled on a hard gasp as the feline launched herself onto her back. She felt the paw that landed on her shoulder, but it was the fanged maw that clamped down on the other, scraping bone, that caused her to cry out.

Luce lost purchase as the goddess's form shifted into that of a naked mortalis woman with two pointed horns protruding from her head. "Wow," Luce taunted, "you are some kind of ugly…"

Anliac's vision caught the subtle shift in Qunadisa's thighs and calves as she prepared to attack. "Watch out," she shouted.

Luce went on the offensive—she charged, but she wasn't nearly fast enough.

Qunadisa downed her head and plunged a horn through Luce's throat.

Red blood gurgled from the wound as Luce fell to all fours.

"No!" Anliac shouted as Luce's glazed stare found and held her own. "No," she cried again, trapped by grief.

The goddess lowered herself until she was eye level with beast, forcing Anliac to watch as Luce's mouth opened to emit her last words. But instead of sound, a blue vapor emerged, and the goddess feasted upon it.

"You…" Anliac began to tremble. "What was that?"

"I feed upon souls." Qunadisa smiled as she licked her lips. "And your friend's was divine."

Anliac shivered, not from fear, from anger. "I…am going to kill you." The ground quaked. Rocks, at random, burst from the terra. Her grief became a physical pain that she loosed in the high pitched wail of an angeli.

"Agh…" Qunadisa covered her ears.

Anliac rushed forward. She grabbed the goddess by the horns, pivoted to her right, and in a spinning motion, launched her into the air. Shoving against gravity, Anliac rose to intercept her enemy.

The ground flowed upward at the goddess's command, pushing her towards where Anliac hovered.

As soon as Qunadisa was again within reach, Anliac struck out with her fist. The blow to her stomach doubled the goddess in half and sent her flying again.

Like a flowing river, the terra moved with them, and Anliac pulled from the element to stay in the air. With her power strengthened by rage, she rained blow after blow upon her enemy, carrying the both of them ever upward.

Through grunts of pain the goddess started to laugh.

It wasn't long before Anliac understood why. She'd never gone so high before. The air was too thin. She couldn't breathe. Lights danced in front of her eyes and then began to fade into a pinpoint that collapsed.

With the last of her strength, she struck out with her fist and then lost consciousness. In a free fall back to the planet, her body didn't feel the impact as she hit something as solid as stone.

***

"I'm going to catch you at some point," Tristan shouted as he spun around the hammer meant for the side of his neck to continue chasing the blond god. He'd learned the hard way that the hammer could appear from any direction, regardless of the one its master took. Within reach of the

———

god, the hammer found its mark and smashed into the back of Tristan's head. It dropped him cold twenty feet from his enemy.

Thor, victory at hand, rushed the Angel before he could regain his feet. Standing over him, Thor raised both of his fists and brought them crashing down. Air gushed from his victim's lungs. Adding insult to injury, he smashed the Angel's face into the dirt with a boot to the back of his head.

Backing away, he said, "It was a good battle, boy. A very good battle." When Tristan didn't move, he nodded and turned to go find Qunadisa.

Tristan's body stirred as it healed itself. He pulled his head from the hole in the terra that Thor had stomped it into, spat out the dirt in his mouth, and then stood. "Is that all you've got, Thor?"

The sound of the angeli's voice turned the god around. His eyes narrowed. "Nah." He hefted Mjölnir in his right hand, bent his knees into an offensive stance, and grinned.

"Good," Tristan said. "Because I'm not finished."

Thor didn't see him move, but the left hook thrown by the angeli drove his left knee into the dirt. He swung his hammer in an upward arch.

Tristan sidestepped and snatched Mjölnir from Thor's grasp. "I've had enough of this cursed weapon," he growled and, with a grunted heave, hurled the hammer in the direction of Dura Mortis.

Dumbstruck, eyes wide and mouth gaping, Thor stuttered. "You…you threw Mjölnir?" He saw the angeli's attack coming, but disbelief slowed his reaction.

Tristan hit first with a right backhand, followed closely

by a left hook. As Thor went down, he followed, pounding his fists into the god's face.

Thor's bloody head bounced off the terra as Tristan mounted his chest. Wrapping his left hand in Thor's blond locks, he helped it hit the terra again.

Thor made a desperate, two-handed push at Tristan's thighs. Finding purchase, he flipped Tristan off of his chest.

Coming out of the backflip before Thor could crawl out of the hole, he met him with a vicious kick to the chest. The force of it lifted the god into the air and cast him, crashing, into the perimeter wall of the grove.

Thor was not quick to rise and he was spitting blood when he did. Blinking to clear his vision, he pulled himself from the rubble, and then pivoted in a slow, full circle. As he surveyed the environs, he called out, "Why do you hide? Show yourself! I would know what trickery you used to control Mjölnir. BOY!"

"One does not need tricks to throw a hammer."

Thor turned towards the voice, only to be spun like a top from a left hook. Driven to his knees, with head slumped, Thor attempted to stand. A devastating blow to his chest caved in his armor; he couldn't breathe, as it tossed him skyward. Desperate, he called out for Mjölnir, but without air it was a vain attempt. He felt a vise grip close around his ankle. He felt the hard pull, and then the Angel cast him down.

Shoving off from Thor, Tristan was carried to new heights. Hanging from nothing, he viewed Thor's magnificent decent. The god plummeted towards the ground like a burning meteor that had passed through the atmosphere, gathering smoke and clouds as he greeted the terra. A hundred feet deep, and three hundred feet in diameter, their meeting created a crater that Superi would never recover from.

The pain Thor experienced upon landing was exquisite. He did not fear pending death. He readied himself to hear the songs of Valhalla.

Assessing the injuries he could feel, he wondered at the extent of those he could not. His helm was crushed beyond saving. His chest plate was caved in multiple locations, forcing him to take shallow breathes if he intended to breathe at all. The pauldrons on his shoulder was cracked, the other missing. The cool air sweeping across his thigh, and the dagger like pain in his calve, said the chainmail covering his legs had been torn and punctured.

He felt, more than he heard, Tristan's landing through the vibrations it caused in the terra. A grin tugged at the corner of his mouth. From the splayed, awkward, position he'd held, he pulled himself into a sitting one….at the bottom of his would be grave…to await the arrival of his worthy opponent.

Tristan slowly approached the crater's edge. Validating his foe was still at the bottom and not rebounding with some new ability.

Peering over the edge Tristan shook his head. "All of that," he said, "and still you live." On the verge of joining the god at the bottom of the pit, something falling caught his attention, and he backed away.

Thor attempted to stand but fell back into the crater, as he called for Mjölnir. His blood ran cold. He couldn't even sense his weapon. "What are you staring at Angel," he shouted.

"Be the man you claim to be, boy," Thor bellowed, "and finish what you've started!"

Tristan watched the object fall faster and faster to Superi's surface. As realization hit him he reached down for a head sized rock and looked back at Thor.

Tristan's markings lit up like white fire, blinding the god. Holding nothing back, he threw the rock finding purchase in the center of Thor's breast plate. Thor's chest armor became his prison, trapping him without breath. Eyes bulging, fingers clawing, the god was helpless.

Tears spilled down Thor's cheeks, to mingle with the blood seeping from his nostrils, as Tristan turned his attention back to the falling object.

Tristan's eye found the falling object again, "Anliac…" He whispered and then disappeared.

Made in the USA
San Bernardino, CA
11 December 2016